The Dark Side of Paradise

The Dark Side

of

Paradise

Anna Winton

BACH DOCTOR PRESS

This first edition 1.0 published in 2022 Bach Doctor Press

This is a work of fiction. While many places are real, the events and incidents are products of the author's imagination. Any resemblance to the behaviour or appearance of actual persons holding positions similar to characters in the story is coincidental and unintentional.

ISBN: 978-0-473-63102-4 (Print)

ISBN: 978-0-473-63103-1 (Print on Demand)

Cover design by: M W Innes-Jones

Contents

The author in Samoa

Anna is known affectionately amongst her friends as an intrepid traveller, always on the move travelling the world. You could bump into her as easily in a bazaar in Cairo, an antique shop in Wales or sipping on her drink at a BBQ in the Cook Islands.

Chapter One:

The Telephone Call

Why is it that the ringing of the telephone in the early hours of the morning makes one so uneasy? Probably because one is usually in a deep sleep, and it takes several moments to decide if you are dreaming or really awake.

Then there is the other problem to remember where one is, well that may not happen to people who stay in the same bed, or the same house. But to someone who is travelling so much, you have to remember where you are, which side of the bed is the wall, or you will try and go through the wall to put your feet on the ground.

This I have done many a time, and the wall gives a loud crack as I try unsuccessfully to push through it. That is why it is a good idea to sleep with a torch under the pillow. So the first reaction is to find the torch, turn it on and then sit up and see exactly the layout of the room.

Very few rooms have a table light, usually the only light is near the door for some reason. Probably as it is easier to turn a switch on as you enter a room, but you have to re-cross the room to turn it off again.

More modern houses have a light over the bed, so the golden rule is to take notice of the layout of the room before you go to bed. Of course if you're travelling this is most important as there is always the fear of fire.

The regular traveller usually looks for a rear room to be away from street noises, and a room near the ground. The stairwell is another important factor. Nearly all hotels say, do not use lifts in an emergency instead use the stairs.

So who wants to run down twenty or more flights of stairs in the dark? Anyway by this time you will have all the floors below you using the same stairs so you may as well forget about it.

The ringing continued and instead of thinking 'is this all a dream', my arm slid under the pillow for my torch. Good I realized that I was in my own bed, putting my feet to the carpet and taking a deep breath, I wandered out into the study.

I think a telephone by the bed is an excellent idea, except when wrong numbers call during the night, better to take it off the hook. This is another dangerous situation as you would not be able to take an urgent call, which this one maybe now. 'Oh dear who is ringing at this time?' goes through my mind.

A member of the family maybe, I hope it is not my daughter ringing to say, 'the calls are cheap from London at this time thought we would give you a ring.' Why do people not think of the time difference between the Northern and Southern hemispheres?

Finally I pick up the receiver and say "Hello. Who is it?" There is a click so this is an international call coming through.

"Simon here Catherine. So sorry to wake you at this early hour, but I have some bad news." I sit down to take another deep breath, somebody once said the extra air helps to oxygenate your brain and keep you calm.

Simon continues, "It is Leticia… she went swimming in the Deep yesterday afternoon, and well… she didn't return. We waited all night and at first light Jack went out in the canoe to the fale out on the edge of the Deep to check there. It was he who discovered her when he swum around the edge of the lagoon. We were lucky that she hadn't been sucked out on the outgoing tide but somehow had remained in the hole. The police were here all night looking of course, and some of the men had been up and down Vaiala Beach, but with no moon out it was useless to go out on the reef."

Simon takes a pause and continues, "Sorry I'm not saying any of the right things, but could you come up on the late afternoon flight? I'd really appreciate it, I realize that this will not give you much time, but I just need to talk to someone in the family. It is useless ringing England as by the time any member of the family decides whether they can come, it will be too late for the funeral. At the moment the funeral will be held here in Samoa, well it seems the best as we are too far from England, Hinton St George and the family plot, and your family are in so many different places dotted around the world. We have lost all ties with Waimate and I can't think of anyone we know up there in the North Island."

Not giving Catherine much time to say anything, he rushes on, "Close friends that is, we seem to have been away for so long.

Everything will be a bit upside down today, so leave

a message with my Secretary at the office if there is any problem with getting on a flight. She will take care of it with Air New Zealand and a ride from the airport from this end. Otherwise if I cannot make it to the airport, Toni will be waiting for you with the car.

I know how you like driving in our DC1 car with the British flag flying, but not tonight, he even may have the Subaru station wagon, just look out for him. I suppose you can attend to everything at your end. Right then, be seeing you later this evening?"

He finishes as quickly as he announced the news with a question finally giving me time to reply that naturally I would fly out and be there but my head is full of thoughts.

Oh dear so many questions were coming to mind, but nothing seemed to be more important than being on that flight. Should I ring the family? No what could they do, one in the States the other somewhere in France. Better wait until later.

I managed to get in with a final reply, "Simon I am so sorry, I don't really know what to say at this stage, of course I will be on the afternoon flight. Oh and leave a message on the answer phone if there is anything you wish me to bring up on the flight."

Simon relieved replies, "Just to know you will be here to help hold the fort makes me feel a little better already. Have a good flight, oh and the best bottle of whiskey you can find at the airport. Single malt of course. Faa," and the telephone went dead.

I drifted back to the bedroom and sat on the bed looking at the picture at the other end of the bed. My favourite picture of two girls in white Victorian frocks holding hands and walking along a beach.

When I first saw the picture in a shop window in Kerikeri in the Bay of Islands, Amanda who was staying with us at the time said, "You should buy that it looks like you and Leticia when you were about ten years old." We stood outside the shop window and looked at it for several minutes deciding, then both went inside.

Amanda insisted on buying it for me, she said it would be her present for the house we had just bought at the time. It looked just right hanging inside the main bedroom and had travelled with me back to Auckland once Fairlight our family homestead in the Bay of Islands was finally sold after my dear husband Stephen had died.

Oh the happy times we had all had at Fairlight, such a happy house to come home to every Christmas. The table in the dining room would always be set for at least eight people.

Then there were always the visitors, somebody usually arrived with friends from overseas and that is what Christmas was all about.

The house would remain empty for those winter months from June to October unless someone was in the country at the time and wanted to go up to the Bay of Islands. Winter or summer the trips out on the Fullers ferries was always a joy, and Russell such a lovely quaint little village to visit. Hard to believe it was once the capital of New Zealand.

All of a sudden I started to cry, was it the happy times we had all had? Or was it because nothing was ever the same? Stephen and now Leticia would never be with us ever again. That is just too hard to think of all at once. I'd better stop feeling sorry for myself and go downstairs and make a cup of tea. Amanda always said "A nice cup of tea is what you need."

Putting on my dressing gown and slippers, as it was still cold, I walked downstairs and turned on the light by the grandfather clock. I passed through the dining room and into the kitchen and filled the jug, drew the curtains and looked out on the garden. The first dawn light had come and the birds were announcing the new day from the trees next door.

I walked through to the living room and drew the curtains, this was a special time of day, as all was quiet in the neighbourhood.

Soon I would hear the train that had travelled all the way from Wellington coming through the cutting in the basin behind the hill. Strange how sound carries, the train track was miles away, but maybe as it was built over water the sound carried.

The jug had boiled so taking my favourite tea Dilmah out of the cupboard, I took a mug I had recently bought while in Brittany on one of my trips to France and popped the tea bag in. On went the hot water, added by a lone teaspoon of sugar and with a dash of milk. Putting this on a tray as my hands seemed to have lost their strength of late I carried the tray into the living room.

We had had two spinster friends years ago, who always set up a tray with such care. I must admit the tea always tasted better but in those days a fresh starched cloth was always on the tea tray. Why had all these fine little extras long since gone? Maybe as everyone was always busy these days, rushing from one thing to another.

The first rays of the sun shone upon the trees next door and was that some buds on the magnolia? Every time a magnolia tree is in flower my thoughts went to that first tree I was aware of.

Stephen and I had gone for a drive one Sunday when I was in the last stages of pregnancy. We came to a farm high up on a hill, we crossed the river beneath and drove up and past the entrance gates to the farmhouse. Here was a beautiful pink magnolia in bud, and the first full blown flowers on the lower branches.

The next day we visited the local cottage hospital. One of the first visitors were my two elderly friends. They arrived with a lovely small bunch of the same pink magnolia. They had also gone out to see friends who owned the farm, and she had kindly given them some cuttings for me.

Sitting there in the living room my eyes glanced towards the pictures on the wall. How is it that pictures stay mostly unnoticed on walls once they are hung? It is the first thing I notice, when going into a house for the first time. It gives you an insight into the people who live there. Sometimes it is of a place that you have holidayed or has some other special meaning. Many prints are available these days, of paintings in galleries all over the world, and these can be bought for very little in some of the larger stores.

Other people buy paintings for an investment, and the wealthy are privileged enough to be able to buy these original works. With so many new artists having the opportunity to exhibit all around the country, more people are becoming aware that they too can afford an original painting.

I looked at the yachts on a lake where we had lived once, now hanging over the piano. We never did swim in that lake, but as we lived inland at the time we would often take the family and drive down to the lake to a children's playground.

The small old fashioned yachts with a line of hills, and

Somes Island reminded me of the days we had lived in the Bay on the far side of Wellington Harbour. You could feel the wind blowing as the yacht had leaned over, sea spray flying up from the choppy water, as it so often was on Wellington Harbour.

The days spent on the Harbour always were a great experience, even though we were only able to land on Ward Island, as Somes had been used to intern Germans during World War II. Later it was used as a quarantine station and it seemed such a waste, to have a natural area not available for the use of the city.

The third painting was all yellows, golds and oranges, a hot looking beach with a boat pulled up on it under a tree. This reminded me of the time we had spent in the Greek Isles.

Having been around the usual islands of Patmos, Crete, Rhodes, Mykonos and others, we were lucky enough to return with small packs and took a boat from Athens to spend a further three weeks island hopping.

Leticia and Simon were stationed in Athens back then and it seemed a good way to spend our time. The cruise ships spent such a short interval in each port. I remember coming into Mykonos early one morning, and by the time all the passengers had been taken ashore by a Lighter, two hours had been lost. Then strolling along the quay and finding a bus to take us around the island had wasted so much time, there was little left to enjoy the waterfront area. We had to be back on board by 6 p.m. to sail overnight to the next island.

It was then I made a promise to myself to return one day, with all the time necessary to enjoy any island at whim. So thirty years later Stephen and myself took the first ferry, and looking at each island as the ship stopped, we would decide whether to leave the ferry boat or go onto the next island.

The island had of course become more popular over the years, and in desperation we asked our landlady on Santorini where we could find an island not yet discovered. She had suggested Amorgos, and so we arrived at the island of my dreams. This ship anchored at the quay, and we were able to walk up a cobbled street and found a whitewashed cottage with a patio and view of the harbour.

We took a bus to another village high up in the hills, and here we climbed one hundred steps to a monastery almost hanging over the cliffs. As we climbed we looked down into the truly blue Mediterranean so clear we could see the bottom of the sea.

Reaching the door of the monastery we knocked, and a monk opened the door with these words which I will never forget.

"Wine or Water." It seemed an occasion to celebrate the stiff climb with wine, so with a nod he asked us to follow him to a terrace.

Here we looked out on one of the most memorable scenes that I can still recall today. How the pirates managed to scale these steep cliffs to take the monastery I could not imagine.

Later I asked for the toilets, and was told to walk to the far end of the terrace.

Here were buildings built almost into the towering cliffs, where the monks lived. What a wonderful place to spend the rest of your days.

Later we were shown into a small chapel, very dark with only one small window. After some time to ourselves we took our leave and were taken back to the door where we had come in.

With a farewell to the monk who blessed us, and wished us safe travels, we walked back down the long flight of steps to the area where the bus had left us.

Every time I look at the picture you can almost smell the heat and see the olive trees which grew in all the small villages on that island. Also the old fishing boats pulled up on the beach, and the freshly painted newer ones bobbing in the harbour.

Suddenly I realized this was not a time to dream, there were more important things to do. Would it be too early to ring Air New Zealand and make a booking for this afternoon's flight? I went into the kitchen and rang Air New Zealand, oh goodness why do we have to wait so long for someone to answer. Well maybe they were just not open at this hour. I better go and take my suitcase out of the garage and start packing.

Opening the door into the garage I took down the brown suitcase that was always already packed for the tropics. Inside was an assortment of colours, my lavalava which I live in while in the Islands as it keeps me cool in the hot climate. And as for the pink, yellow and blue colours. Well where in Auckland would you wear such a brightly-coloured lavalava? My other Samoan clothes tucked away in my suitcase were equally more colourful than the drab colours I wear when in Auckland. With just the addition of my sponge bag, some black shoes and of course my funeral frock.

This frock had jokingly been bought several years ago. Leticia had said we really must have a frock in the wardrobe in case one of our friends die in New Zealand

and we haven't time to buy one. This was quite likely the way she flew in and out to and from New Zealand with a few hours' notice. So we had gone out one day especially to buy a frock each. Not entirely black, neatly decorated with a small pattern of flowers, but quite correct for the occasion when it arose.

Little did we realize that the first occasion our frocks would be seen was Stephen's funeral.

It was all so sudden and with no time to think of doing anything else but putting on the frock at the back of wardrobe.

Now it would be worn to Leticia's funeral, so strange how things turn out. Goodness knows who would be the third. It's strange how everything seems to go in threes, or so the old saying goes.

I lifted the case into the hall where all packing naturally seemed to take place. Why carry it all the way upstairs only to carry it down again? Much easier to have it packed and ready to go straight out to the car.

That was another thing, I must ring Amanda and ask her if she is free to take me to the airport at 4 pm. We had an understanding not to ring each other until 8:30 am, which was too late for me really as I would have already had my morning walk by then, but Amanda was a night person so she lay in bed until late.

I better try Air New Zealand again so rang and this time there was a bright voice in reservations answering, "Well you are the first call of the day, so how can I help you? You're speaking with Terry."

"I would like to make a booking for this afternoon's flight to Samoa please."

"Apia on the 5:15 pm is that the one you want? Business

or Pacific Class?" asks Terry.

"Pacific Class thank you and maybe there may be a chance of an upgrade? Is the plane very full?"

"No the plane is not very full, and I imagine from your early call this is an emergency, is that right?"

"Yes, well actually it is…" I pause, "My sister has accidentally drowned there."

"Oh my, I am so sorry, I will put a special remark and see if you can be given an upgrade," Terry replies very kindly. "Now what is the name please, and how do you wish to pay for your ticket? It will be at the airport for you to pick up if you wish."

I gave him my name, and telephone number, then my new Visa number. Thinking 'Didn't it make it all so much easier since the plastic cards had come out.' No more worries with local cheques having to be cleared, or picking up travellers' cheques.

When all was finished I put down the telephone. Those travellers' cheques were such a nuisance in the old days when I used to travel to see Leticia. Firstly you would have to go to the Bank and spend ages applying for the funds, and usually told to return the next day.

On returning you would be shown to some clerk, who had a bundle of cheques to be signed. I always remember when after one of Leticia's calls it all seemed such a rush as I thought everything was in order until the arrival at the bank on the second day. Here the stupid girl said quite brightly, "And here is your $5000 dollars you have asked for." In front of her was a huge pile of cheques.

"Those are not all for me are they?" I asked.

"Yes," she said, "you did want $5000 dollars did you not?"

"Yes, but I will be travelling for three months and how will I carry them in the countries I am going to?"

She handed me the cheques and to my horror she had not made them up of the usual $100 each, but in $20 bills.

"I want them in $100's and a few $20's thank you."

"Oh we cannot do that, this is all we have you know." The woman pauses looking at me blankly and then continues, "Not many travel for that length of time you know, or if they are going overseas for a long stay, they usually remit money and open a local bank account."

"Well I will be travelling the whole time from country to country and do not need to open a different bank account in each country, if I have travellers' cheques."

"You will have to take them now as we have nothing else."

So off I went home with this bundle of cheques, and in the end only took $2500 as that is all I had room to put in a small travel bag I had made to put around my neck.

In those days we did not have travel bags around our waists. Mine was a large man's handkerchief, sewn down the sides with room for passport, airline ticket, and money.

Now it was time to ring Amanda. "You are early this morning Catherine, no trouble I hope."

"Well yes, there is, I have some very bad news..." I pause taking a deep breath, "Its Leticia, she drowned in the Deep yesterday in Apia."

Oh good I had managed to say it for the second time today. But I had the feeling I was talking about someone else, not my sister.

"Goodness how awful! Can you speak about it Catherine? Now just take your time," Amanda sympathises.

"Well there is little to tell, Simon has just rung and

asked me to fly up as he thinks it is better that she is buried up there."

"Whatever for, why not back here?"

"Well, we do have connections with Samoa you know. It goes back to the First World War. Actually our Uncle was one of the first New Zealanders to come ashore at the beach right outside where Simon and Leticia live. It was a German Protectorate until the War and then New Zealand took it over. There is a relation of Simon's buried there also, sometime in 1899 I believe."

"I am so sorry, I know you were close. But I just cannot believe it! Leticia was such a strong swimmer at school. She used to win all the school swimming races. This is hard for me to take in, I don't quite know what to say. Now what can I do to help, need a lift to the airport do you?"

"Oh yes, could you pick me up about 4 o'clock, or earlier if you like we could have a drink at the airport."

"Taking you to the airport is no trouble, but I would like to come home straight away, I'm going to play bridge tonight with an excellent new partner, hope you don't mind."

"No that is fine, I will just go up to the lounge and have a drink or two myself, it is so peaceful up there in the lounge, and I suppose I could make a call or two if I'm brave enough."

"Well, see you at four then, unless you want me to come around now," Amanda offers.

"No that is fine, I'll go for a long walk around the Bays and maybe up to Bastion Point to the lookout. Don't want to sit around thinking today, otherwise I will only feel sorry for myself, thanks so much, do you think I should ring anybody now? I don't want people to feel they should fly up, it makes it so difficult, better to leave it until I have gone, and then maybe you could ring one or two for me."

"Of course, anything you want. I'll see you at four and remember, just ring if you want me."

With a click she was gone, and then I really did feel sorry for myself. So I hurriedly put on tights a top and then found my sneakers. Sat at the bottom of the stairs put on my socks, sneakers, and jacket, and opened the door to a cold blast from the south.

Never mind, a brisk walk would do me good, and so down to the road I went and crossed over and onto the waterfront and turned towards town.

Around the point to Mission Bay, the pavement clear as it's too early for the café tables and chairs to be set up yet. Walked along the seawall and crossed the bridge, then the road and up the steps, a real stiff climb I could feel in my calves and finally through the gardens to the monument.

Everything looks so dull in winter, even the view of the harbour did not help, may be it was my mood. I turned and walked back and up a side street, amongst the houses, out of the wind. Continuing up the hill and then a short cut through to the Anglican Church.

I had not been in this church for a very long time, so on impulse went to the door and found it open. Walking inside, I found myself sitting in a rear pew, gazing at the altar. It seemed so right to be sitting here and so my mind drifted away to other churches that I had sat in.

Should I have suggested that Leticia came back to her beloved Church at Waimate? She always said 'If anything happens to me this is where I would like to be buried.' How many years ago was that?

We had always gone there at Easter and Christmas,

firstly as quite a large congregation and then fewer people each following year. Most I suppose had moved to Auckland, it was really a Church of the elderly by the time we had sold Fairlight.

Better walk home it was really too cold to be sitting here, keep busy that is the answer, I will go home and clean the house.

But by the time I reached the house, the energy had gone, and I decided to park myself on the couch and finish a very good book that I had found in the library earlier in the week.

The morning went by quickly, and in no time at all it was time to think about tidying the house, and being dressed and ready for Amanda when she arrived.

Four o'clock came around quickly, and a ring on the bell told me she was here.

I opened the front door and we gave each other a big hug, stood for a moment which said it all, and then Amanda said, "Well, let us get this show on the road. Only one suitcase this time where is the chilli bin you always carry with the frozen chops and roasts?"

"Goodness! I completely forgot all about that, poor Simon will be looking for his chops for his BBQ."

"Never mind, let me look for the chilli bin, in the kitchen is it? Or the garage?"

In a moment Amanda had the chilli bin from the top shelf of the kitchen and it was loaded in the car.

"Come on I have done this so often we will stop at the supermarket on the way. We have time, I knew I had to come early."

We stopped at the supermarket and with the chilli bin in the trolley, Amanda and I whisked our way down to the meat section. In no time at all she had packed roasts, with chops on top, and some fillet steak and had us back to the check out.

"We are flying in an hour, would you girls be kind enough to take these packs of meat out, and repack as carefully as possible, then if you have some heavy tape, seal it on all sides and over the top so that it will travel on the plane."

Again it took only a few moments more, she paid for it all, and whisked it back to the car in the trolley, dropping it into the boot and we were off to the airport. We didn't much feel like talking, so she put a tape on in the car and we just sat back and enjoyed the classical music.

On arrival at the airport she took over again, parked right outside in the No Parking area, and unloaded the car into a nearby trolley.

"Do you want any more help, I think I had better come into the weighing area with you."

"Yes please," I said a bit dazed, and we walked to the check-in.

In minutes the luggage was gone, and Amanda gave me a long hug and said "You had best be off to the lounge and have a large brandy."

Another final hug, and she was gone. So off I went up the stairs and over to the duty free to pick up that bottle of single malt for Simon and a bottle of brandy for myself. Brandy for medicinal purposes especially if I see one of those mogamoga's flying around the house!

As I take my carry-on bag and portable typewriter on the trolley over to the Koru Club counter, who should be there weighing in front of me but my old friend Pierre, thank goodness for him we can have a champagne together.

He thinks of champagne like water, especially if someone else like Air New Zealand is paying.

He turns and sees me, calling out "Kia Orana", rushing over to give me the traditional Polynesian welcome. We stand laughing and hugging as the rather bland girl stands behind the counter as if she is quite beyond human warmth. I do wonder why these girls take on such a boring job as tickets and weighing, I suppose it is for the free perks of travelling around the world on standby for a few hundred dollars.

Weighing in finished with, we move to the escalator and up to the next level to put our bags through the security. My new portable typewriter is taken out of its case and with the other personal effects is soon through the barrier. Suddenly it rings the alarm bells, some poor person has gone through with his house keys or has a new hip probably.

Into the duty free for that bottle of whiskey, brandy and maybe some perfume. Nothing like some perfume to brighten the day. Sometimes there is a special on my favourite, two bottles for the price of one. Well the extra bottle is always good for a special thank you to someone who has done something nice for you.

Pierre is looking at the wine, his passion, but he should know better than to buy wine at the airport as it is always more expensive, better to take a bottle of liqueur, Tia Maria or Drambuie. It is a lovely gift and lasts so much longer than a bottle of wine which is gone in one sitting.

Purchases made, we are off up the escalator to the lounge. Soon we are sipping champagne and a plate of fresh sandwiches is brought over, being most welcome as I don't seem to have had time to stop for a bite to eat in the last few hours.

We sit and look out at the airport and the fading light on Manukau Harbour which is always beautiful and not really appreciated by people who live on the North Shore.

Finally I take a deep breath and say. "I have two things I must tell you Pierre so here goes. Firstly my sister who you have only met once while we were in the Cooks drowned yesterday in a lagoon in Samoa." Almost choking on the words, Pierre immediately puts his hand across the table and holds mine.

Then he gets up and comes around the table to sit on my two seater chair. We sit for a few moments holding hands, then he gives me a hug and returns to his chair opposite.

He feels I want to talk and it's better to sit across from one another for that.

"Secondly I am sure it was not an accident, she was always the strongest swimmer when we were younger, and she still can swim forty lengths of an ordinary pool. So why should she drown? The "Deep" as we call it is very deep, I'm not sure how deep it actually is, but it is really just a large hole which you can swim to the edge of and there is a little fale built out there."

I take a pause as I prepare myself with the next part of the story, "She used to spend hours out there, just to swim at high tide or a walk at low tide, climb up the ladder onto the little deck and sunbathe, then when the sun was too hot, she would go and sit under the thatched roof of the fale. She would be there for hours, you could see her from the shore, or others if there were a few people out there. It just seems so strange, but then I suppose all will be made obvious once I talk to Simon."

Pierre sat there looking puzzled with those deep blue eyes and looking very concerned. "Keep in touch when you arrive and tell me what the post mortem says and maybe there will be an explanation. You see when someone drowns their lungs fill with water. It is most important that you find out if this was the case if you think it might not be an accident."

"You may have forgotten when that drug dealer was drowned in Fiji, I had to go over to investigate as my position as French Consul and make arrangements for the body to be returned to France. Well the post mortem showed that his lungs were not full of water, and of course there was a large bruise on his head. He obviously had been murdered and then put into the lagoon hoping to be taken far out into the deeper waters. It was fairly obvious as the girlfriend said they had been snorkelling and he had disappeared. Instead of coming ashore standing on the road and stopping the first car and reporting what had happened. She said she walked five miles back to the motel and then reported it. Once she did that she took the bus to the airport and flew out on the ll.30 pm plane for the States. Not a normal reaction from a girlfriend who has just lost her best friend."

At least she could have stayed until they had tried to find the body and waited for the funeral. It was hours before they found him washed up on the beach opposite the gap in the reef. If the tide had been right he would have gone out on the outgoing tide but that is where she or they had made their mistake.

We knew he was murdered as not only was there a head wound but his lungs were not completely full of water. It took some time for the authorities in Fiji to release the body and the French Consul had to come from Wellington in the end to sign the right papers. Do you think your sister will be returned to New Zealand? Or will she be buried in Samoa?"

"We have a family connection going back actually to the turn of the century, and yes I think it would be appropriate for her to be buried in the cemetery a little out of town, where there are other members of the family. Do you really think there might be some foul play with Leticia's drowning?"

We were interrupted by a voice saying that flight NZ56 was boarding now and would all passengers go to Gate One. All too soon my comfort zone had been broken and Pierre took me to the door and with another hug and Au Revoir, topped with a smile from the girl behind the desk, I walked off behind the other passengers. He departing on another flight to the Cook Islands.

I find it's always better to follow someone, my mind drifting as I boarded the plane, to the time I got lost and found myself in an airport chapel and for several minutes could not find the way out to the main passage to the Gate.

Chapter Two

The Flight

I make it down the last walkway to my departure gate around the corner to be greeted by the chief steward. "Your seat madam is second on the right by the window." Once years ago you would be greeted by your name boarding the plane, but no longer, so many people fly and no longer was I a regular on this Pacific run.

Someone kindly opened the hatch above me, and handed up my carry-on luggage and typewriter. I moved into the seat, sat down and waited for the hostess to offer orange juice, or champagne. Champagne for me again that might make me relax, or even feel festive as it was my third glass for the day.

A fellow passenger introduced himself and sat down next to me. Maybe he was another consultant, I think the Pacific is full of consultants they have a certain look about them. Not on holiday although they give themselves away by the black business trousers and white shirt or coloured shirt. A traveller usually travels in beige trousers and shoes, funny to notice a little thing like clothes.

We drank our different drinks, mine champagne and his orange juice. Maybe he was a courier for one of the High Commissions? They always sent up a police officer with the diplomatic bag. Maybe that rather large black bag he put above us was carrying important documents, mail for the staff, and probably some fresh cheese unobtainable in Samoa.

If he asks me why I am flying to Apia I will just say I am having a quiet holiday in Samoa as have had a busy time at work. That should keep things on an even keel, I will not mention my reason for going to Apia this time.

My travelling companion then turns to look at me asking, "On holiday?"

"Yes, I just saw one of those package holidays and decided on the spur of the moment it would be good to leave the cold of Auckland and have sometime at Aggie's and then take a few days at the Vaisala on Savaii my favourite hideaway in Samoa. And you? I suppose you are on business."

He responds, "Well yes, but between you and me there has been an unfortunate accident with the wife of the British High Commissioner and they called me to go up and investigate on behalf of the Department. We do not like accidents with our own citizens and we like to assist the local police and make sure that everything is above board."

I nod trying not to look too shocked.

He continues, "Oh she drowned, seems she was out swimming in front of their home and didn't return as usual at 4 pm when most of the offices close. Her husband didn't worry at first as she often went off to Aggie's to play bridge with a group of friends. Evidently it was known that sometimes when they needed an extra at the last moment they would ask her to come along, she only lived a few minutes from the hotel."

He then realises he has said too much. "Oh by the way I should not be telling you, but you are not a reporter are you? Well if you are, you don't have a reporter's face."

Feeling a little offended I say, "OH and what sort of a face does a reporter have? I think the girls on TV 1 and TV 2 look most attractive."

"Oh no a reporter has a sort of what are you going to say next and I won't believe you anyway face." He continues on, "In fact you look rather sad, thought you might need cheering up I don't usually talk to my fellow passengers. They are usually so boring talking about where they have just come from and where they are going next, and how many flights they have done like this before, and the hotels they have stayed in, and how long the flights are."

I was keen to hear where this conversation was going so I decided to sit in silence and let him continue talking.

"If only they would tell you about how beautiful the last country was, and the places they had discovered off the beaten track and the people they met. Like talking about the man in the country store, or the man at the petrol pump who gave them directions to some unknown local beauty spot."

He then stopped waiting for me to reply.

"Well, I must be very careful not to say any of those things. Would you like to hear about a very boring art exhibition I went to yesterday with a group of people who all pretended to be very interested in every picture? Why were they not honest and say either they did not understand the art of Victorian times, or that they just did not like it?"

"Having visited some of their homes, you usually find one or two lovely paintings in the lounge, local scenes of some favourite place, where they have lived previously or holidayed at. Or even a family painting handed down from Father or Grandfather."

"Even a print they have bought at the warehouse, or a scene that either has the colours to match their decor or a copy of an art work they have always admired in some art gallery they have visited."

"Unlike the wonderful exhibitions of previous years of Monet or Rembrandt, this was Victorian paintings in the most hideous gold gilt frames of women walking around in Grecian frocks, followed by tame lions and tigers. It was just too much trying to understand why we were sitting in front of these horrid works, and having colours of backgrounds pointed out to us.

When our hostess turned to yet another ghastly painting I ducked off into another gallery and asked one of those poor bored people who watch for us to touch or steal a painting how to get out of the place. She came to life smiled and pointed to an exit sign. I returned my stool, it was to have been used for the next two hours, to the usher who smiled and said "So how did you enjoy the exhibition?" She had a twinkle in her eye while asking."

"I didn't, it did nothing for me at all. I love the art of the impressionists, early New Zealand. I can spend hours in the Wallace Collection or the National Gallery in London, but sorry not this."

"She responded heartedly with, "Good for you, we do like people to be honest it is good feedback. It has cost the gallery a lot of money to stage this exhibition and some of us think by the numbers turning up it will not be a financial success."

I too realized I had said a lot so I took a deep breath and turned to my flight companion, "Enough said."

He laughed and leaned back in his seat "Very interesting. I feel the same about Art. Anyhow on that note, let us have another drink and see what is on the menu for dinner."

Having set the scene, I noticed he was quite good looking and my heart was racing a little, I thought I would give him some time, and then ask him some more questions.

I then realised with a start, my sister's drowning had come to the notice of the department in Wellington already and they had sent somebody up to investigate, might there have been something else to her drowning? It would be better to tell him who I was now, as he no doubt would turn up at the house tomorrow, and it would seem strange for me to have sat with him for three to four hours and not mention we were going to Apia for the same reason.

He may even be at the funeral, and he may tell me more than would be normal, having met me on the plane.

The drinks arrived and I turned and gingerly said, "I have a confession to make. It is not really a holiday for me. My sister is the person who drowned yesterday in the lagoon and Simon her husband, has asked me to fly up and support him and to help out with the cultural side of her death."

He doesn't appear to look that shocked. I continue while I have the courage, "You see when we were younger we used to travel to and around the islands with our parents. My Father worked with Burns Philip in Samoa."

Feeling a bit stupid about not telling the truth right from the start, I felt quiet relieved.

We clinked glasses, and he responded kindly back to

me, "I'm glad you told me, although now it's my turn for a confession. I actually already knew who you were. The office said that you would be on the flight, and arranged for my seat to be reserved next to yours."

I felt even more embarrassed that I had let the charade go on for so long.

"Where are my manners, I had better introduce myself as we have nearly three hours to sit together, my name is David. Sorry for acting like a policeman but I thought it better that for you to tell me in your own time, rather than me upsetting you, and maybe you might tell me anything Leticia may have said or written to you in recent weeks? Don't worry yourself at the moment but just try to remember and I will keep in touch with you when we arrive in Apia."

"Now sit back and relax, we will see what that hostess can suggest for our dinner. Frankly with such a rush to pack and catch a plane from Wellington, lunch went by the board today, and it has just been cups of coffee at the office, and at airports."

"They have had some good wines on board lately some of our best wines are now coming from Marlborough since our best vineyard has moved from Kumeu to somewhere just out of Blenheim."

With that the waitress appeared with a menu and stopped to see what we would like. There was not much variety but then it was either chicken, meat or fish, and it didn't really matter to me. But not feeling that hungry I left it to him to order for both of us.

He seemed such a friendly person and quite open, and when I had a quiet look again, he was surprisingly quite good looking. Probably married, the nice men always were. Well you cannot get to our age, and not be married, or divorced and some widowed such as myself.

The waitress must have thought so also, as she soon was off to bring us our meal.

I then realise that I haven't introduced myself and hesitantly say, "Sorry, where are my manners, I'm Catherine, although you know that, Oh and thank you for ordering, come to think of it I have not eaten a proper meal today either. I hope the wine is good, although they do say you should not drink alcohol on planes just lots of water. What a boring thought isn't it?"

He laughed and said, "The only thing that makes a flight bearable is a drink or two, some people can read, but I try to relax, think about what is going to happen at the other end, or what I should have done before leaving."

The meal came all too quickly and the waitress was putting a large dark blue napkin on our tray and setting down an attractive setting of a small fish dish.

The steward appeared with the dry white wine that I liked and I found that I felt quite hungry. The main course of chicken came and went, followed by a peach tart. The thought of coffee or tea did not appeal and so the tray and glasses were removed.

Perhaps I should go for a walk to the rear of the plane, just to keep the circulation going. So I excused myself and David stood up so I could pass him and I walked down into the Pacific Class.

The plane looked half full as I walked down the aisle, and other than lots of Tongans and Samoans there seemed few tourists on the flight.

A man dropped his book as I passed and bending down to pick it up I noticed how dark his hair was. Definitely not a Pacific Islander his face was more that of an Italian or Spanish. He said "Pardon Madam" and definitely had a foreign accent.

It was good to see tourists coming this way, so often after visiting Australia and New Zealand they took the direct flight to Los Angeles. The Germans still visited Samoa as there were still many German names in the telephone book there, not full Germans any more but definitely a Grandfather would have been German.

That jolted me into remembering Leticia saying on the telephone that she thought she had seen an old childhood friend on the island. But our conversation had been interrupted by the satellite noise that often interrupted our calls from Apia.

There was a sudden bump of turbulence and quickly grabbing the nearest seat back, I thought it better to return to my seat. Just before an announcement was made, "Would all passengers return to their seats, as we are due to land in fifteen minutes."

I hurried back and as David stood again to let me pass, I advised him, "I think we better buckle up now, it is often bumpy as we come in over the reef."

David responded as he sat back down, "Now you remember I will contact you as soon as I have a moment and best of luck for whatever comes up when you reach the house."

With that we sat still waiting for the landing and as always I held my breath until we finally hit the ground, ran along the runway and turned towards the terminal building. It was only a few minutes before we came to a halt and then everyone got up and took their luggage down from the overhead locker.

We hurried across the tarmac with the hot air enveloping us as we went. It took only a few minutes to have our passports stamped for thirty days, the usual procedure and then onto the arrival room to wait for the luggage.

Seeing my bags, I picked them out from the masses onto my trolley and went over to the customs officer to declare the meat. I think it must have been Tina's husband as he smiled at first and said, "Welcome back, do you have some meat there for Mr. Simon?"

I replied, "Yes his favourite steak for the BBQ and also a bottle of whiskey for him and a brandy for me."

"That is fine" he said, "But Miss, we are all so upset about Miss Leticia we will all be at the funeral tomorrow. That is the office and their wives and husbands."

"Thank you that is most kind, well, until tomorrow," and I wheeled the trolley out into the arrival hall. I was scanning the waiting people looking for Simon, when a light touch on my arm and there was Toni. "Talofa, let me takes those bags please Miss Catherine and you just follow me to the car."

Well I had arrived in Apia and now I was to be brave for my sake and everyone else.

Chapter Three

Drive into Apia

Toni opened the door of the station wagon for me, and then put the suitcase, typewriter and chilli bin into the boot. Oh it was good to be in the cool air conditioning again after being in the hot humid temperature of the open airport. Toni must have had the air conditioner on for some time to make it so cool.

It did not matter how many times I came to the tropics it was always difficult for the first day, accepting the higher humidity. So I sat back and looked at the rest of the passengers coming out onto the road.

In no time we were driving through the gates and out onto the main road for the forty minute drive into town. It was very dark and there was nothing to look out at. "Toni, is Mr Simon still at the office?"

"Yes Miss Catherine, he was still there when I left the house, and he said if he was not home one hour before the flight was due, for me to go and meet you."

"May I say Miss Catherine we are all so very upset with the disappearance of Miss Leticia yesterday and only a little relieved when she was found this morning. It is such a shock and the police keep coming around to the village asking if anyone saw her late yesterday afternoon."

"But none of us had seen her since early afternoon, when she was sitting out on the patio as she often did after lunch. She just reads for a while, doesn't go down to the Deep usually until around 3pm. Then she stays there until just before Mr. Simon is due home, and sometimes he goes back out there with her if the tide is in."

"But yesterday nobody noticed her go, and we thought she must have been picked up by a friend and gone down to Aggie's. What do you think could have happened to her, she was always so careful about swimming in the Deep?"

Catherine listens intently to what Toni has to say.

"Miss Leticia said she would never swim unless somebody else was out there just in case of difficulty with the tide and she would never swim on the outgoing tide."

"There is some talk in the village that she was not alone out there that afternoon. Lesi's father said he saw some tourists arrive sometime before Miss Leticia went swimming."

"Lesi spends as much time in the village as she does down on the beach to collect shells and then she leaves them to dry on the beach in front of their fale."

"She also saw a tourist swim out to the fale on the edge of the Deep, and then later Miss Leticia swum out there and then another tourist arrived and swum out after her. But I don't know what to believe."

"Did you mention this to Mr. Simon today?" Catherine asks.

"Well no Miss Catherine, I did not want to worry him with gossip," Toni replies.

"Well did you mention it to the police?"

"No they did not ask me that, just had we seen Miss Leticia go out in the afternoon, and none of us did," Toni replies. "Mr Simon had given me the afternoon off, as he didn't need me and suggested that I went to Falefa to visit my mother. She lives there and there are not many buses that go that far. So he kindly lent me the Subaru if I promised to be back in time to pick him up from the Office at 5pm."

"Pae said she would like to come, and Miss Leticia said what a good idea, so we both left after lunch. If only we had not gone, but Mata said she would be there, so with someone in the house it seemed a good idea."

"We had had a busy week last week, with all those officials coming from Wellington, what with picking them up from the airport on the very late flight, and then departing on the early morning flight. We had to take them around the whole island so they could look at all the hospitals. Then they wanted to be driven around Savaii, so it seemed easier to take the Subaru over on the ferry. Then I was able to pick them up from the airport at Salealonga."

"I did enjoy seeing Savaii again, the road along the north shore is sealed now, and so it makes it an easy drive right around the island," Toni concludes.

"Yes, I remember the early ferry boat, and catching the bus from the market at 4:30 am and taking the ferry across. It was not very good for cars in those days, if you liked your car."

"Then rushing to catch the bus to Vaisala, the southern road was good though after the Australians sealed it. We would be at the Hotel at 9:30 am in time for a late breakfast."

"That is still one of my favourite places in the world, pity they built that wharf of rocks, they all ended up on the beach in the cyclone."

We came to the first village, and I remembered to start counting the churches. I had been told there were forty churches between the airport and Apia, but had never managed to count more than thirty eight of them.

With the advent of T.V. there were quite a few screens glowing through the local 'venetian blinds' as I called them, one could see into most of the fale's. Such a good invention to make, using many pieces of coconut matting in long narrow strips and then tied together so they could be pulled up during the day, and closed for warmth and privacy at night.

I had never had to sleep more than a few nights in a local fale, as it always reminded me of that one time when a rat that crawled in during the night waking me with such a fright that I started screaming.

Stephen said after that he would rather sleep on the beach, and that is exactly what he did. He took our mattresses down onto the beach with a sheet and we slept there for the night. When we woke in the morning we found our neighbours were there also. The rat had visited them as well so we both were down there to watch the dawn breaking.

It was a wonderful weekend to go to the northern side of Upolu, the main island of Samoa and take a little open motor boat from the mainland over to the small island. It only took twenty minutes and the lagoon was so shallow we could see all the coral heads all the way down to the bottom of the beautiful turquoise lagoon.

We were a little surprised when shown our primitive

fale by Lily the Resort owner, we had one of the four fale's on the beach. It had some steps up to it, but it was just as easy to sit on the edge and swing your legs up.

We were only given a foam mattress each and sheets and pillow to sleep in. So this was ours for the weekend. Further along the beach was a large fale where we were to eat. Along a path up the hillside in the trees were two toilets and two showers.

Well everything that one needs, except I could see from Simon and Stephen's faces it was not quite what they had expected.

Lily insisted on making a cup of tea, and served it with some banana cake in the dining fale. She was so sweet we could not let her see our disappointment that it was not quite what we expected.

So we all made the best of it, and with the next boat arrival found we had some good companions for the weekend.

We spent the time reading, and lazing on the beach when not snorkelling around the island.

Catherine reminisces of happier times and with the screech of the brakes, brings herself back into the present thinking, 'Goodness how many churches is that we have past?'

"Toni is that the fourth or fifth church we have gone past?"

He laughed. "Miss Catherine you always forget to count and now you have me counting every time I come out, it is the fourth. Don't you remember this is the village that you gave the 'Best Village' award when you were here?"

"Oh is it? I had quite forgot. I did enjoy that week, especially been driven into every village, on Upolu and

Savaii. Some of them I could never find again."

I remembered having been asked by the head of the UN, to judge at the last minute as his wife had fallen ill, so I was hurriedly invited to take her place. Each morning I would be picked up by a Government car and with Mr. White and Willie, a Dutch woman whose husband was working on an aid project, were driven to another starting point.

Mr. White with his usual efficiency would hand out papers for the day, each one marked with the villages we were to visit, and a column for First, Second and other Prize holders.

We always started with a good heart and motivation, but after a good lunch in a village, we returned to the car, and had difficulty in keeping awake. By the late afternoon we had to ask one another what they thought of each village, to make sure everyone was awake.

We went from Falefa in the west, to the village at the end of the road where the ferry left for Savaii. Another day we went over the Cross Island road and turned right and followed the road to the end. We visited one village that had flowers all along the road through the village.

We were met by the Head Matai and walked in procession to the beach at the far end. The beautiful little beach had been used for the film "Blue Lagoon" many years previously and had become quite a tourist attraction for day trippers.

It was such fun, and having my first video camera I broke away from the procession so I could film it. Just as well as I guided Simon and Leticia back there the next day and all the flowers were gone. The villagers had been very clever and had decoratively placed freshly cut flowers there just before our arrival. If this had not happened we would have given them first prize instead of the village near the airport. The prize was $500 which was a lot of money for the village, and I always wondered what it was used for.

Savaii was an experience in itself. We flew there and this time the pilot took us right across the middle part of the island and we looked down into an extinct volcano. The plane was small and I had to sit at the rear of the six-seater plane, where there was no window, I think I closed my eyes on quite a few occasions.

We stayed at the Vaisala Hotel and visited the Northern Road first. It was in a terrible state and you could not really call it a road, it was more like a donkey track. In one place we drove down a dry river bed and the 4WD was the only vehicle that could have done this. We had borrowed the vehicle from the New Zealand Forestry Department.

They were busy replanting plantations of pine and Australian Eucalyptus trees. It was an area that had been torn to pieces by an earlier cyclone but the trees were growing very quickly in the two years they had been planted.

None of us were to realize that it would all be torn to pieces yet again in a few years' time in one of the worst cyclones they had ever experienced. However this time the cyclone would destroy the lovely little Roman Catholic Chapel on the tip of Faleolepo village. The last village to see the sunset in the world. From here you could see the sunset in tomorrow, as the International Dateline was out there on the horizon.

My two favourite churches were on this road, and I named them the Twin Cathedrals. Two huge white churches almost next door to one another. One of which had a definite French influence.

I had asked Mr. White if we could stop for a few minutes, and he said of course, he was just as interested in going inside as I was.

It all seemed so peaceful here, and we thought how strange to be here in a church very like a European one, but know we were on an island in the Pacific that not many people would ever visit.

The driver told us as we drove along about the myths of Savaii. They were not myths to him but very real legends handed down from generation to generation.

One was of a young girl who had been buried in the village. When the eruption of 1916 came the lava flowed down the mountain to the sea. It covered the ground all around the village with its hard black rock substance, everywhere but around the grave.

So even today the villagers will take you to this small area and show you where the girl had been buried.

It was an exhausting day, and once we reached Salealonga we drove quickly back along the southern highway. The next day we returned and visited the villages along this road. We stopped with a picnic lunch at the famous blow holes. Lucky for us the tide was in and it was a magnificent display. I had seen the blowholes in Tonga, and it was equal to those but did not have the same rock terraces along the coast.

Here again we were told the story of a young man who went a little too close to one of the vents and was sucked down underneath. There was no hope of him surviving, so the people in the village had a service for him the next day.

The whole village was in mourning and had held the service on the rocks nearby the vent, and then returned to the village. It was quite a long walk and so they were very surprised later that day when the so called drowned man returned to the village.

He told them he had been sucked down into a cave, deep under the blow hole. He had managed to keep his head above water and eventually found a ledge to sit on. He had actually heard echoes from his own funeral service far up above.

Later when the tide went out he was able to swim out of the cave and make his way along the cliff until he eventually found a place he could climb up. What an amazing story.

Toni, my driver brings me back to the present, asking, "Miss Catherine, have you lost count of the Churches again?"

"Yes, how did you guess? I have been going down memory lane while sitting here thinking of Savaii and how I went there to Judge the Village of the Year. It is still my favourite island and I try to visit it every time I am here, but don't think I will visit this time, Samoa will never ever be the same to me again without..."

"Now don't you fret Miss Catherine, you must be brave for us all, especially Mr. Simon. He is so upset his family from England will not be coming."

"You know he rang them straight away, thinking they may be able to drive to London to catch a plane in time. But they would have needed four hours to catch the plane from Heathrow, and then wait for a connection in L.A."

"It would have meant a long wait for a connection so it was decided they would not come. They said they would come next week, and maybe it would be more of a help then as Mr. Simon did not know how long you could stay."

I knew his mother did not like flying, and people always said the month after a death was the worst. I had found this in my case when Stephen my dear husband passed.

Everybody was just marvellous when Stephen died and the week afterwards. People ringing to see if I would like to come and stay or have a meal. Then almost to the day one month later the telephone stopped ringing as did the flowers stop being delivered.

That was when I had decided to visit Leticia and Simon in Bangkok. It was the best thing at the time, and Leticia and I went up into the Golden Triangle where we had always wanted to visit.

The first lights of Apia flashed by as we passed the Mormon Temple with that large Gold figure shining under the spotlights in the dark.

"Which way home Miss Catherine. The back road or the waterfront?" Toni asked.

I agreed as it would be good to finally be by the sea again. As we turned the corner at Four Corners I looked at the coffin shop. Oh dear I suppose that is where Leticia's coffin will come from, or maybe Lesi's father had a suitable one in stock.

My mind drifted back to the time that the Norris's, a couple from Blenheim in the South Island, had gone to a lot of trouble to especially choose the best timber for their packing case. Peter was a builder and thought he would build a boat while in Apia, working for Morris Hedstrom's Hardware. So he had made his container out of the best wood he could find.

This was packed and duly sent by ship via Fiji to Apia. When the ship arrived they received no ship's message to say it was on board. Having the ships documents with them, they went down to the wharf to see why it had not come in.

Somebody had seen their possessions stacked in the back of the shed. Upon looking, they confirmed that they were all their possessions. They were told someone from the Customs Department had come and removed the contents and driven off with the packing case. These packing cases were very sort after, as most people keep them until their return passage to New Zealand. So where had their packing case disappeared to?

On making enquiries one of the staff at work had told Peter that they had seen a beautiful new coffin in the shed when they had gone to look for one for an aunt who had recently died. They were immediately taken with this unusual coffin and upon opening it, saw the name Peter Norris. C/- Morris Hedstrom's, Apia, Western Samoa stamped inside.

They went straight back to work and told Peter who went to see it for himself. The poor owner of the shop said he had bought the packing case in good faith. He had let it be known he would buy any unwanted packing cases. This was not the first he had bought, but definitely the best wood. It was a deep Matai and not the usual light thin cork board type wood used.

No matter how much they questioned him he would not say who had bought it in, in fact he didn't seem to remember as he paid cash for it.

The lights of the main street made it look uninteresting until we turned at the market. Here were quite a few lights from people who slept in the market overnight with their produce. It was a place that I enjoyed shopping in, and especially the handicraft section. But you had to be early as the heat came very quickly in the morning, and I had found shopping by 8 am a must.

The waterfront was quiet just a light at Otto's Grotto for the late night drinkers. A great meeting place for ex pats after work, with a sea shanty theme which had an added bonus being on the seaside as it had a little breeze.

In moments we were outside Aggie Grey's and the welcoming lights at the front entrance beside the large tree showed a group of people chatting outside.

It must have been quite a place during World War Two when the Americans used it as their Club. Aggie and her sister Mary had been great hostesses at the time, serving the G.I.s with hamburgers.

It was always a great place on a Tuesday night to go to their traditional dance night and see Auntie Mary still dancing the graceful Siva, for at least one dance. She was so elegant with her dark Samoan outfit and her dainty gold evening shoes. She danced well into her eighties and played a very good game of bridge.

I saw her once open her hand on six points instead of the usual twelve or thirteen, when we asked her why. She said. "I felt like a gamble, and it put the opposition off bidding didn't it?"

I wonder how she has taken Leticia's death, she was so fond of her. They had become such good friends. I know Leticia would take her for drives sometimes along the coast to Falefa in the morning when it was cool.

We slowed down and as we past the Seaside Inn, a dog rang out barking at the car. Too many dogs in Samoa roaming aimlessly these days, they always frightened me.

We entered the familiar village, drove past the church and rounded the corner, past the entrance to the Deep and in through the gates of the Residency.

Chapter 4

Vaiala

There were lights on all along the patio, and as we drove up Pae hurriedly ran out to greet us waving, with Simon a few steps behind. Pae is Toni's wife and she must have been waiting for the car at the front door, and then she stepped back to let Simon come down the steps first.

Toni went around to open the door, and as I stepped out Simon was there to help me. I stood up and we hugged one another for a few moments, and then he walked back to the house and I followed.

Pae was on the steps and she threw her big arms around me and hugged me close. We didn't speak for a few moments and then she said, "Oh Miss Catherine, I prayed you would come, now everything will be alright, you will help us all won't you?"

Trying to act braver than I actually felt I replied, "I will try Pae, I will try. But we must all help one another."

We went inside and there in the hall was that large oil painting of Leticia that had been done so many years ago. It was as if she was welcoming me, I stopped for a second and smiled at it.

'Yes,' I thought, 'we are all here together, you have just gone out of the room for a moment.'

Simon seemed to be keeping it together with his stoic British stiff upper lip, invites, "Why don't you go with Pae and freshen up first, then come into the Garden Room and have a nightcap, or would you prefer a cup of tea and something to eat? Mata is still up and has some of your favourite cucumber sandwiches made, and I think there is a banana cake freshly baked, I can still smell it."

Toni came in with the suitcase and chilli bin. "The chilli bin for the kitchen is it Miss Catherine? And your suitcase I suppose in the Blue Bedroom that you usually have?"

"Sorry Catherine," said Simon, "Of course Pae will have made up your room."

Pae was already walking down the passage, across those black and white tiles that were laid throughout the house, "I'll be with you in a moment Simon," I said, and followed behind her.

I loved the blue room with its Laura Ashley curtains and matching bedspread. Everything was in place as usual and a small lamp was on by the bed, a small vase of Cecil Brunner roses also and the latest English House and Garden magazine.

Pae laid the suitcase over by the wardrobe and asked, "Do you want me to unpack?"

"Oh yes please Pae, just hang up the frocks that is all and the sponge bag in the bathroom. Is there enough hot water for a bath tonight it may help me to sleep? Of course I won't run it now. Mr Simon will want to talk."

"Oh dear Miss, none of us can really accept that Miss Leticia will not come back," a saddened Pae walked back over to me and we hugged again.

"Now Pae you said we must be strong, especially for Mr. Simon and tomorrow will be a difficult day. Why don't you go to bed now and we will see each other in the morning?"

Pae dutifully left the room and I splashed some cold water on my face, washed my hands and walked back to the Garden Room to speak with Simon. I found him asleep, slumped in his chair and I had to wake him.

"Come now Simon, you better fix me a brandy and then tell me all about it."

Simon opens his eyes and steadies himself in his favourite chair, "Well I do not know where to start, I seem to have gone over it time and time again, looking for any missing pieces. When I came home Leticia was not here. I asked Pae and Toni who had been out for the afternoon but they had left Leticia reading in the Morning Room. Then Mata came in and said Leticia had gone off to the Deep she thought about three or four."

"She didn't really notice as Leticia said to take the afternoon off, but Mata went back into the kitchen to make a banana cake. Later when she came in with afternoon tea, Leticia was not there. So she thought she must have gone down to the Deep."

"It was not until later, when I went over to ask Jack if he had seen her, that we realized she had gone out to the fale, but nobody saw her return."

"Jack went out and as it was the end of the day he didn't wait for any more tourists to come. I rang Aunty Mary and all her bridge friends to see if she had gone into town afterwards for a drink at the Club. But nobody had heard from her at all. That is when I became concerned and thought I had better ring the police."

"Sergeant Tui came around immediately, he must have been at a Function and was not in his usual uniform. In fact he had an island shirt and lavalava on, so someone must have said that it was Mr Simon on the telephone. I cannot remember when we last spoke."

"I noticed that he had another police car behind him so he must have thought there was some trouble. He came straight to the point and asked if he could be of help."

"Well what could I tell him, Leticia was late home, it was unusual and it was dark and the curfew had long since finished. Anyway she was used to the curfew and would not have driven into the village unless it was an emergency, she would have left the car at the church and walked in on foot from the beach end."

"I must say she always respected the curfew but I found it a darned nuisance. Pae would never leave the house in the middle of curfew and would rather wait the extra thirty minutes until it was over."

Simon takes a sip of whisky and then relays verbatim the conversation with the sergeant.

"The sergeant said, "Let us take this slowly and in your own time. So Miss Leticia was not home when you arrived home, what time would that be Sir?"

"I responded with "The usual time 6 o'clock. I like to be home well before curfew. They are good about it in the village, but we do not like to break the curfew unless absolutely necessary. I must have dozed off in my chair for longer than expected and I think it was the church bells that woke me up."

"I thought it odd Leticia was not around so I asked Mata and she said Miss Leticia was not at home. Then she told me she had last seen her going down to the Deep around 3 or 3:30 pm. I do not know why but I thought I will walk down and ask Jack what time she had left. Well he told me he did not see her leave."

"So I walked back and rang Aunty Mary to see if she had gone into see her and maybe had stayed on for a pre-dinner drink. She often took the old lady down to see the sunset at Pilot's Point and then they would have a drink before Aunty Mary went into dinner. But no she had not seen her, so then I went through the ringing list near the telephone to see if she had gone to friends."

Simon falters and is on the verge of tears, so I as calmly as I could say gently, "You don't have to recall all the story with the Police right now."

Simon looks at me through his sad brown eyes. "It's okay I would rather tell you everything now and get through it," so he continues with his encounter with the policeman.

"I remember coming home and when I rang her bridge group up at the top of the Hill. Jill Taylor told me her husband was late coming home that night, and as the staff had gone she was nervous as they had had villagers in the garden. So she had made the girls promise they would not come home until Mark came home. The girls did not arrive home that night until after 7 pm by the time they dropped the other two off."

"But nobody had seen or heard from her since the day before yesterday. I'm sorry Tui that is when I rang you, probably some reasonable explanation and she will tell me off for troubling you."

"Tui was so kind and said to me, "No trouble at all Sir that is what we are here for. We have had some tourists enter the country during the last week, and we are checking up on them."

"Nothing at the moment but we do look over the arrival list just to make sure that nobody on Interpol's wanted Red List uses Samoa as an entry into Australia and New Zealand. It has been known of late that people from the States are using different Pacific Islands as a stop off. Then several days later they take another flight onto their destination. So our turn around flight is not checked on arrival to the same extent as the flights direct from the States."

"Now I will ask some of the boys out in the pickup to check on all the bars, and restaurants in town in case she has met some friends and called in there. Also see if her car is in the garage. And I would like to ask Toni, Pae and Mata separately to have a word with me. Is there somewhere we can talk to them in a relaxed manner so they will not become nervous and think they have done something wrong?"

"And I replied, "Of course use the Morning Room everyone feels more relaxed in there."

"So he went over the afternoon again with them and returned to me in the dining room where I had gone to the bar to pour myself a very stiff whiskey."

"Would you like to join me?" I asked Tui."

"No sir I am on duty, maybe another time. One or two more questions if I may Sir?" he asked."

"Was your wife upset by anything lately? Had anyone upset her? Was she quite happy?"

"What do you mean Tui, she is always happy, a little too much sometimes, she wears herself out, running this house, entertaining people, and keeping an eye on the British women in the community especially the new arrivals, or the young mothers."

"Quite so, no offence Sir just trying to make a mental picture of her movements in the last few days. Did she say she had seen or heard from anyone new to the community?"

"Well yes she did mention she thought she saw someone she and Catherine used to know when they were twelve or thirteen. But she said that it was at a distance, so she was unable to know for sure."

"You see we are always aware of people around us, you have to be in this line of work. You never know when you will meet them again and we try to remember their name and where we have met them as part of the job so to say."

The lengthy interrogation came to an end and Simon took a large sip of his whisky to steady his nerves. He had spent some time catching me up on his conversation and chain of events with the friendly local policeman when I interrupted Simon and said, "She told me the same thing on the telephone just the other day, but the satellite interference cut us off and I didn't catch the name. Simon, did she mention the name of our old friend?"

Simon thought hard, "I did think it was odd that an old friend didn't look Leticia up. Most people do ring from Aggie's and ask if we will go along and have a drink for old times' sake. If we hit it off, of course we ask them back here for dinner, or take them over the hill to one of the beaches for the day. I think his name was Alberto or Roberto, some Italian name like that."

A shiver ran down my spine, Alberto lived quite close by us just after the war, he and his parents came out from Italy and rented a little cottage in the orchard next door.

Simon continues, "Anyway Tui took some notes and then went out to speak to his men. They went off in the pickup and Tui asked to use the telephone."

"Tui informed me, "There is very little we can do until it is light Sir, we must not rule out the possibility of course, ah I don't know how to put this. Maybe Miss Leticia had trouble in the Deep and couldn't make it back to shore. The tide was going out I believe and if she was unable to reach the coral walls of the Deep, she may have gone out through the gap."

There the unmentionable had been said. Just what I had put to the back of my mind, and every time it came to the surface I had hurriedly thought of something else. My brain wouldn't accept that explanation, as Letitia was such a strong swimmer.

Simon had finished relaying the story and with that he put his head down into his hands, gently sobbing. I walked over to him put my arm around his shoulders and let him take his time to look up again.

"Well of course I hardly slept, maybe I did for a few hours until the church bells at 5 am woke me up. To be truthful I don't remember going to bed, but I do remember Tui gave me a whiskey and then he must have gone, maybe it was several whiskeys later, it's all a bit of a haze."

"Then of course I waited to ring you but I needn't have worried as you are always awake early. By the way I'm sorry I haven't mentioned it, but I am so pleased you could come straight away, just not sure of the procedure from here on."

I smiled at Simon and then he says something else, "There is one worrying thing that Tui told me today. They insisted on a post mortem when they found her."

"Jack went out at first light and there she was near the fale. He could not lift her into the canoe so came ashore and rang the police straight away. He was worried she would go out with the tide and had put her on the edge of the Deep."

"They came immediately as they were in the pickup further along the beach as they thought she may have drifted along towards the gap in the reef. They bought her in and took her straight to the hospital. Then… well you know what, they insisted on... and then Tui came to see me, to say that there was not very much water in her lungs, whatever that means… seems there should have been more. It looks as if she may have died before she drowned but that doesn't make any sense."

The room fell silent as we both sat there thinking through what the Police had said. Reflecting to myself, 'What could have happened out there?'

I then plucked up enough courage and said to Simon, "She was always so careful and never went out there unless other people were around. Although she was a strong swimmer, Leticia did get cramp sometimes and she told me she would make sure there was somebody else out there in case she needed help."

"So there must have been someone maybe a tourist who talked to her while out there. Probably it's too late to find out who, as people come and go so much in this place. But I am sure Sergeant Tui will have looked into that."

Simon in deep thought reveals, "I must say, she has not been herself over the last few days. When she went for her jog around the village, she said something about going at different times. It seemed strange at the time as she preferred to go as soon as it was dawn when the village was out and about."

There was silence once again and then Simon said, "Look it has been a long day for us both, I suggest that we go to bed. I do not say to sleep but there are sleeping pills in the house if you would like one?"

"Leticia used to say just half a tablet will give you a good sleep and you do not feel too tired in the morning, better than lying awake half the night waiting until the first light."

"I will find them for you and suggest that you take a half, and maybe the other half tomorrow night. What do you think? Would you like another nightcap, although that may not mix too well?"

"Yes, good idea Simon, it has been a long day, and you are right, I will probably lie awake thinking, a sleeping pill would be a good idea."

He stood and went out of the room, a little hunched I thought, what a time he has had, and worse to come tomorrow.

He returned so quickly with the bottle in his hand, "Now be careful won't you, just a half tablet."

I laughed "I promise you that I will not sleep through my own sister's funeral, you take care also."

I walked up to him took both his arms, and said, "I cannot say sweet dreams, but I know from experience that day by day it does become easier. It took me a long time, there are so many stages for you to go through yet. But believe me you are not the only person out there experiencing grief, there are many before you like myself, and unfortunately there will be many more people following your path."

I turned and hurried out of the room, better for him to be on his own now with his thoughts and memories, at the moment it is all too unreal, he probably felt numb and he would need to find his own path to follow as best as he could.

The flowers in the hall had a lovely perfume, maybe it was my favourite 'Yesterday, Today and Tomorrow.' The lovely little purple, mauve and white flowers. Yes, what a lovely thought Yesterday, Today and Tomorrow and then we will see.

It took no time to prepare for bed, and how inviting it looked, Pae had turned the covers down and plumped up the pillows, and even a thermos of iced water near the bed.

I undressed and into my favourite lavalava and reached out for the bottle with half a tablet, and a glass of water.

Turned out the light, and try to relax, don't think about tomorrow, it will come soon enough.

Sweet dreams Leticia wherever you are, maybe somewhere out there in the sky.

Our Mother used to tell us when someone died, they actually had gone on a wonderful trip. They took a plane up into the sky to another place. Leticia thought it a wonderful place to go to and called an aeroplane a car birdie and that is exactly what it was to a small child.

The last thing I heard was a clock chiming somewhere in the house, and I would not hear another thing until the Church Bells woke me the following morning, calling the village to prayers.

Chapter 5

The Funeral

I had not slept very well, maybe it was getting use to the bed again or the unfamiliar heat. However the fan had been gently turning all night and at least there were no mosquitos. Normally I was woken by the gentle call of the first birds at dawn, there are no other birds like that in the world. I felt quite at home in my favourite Blue Bedroom.

Then I sat up with a start, this was not my first morning on holiday but the funeral of my dear sister. What a terrible day ahead of me, just how does one get through a day like this?

Some people take pills, others start to drink early in the day, and others sit, weep and look into space. Well I was not going to do any of those things, I was here to bring support to Simon and the household. Let's pray that I had the strength to do just that. With no other family around it was going to be hard.

There had not been enough time for people to fly out from England, and the family in New Zealand would never had made the plane in time like me. Or was it that Simon didn't want them at this time as it would be more trouble looking after them?

Well most of them were getting on in years, and the heat always affected Aunt May but she would have made an effort. Knowing her she probably would have gone straight out into the kitchen with Mata and wanted to bake a cake. She loved baking cakes, and I must admit nobody could make a trifle quite like my dear Aunt May.

I looked around the room and thought of the time Leticia and myself had spent shopping for the curtains and bedspread for the room.

"Everything must be like a country garden," she had said. "I want my visitors to wake up with flowers everywhere, on the covers, curtains, and vases of flowers from the garden. Everything must be pink and blue," and that is what she planted in the garden.

Pae's gentle knock on the door bought me back to the present and I called out, "Come in Pae, you are a mind reader, that is exactly what I need to start this day, with a strong cup of tea."

She had thoughtfully put some bread and butter on the tray also, something that Leticia and myself had grown up with. We would go downstairs as soon as we were old enough to carry a tray, and make tea for our parents.

It took longer to learn to cut and butter the bread but that was something they always did in the hotels, when we were on holiday. Although the tray would be left at the door, and we would race to see who could bring it in.

Then if we were good we would be allowed to put sugar on the bread and eat the little triangles if we promised to go back to bed.

Pae greets me with her usual cheery voice but today it

sounded a touch sombre, "Good morning Miss Catherine, but I cannot say that it is a good morning for any of us."

"I know Pae but we will just have to pray that we will hold up together. Is Mr Simon up yet?"

"Oh yes," responds Pae, "He said not to hurry but he has been on the telephone to England."

I remember all the calls I have ever had from the other side of the world and most of them at the wrong time of the night. "Pardon me for saying but people never remember the difference in time do they? Well would you tell him I will not be long and make sure Mata makes a cooked breakfast this morning nice and early, and would she have any porridge for me? That will give me a good lining for the morning, and Mr. Simon may just eat it if he sees it on the sideboard."

"What a good idea," said Pae, "I will go and tell Mata straight away."

I jumped out of bed and hurried across to the bathroom.

A long shower would do me good, ended with a cold blast to fully waken me up.

When I came out of the shower there was little hesitation as to what frock would be worn today. The times we had joked about the purchase of a funeral frock, in case a neighbour or relation should die.

I can remember the day we went shopping and laughing at the thought of buying a frock with no occasion to wear it. Little did we realize at the time the first funeral would be Stephen's. Oh I simply must not think of that, not today.

Perhaps Stephen was there on the other side to welcome Leticia when she arrived. Evidently there was always a friend or family member to meet us when we die. It would be good to think that she would not be lonely, but have someone to greet her. A bit like arriving at an airport with somebody waiting for you, and to look after you until you settled in. Strange I had never thought of this before, but maybe it was like going to live in a new country and learning new ways.

Thinking to myself, I will just put on a lavalava for comfort until we change for church.

I hurried down the hall. I had always liked the black and white tiles it gave the house a sense of grace. Of course the large portrait of Leticia in the hall gave it the air of a country house.

It was the one item that always travelled with them. She had been greatly touched when asked to sit by a young artist. It had only taken six sittings, and he had caught the gaiety that always went hand and hand with her. She was such a bright, happy loving soul and I loved my times with her.

None of us, least of all the artist realized at the time he would become a most sort after portrait artist in England. I had heard recently he had been commissioned to paint one of the young newly married royals. I hope he had been well paid, it must be a dream for an artist to receive a commission to paint royalty.

He would never have to worry again about work, and could charge whatever he liked after that.

I walked into the dining room and Simon was already at the table with a plate of porridge.

"Good morning Simon I am pleased to see that you are starting the day the right way. Wouldn't the relations in Scotland laugh to see us having porridge for breakfast in the Tropics?"

I helped myself and sat down at the large well-polished

mahogany dining room table, a well preserved and loved piece of Antique furniture. Both Leticia and I loved anything that was tasteful and over one hundred years old, we had spent many hours looking through Antique shops together selecting furniture for each other.

Simon stood up from the table like a true gentleman and came around the table to lightly touch my shoulders.

"It is giving me strength just to know you are here, thank you for coming Catherine. I seriously don't know how I would cope with today if you weren't here."

There was a long silence. Neither of us wanted to speak, what was the point we would probably both upset one another.

Finally I said, "Today will be terrible for both of us, but we have each other to lean on, and the staff will be watching us closely for guidance also, so come, where's our English stiff upper lip." I don't know why I said it, it really is ridiculous how we are taught to hold all our emotions, good and bad deep within. It can't be good for us in the long term. Nevertheless as they say, one must soldier on.

However, it did break the atmosphere and he sat down again and finished his first cup of tea.

Pae came in and said, "Mr Simon and Miss Catherine, can you come out here please, I don't want to hurry you but Father Tala rang to say he would be here when Miss Leticia comes from the hospital at 8 am. Also some of the village ladies will come soon with food and they will wonder where you would like us to set up the tables. Do you want the food to be served under the trees, or do you want it on the rear verandah?"

Pae then withdraws a little, embarrassed about what

she is going to say next. "Also do you want Miss Leticia inside in one of the main rooms, or would you like her on the front patio? I only ask now as we will have to make plenty of room for the people to be able to sit around the coffin. Shall we go and look?"

"I am sorry Mr Simon but we want to make sure everything runs as smoothly as possible as this is a first time for us all to be involved in a palagi funeral. We just want the best for Miss Leticia."

We followed Pae out to the patio, where Toni was waiting to look at the space together.

I saw the pain on Simon's face as he replied, "It is best to do what you feel comfortable with, this is a first time that the village and the people in the house have had a shared death together."

"Remember we are the palagi and whatever we do will be respected, but it is their wish that we bought Leticia to the house so they can say their farewells in their culture. It is a mixture of both cultures, and so we must help one another at this time."

Toni came forward, and said, "We will move the furniture Mr. Simon and then it will give plenty of room for the mourners to come and sit around Miss Leticia."

"Oh good Toni you do what is necessary Miss Catherine will go inside until you are ready," Simon replied.

We walked back inside and returned to the dining room although neither of us wanted to eat another thing. After sitting over a cup of tea, Pae soon returned in her black frock and looking around I thought we do look a sad lot, all in black it is most depressing.

Thinking a moment, I broke the silence, "Now come on you two we all have to stand together as family today and each one must help the other so that we do not let Leticia down, she would want us to be brave and that will also help the people around us. Right so chins up and think how lucky we all are to have such a lovely place to share our sorrow together. Pae don't forget to water the plants as usual as plants need water just like we all do."

Pae looked a little taken back, "But Miss Catherine that is the first thing I do in the morning when I arrive, and they have all been watered as usual."

I felt a little guilty as of course Pae would carry on as always no matter how difficult it would be for us all in the days to come.

Toni was soon back in the room. "All that is taken care of and the patio is ready, Pae would you like to put the fine mats out now, or shall I do it?"

"We will do it together," said Pae. "The mats are all in the spare bedroom where I slept last night. Just ask the girls to help bring them around the front and I will lay them out."

"Oh I simply must get ready!" I realised to my horror and raced to my room to change into the funeral frock.

Soon enough we all went through the house to wait outside for Leticia's arrival. The Black hearse backing slowly into position, and Simon leading us over to stand near the hearse as two men opened the rear door and slid the coffin out.

Toni and Simon took their place at the head of the coffin, the two men who had helped slide it out next, and two more from Vaiala village that had been waiting under the trees, came and took up the rear.

Gently they lifted it together and walked up the front steps of the residency to the patio. Pae stood here and showed them where to place the coffin. She thoughtfully had it placed long ways, therefore giving plenty of room for people to come through and out the far end of the patio onto the lawn.

When the coffin had been placed in position Pae and her two daughters put the fine mats around the coffin and one on top. This was her special family mat and onto it she placed some fresh Bougainvillea from the garden, pink of course and some small fern leaves.

She then sat down at the head of the coffin and bowed her head. We felt a little left out, but now was the time for Pae to take over and we would be guided by her.

As if a signal had been given some of the village ladies appeared from nowhere and waited at the bottom of the steps.

I came forward and asked Pae if they should come in.

"Yes," she said, "they will join me now and others will come later to replace them." With a nod from her they came forward and kissed myself and Simon on both cheeks in Polynesian manner and then walked over to Pae. They embraced her and her daughters and then sat cross legged on both sides of the coffin and prayed.

After that a succession of people came in twos and threes giving us the same acknowledgement, with each of them sitting for a few minutes by the coffin and then moving forward and along the patio and out into the garden.

We were pleased the coffin was closed, and this was the only time there had been a slight disagreement with Pae, as she had wanted it to remain open. We both found this too distressing and Simon insisted that it was to remain closed. He had said his farewells to Leticia, and I wished to remember her as she was, not a lifeless unknown unsmiling person. My memory of her was to remain the bright golden girl that I loved, always smiling and running from one important issue to the next.

It was beginning to warm up now that the sun was higher in the sky, and only the shade of the huge flame tree was giving us shelter in the garden from the sun. I felt out of place not knowing whether to sit, or stand or kneel so I decided to sit to one side on one of the large cane chairs.

Simon seemed out of place and he also sat for a while until the Vicar came.

Father Tala arrived late as usual, a little like his services. Today he was dressed in white and the only one who looked cool in the rising heat of the morning. He came up the steps puffing as usual and immediately went to Simon.

"Mr. Winchester…" the Vicar started.

"Mr. Simon please, just like the rest of the village Father Tala," Simon corrected.

"Mr. Simon, it is a sad day for us all and Miss Catherine welcome to the island. We will all have to be brave and remember that Miss Leticia would not want us to have long faces all day, she would want us to remember her kindness and enthusiasm for life."

He then continues after acknowledging both of us with, "We must thank the Lord for the good times we have all had together, and now that she has gone to a better place, we must think of her being happy there, and kindly watching over us all."

"I can just hear her saying, "Oh Father Tala do not be so serious. We are all so lucky to live in such a beautiful place, a place full of flowers and mostly happy faces. There are a lot of unhappy people in this world, hungry which none of us here will ever be. Let us enjoy what is around us and think we are some of the chosen few. Why the Lord would have said, 'While there is fish in the sea, and coconuts in the trees we will never starve,' and how right he was. So we should all rejoice today for having known such a positive person."

With that he went over to Pae who by this time was standing and knelt down beside her, and started with the Lord's Prayer. We of course knelt also and although the mats were hard on our knees stayed in this position until he had finished.

Thankfully it was not the longest prayer he had ever made, maybe he was thinking of his knees also.

The morning went by as more of the village appeared and then people in businesses on the way to work stopped to offer their condolences.

Mata was on hand with jugs of cold coconut milk and ever ready cups of tea, for the palagi's who looked a little self-conscious with the large number of locals, as they were greeted by Simon.

I was quite amazed at the people who did come firstly to the house, most would come to the funeral of course.

For most this would be a first as far as a funeral for a palagi was concerned. Of course many years ago it was the normal procedure but now only in special circumstances such as the spouse of a Samoan.

Or as we had always jokingly said, "Don't be seriously ill on a Saturday afternoon after the plane has gone to New Zealand as you cannot fly out until Tuesday and that is often too late."

Leticia would have appreciated it that she was to stay on the Island. But had often said. "When I visit the cemetery with Auntie Mary if there is one spare plot there I would like to go there, but make sure it is when the Frangipani come into flower as it is like blossom time in England." Well she was to have her wish in the most unexpected manner.

Shortly afterwards around 8:30 am, Sergeant Tui arrived looking quite different this time in a black coat, white collared shirt and dark tie and a white lavalava instead of the usual blue the police always wore here in Apia. He went up to Simon and said, "May we have a private word, and of course with Miss Catherine if she wishes?"

We both looked at one another and went into the house and of course to the Morning Room. It was cool in here and everything looked as inviting as ever. Pae had placed new flowers in the vases and a sweet smell of one of the flowers made it almost like a florist shop.

"To come straight to the point, Sir. We are watching the airport. I know there are only the local flights to Savaii today, but there is a yacht there at the far end of the island and they have not come ashore to clear Customs yet. I have sent someone out to go aboard and see who they are."

"They are flying a flag but nobody was sure what it was, it is always difficult to distinguish a flag from the shore if there is no breeze. It is easy for a yacht to come in and anchor near the airstrip and then with the motors of today, to leave without actually coming ashore."

"There is also the inter-island boat going back and forwards, but it's very obvious if a foreigner sails that way as you can appreciate having done it so many times before. The other possibility is the Salamasima to Pago Pago but it doesn't go out again until Friday night so we can forget that."

"The next flight is Tuesday, but that doesn't say

unfortunately that someone didn't fly out on the plane that Miss Catherine came in on, so we are checking on all the passengers on that flight."

"We have also been down to the two hotels Aggie's and the Tusitala, and of course the two guest houses, any foreigner staying in those would be just too obvious especially at the Waterfront Inn. People who want to remain anonymous would be better to stay in one of the two hotels. So many tourists and business men come and go and the staff do not take much notice, and neither do other guests."

"Sorry, I'm following up on what you told me the other day, we are looking for an Italian looking man probably in his late 60's so that should not be too hard. But then he has lived in Australia or New Zealand for many years, and his manner and speech would be normal. Maybe if he had friends they would be a little more obvious."

"The staff have mentioned there is a tall grey haired man staying at the Tusitala who has asked a lot of questions about quiet places to go to on the island of Savaii, seems he would like to stay over there for a few days, or he may be already over there."

"The Vaisala is the obvious choice as there really is nowhere else to stay."

Looking towards me he says, "Miss Catherine could you give me more of an idea of this man Alberto? I know it is difficult as you have not seen him for a long time, but maybe he had some interesting features, or a way of speech, or hot temper, or something like that."

I cast my mind back to my memory of him as a teenager, describing, "He was rather heavy for his age like a very stocky chest, black curly hair often slicked back with lots of hair oil, and ice blue eyes that seemed to look right through you."

"Sorry Sergeant Tui but I think that's about all. Maybe he is not here at all. Although the island is large it is not when you are a tourist looking for somewhere to go. Maybe he did leave on the plane I came in on, that should not be hard to follow up. That is if he is travelling on his own passport."

Sergeant Tui was happy with what we could tell him, replying, "Thank you again, just let me know if there is anything the police or myself can do? We will of course see you soon, at St, Mary's at 9 am. As a precaution, we will have some plain clothes men there, who will look like members of the congregation."

"Because there are a lot of local people it will be easy to pick any foreigner out. Maybe there could be a reporter or two, and I have heard there will be quite a following from the Diplomatic Corps and the United Nations."

"Also there is a New Zealand detective David Harris who will be helping assist our investigation, I believe he was sitting with you yesterday on the plane coming up Miss Catherine. He came in with the diplomatic bag for the NZ High Commission so he has a security clearance from Wellington. Has he made contact with you Mr. Simon?"

Simon looked at me and then said "No" to the Sergeant.

"I'm so sorry, I had completely forgotten about him," I felt guilty immediately upon not having mentioned him before to Simon.

"As a matter of fact he did sit next to me and we had an enjoyable dinner together. I told him I was upset, and yes he did mention he was from Wellington travelling with The Black Bag."

"That is fine," said the Sergeant, "If he makes contact let us know, he will probably be at the funeral with the rest of the staff especially as he has already met you Miss Catherine. Now if you will excuse me I better head back to the office in time for the raising of the Flag, I must see that the men go out on time. Mustn't keep the tourists waiting, must we?"

Off he went and looking at my watch I thought he would have to hurry to be at the police station on time. But surely they were organized enough every morning to be at the corner by 8 am.

The times that Leticia would race to the market and try and beat the 'Turn Out' at the corner on the way home. If we missed we still had time to go the back way over the bridge and past Mr. White's house. But it was such a nuisance, better to time ourselves to stay longer in the market or go to the supermarket.

I suddenly felt very tired and thought a little lie down would be in order, and so excused myself. I'm sure Pae would come and tell me when it was time to leave for the Church. Or would the hearse come back early? I hoped so and then we could drive to the Church and find the coffin already in place when we arrived.

It was wonderful to put my feet up on the bed and in a few minutes I was sound asleep. In no time I was back at the Bay thinking of Alberto, but mostly of the lovely Queen cakes his Mother used to make. She was always so good and sent them along when we had a party. In fact I think she always had some in her cake tin. Just so light and airy nobody could make them like her.

Suddenly I woke with a start, Pae gently shaking my arm. "Time to get ready," said Pae. "They will be here in a minute with the hearse, and you will want to see her leave I am sure."

No I didn't really but of course I must put on a brave face.

I quickly combed my hair washed my face and was down the hall as the hearse arrived in the drive bang on 8:50am. The same procedure again with the six men taking their places and the fine mats on the floor had been removed.

I stood back as they walked by somehow it didn't seem that we were looking at Leticia's coffin going by. Should I have seen her in it before they closed it? No better not to think about it.

A little hesitation as they walked down the steps, and then a sad prayer from Father Tala as much as to say goodbye from the House and the garden. Then the door was closed and the driver quickly took his place behind the wheel and the hearse moved in a circle under the flame trees not yet in flower and then through the gates and out onto the main road.

I wonder if you should wave, silly but thought that is what I want to do, so I did so.

"Inside," instructed Simon, "and let us have a quick drink to fortify us. Toni is sure to have put the drinks out for us."

Should we? I thought, but yes Leticia would have approved. I hurried in after him and in the dining room on the sideboard were the two decanters ready with square cut crystal glasses and a jug of iced water in a thermos. Simon poured the drinks and handed one to me, raising his glass toasting, "To Leticia, safe travels to where ever you are going."

We gave a silent acknowledgement to her portrait which hung over the sideboard.

We drank our drinks quickly, and strolled out to the car which Toni had bought around to the front door.

The car, named after its number plate 'DC1' shone gleamingly in the bright sunlight, Toni must have given it a quick polish while waiting. The cream car was cool inside as the air conditioning must have been running for a few minutes.

As we pulled out, the White Subaru station wagon pulled in behind us driven by Pae's son, the girls and Mata all dressed up sitting inside.

As we slowly passed through Vaiala village, to my amazement some of the villagers stood with heads bowed and it made me feel a little sad that Leticia could not see this final salute of respect from the people she had done so much for.

As we went by the entrance of the Deep there was Jack with his wife and children all dressed for the funeral. Behind him stood two male tourists in shorts and shirts, and then I felt a cold chill as both men looked dark and heavy not like the locals but more Italian or was my mind playing tricks with me? Is that the man on the plane who dropped his book? Should we stop the car? But then what would I say? Maybe it was a trick of the light from the coconut trees and it wasn't the man on the plane?

As I hesitated they turned their backs on me and went off down the path amongst the trees. So that was the end of that, and now I must give Simon every bit of support for the next few hours, or would it be the other way around?

We drove slowly along the waterfront and turned up the road by the little church on the corner, past the bakery and then up past the school grounds, turning into the entrance to the Church. The Anglican Church had always been a favourite of mine, and recently painted by the men from one of the Australian Naval ships. Such a good idea of Father Tala's to ask the Australian High Commission if the men from the small frigate that came once a year to help with the Church Fete, could they while in port, take the Church over as an interest and keep it painted. They not only did that but they also raised some bar funds and kept the Vicarage in order as well.

Lately they also had renovated the Church Hall and put a little seat out under the trees. The tennis court was in better order than it had been for years, and the crew would come here and play in the late afternoons. Mrs Tala would make them tea at the Vicarage with her favourite scones. The men said they felt so at home at the church, no matter if they belonged to different churches at home, they always were part of the family of St. Mary's while in port.

There was a policeman at the gate directing traffic, as there were too many cars today to park in the church grounds. So many of the cars were directed further up the street and around the corner near the supermarket.

We of course went straight in to the grounds and parked in the usual place under the trees near the Sunday school. Toni came around and opened the door allowing us to walk around to the front of the church, thank goodness the hearse had moved towards the Vicarage.

We climbed the steps decorated with pots of flowers and past the usual two dogs that seem to spend most of their time outside the church, sometimes we would catch one of them wandering down the aisle during the service.

We walked down the aisle and found the church full

on both sides. Most of the congregation would be the members of St. Mary's but there were others from the business community and the expats from different walks of life. We slipped into the front right hand pew and knelt.

Goodness it was already so hot in here at only 9 am, although I noticed the fans were going at full speed. The brass gleamed on the altar, and the plague for Sir Guy Powles gleamed on the wall next to me. The young choir were all seated to the side and in front of us, and the organist on the other side was playing something quietly.

Suddenly Father Tala came out and stood tall beside the altar in front of us and looking down at both of us, spoke the first words of the service.

From here on it became difficult for me to concentrate on what he was saying, my mind started to wander and my eyes were drawn to the sun coming in through the stained glass window above the altar, highlighting the attendees of the Last Supper.

How many times over the last few years would Leticia look up as I was doing now, and never thinking that one day she would be here in her coffin with us all sitting and listening to Father Tala giving her this service.

Suddenly I came out of my dreams to hear his special welcome to Miss Catherine in this sad time, and that at the end of the service we would be going to the cemetery, and afterwards all would be welcome at the Residency.

Goodness I hope they don't all come back to the house I thought. Will there be enough tea cups and food? But then why worry everybody would arrive with a plate as usual. After all it was the Tropics.

Half way through the service Mr White stood up and headed up the front steps. Goodness was he going to speak, we had always wondered if he was a Christian or not. Well at times like this did it really matter?

He started by saying, "It is an honour to speak on this occasion and on behalf of my family and friends of Apia, I have been asked to say a few words about out departed friend."

"We came to this island unsure of our position within the community, we were told it could be difficult as people from our country were not always made welcome here."

"The first official function we attended was a cocktail party at Aggie's for some dignitary here for one of those flying 24 hour visits. As he arrived and crossed the room with his aides I found myself standing alone with one blonde palagi. It seemed that we had not moved in time to one or other side of the hall. So here we were stranded until he moved on."

"Leticia had a camera which later I realized she always carried.

"Oh goodness," she said turning to me, "I will be in trouble again with Simon by making an obvious mistake. It is just that the camera was left in the car, and as he would not go back for me I had to. Then arriving at the door with whatever-his-name was I was then stopped by one of the guards, and was almost asked if I could show them my passport. 'Don't be silly' I replied, 'What Lady goes around at a cocktail party with a passport."

At the moment the dignitary having nowhere else to go between the two groups stopped in front of us.

"Good evening," he said, "And who do I have the pleasure in meeting?" Quickly Leticia took over."

"May I present the Head of the United Nations, Mr White. He has recently arrived from New York. And I am the unfortunate wife of the British Consul Mr. Simon Winchester. Well no I have put that quite wrong, my husband will be quite upset that I am not with him at this moment on the right side of the room, instead of being stranded here, but this kind gentleman took pity on me and stood with me."

He laughed heartedly and said, "This is so refreshing in a situation like this. Do you realize that you will now be seen on US television tomorrow, and everyone will wonder who these delightful people are causing so much attention," and with that he moved on."

"That was Leticia's introduction to me, she had done her homework as always, and made the most out of an embarrassing situation. I am honoured to say that she and Simon became our closest friends on the island from then on," Then turning to the casket, "Thank you for your kindness Leticia."

He then took his seat and sat down. There was another hymn and then the service came to an end. Well what I remembered of it.

Suddenly everybody stood and Father Tala gave the committal for those that would not come onto the cemetery.

Then the pallbearers came forward, this time not Simon but his Deputy from the office Peter Stevenson. Then the organist started to play 'Tie a Yellow Ribbon around the Old Oak Tree.' I thought I must be hearing things. But no that was it alright, I looked at Simon and saw he was smiling.

So I walked out into the aisle and with his arm on mine we walked behind the coffin and out towards the door, down the steps and waited for the coffin to be lifted into the hearse. Then when everybody was out of the church it moved off and down the drive.

At once people came up and kissed us and hugged us if they were close, while others looked embarrassed and men came up and shook Simon by the hand, and said those condolence words that everyone says at times like this.

Unexpectedly I felt someone take my arm and there was David, my companion from the flight from New Zealand. "How kind of you to come," I said automatically.

His reply, "But of course would you have wished otherwise? I would have called at the house this morning but heard it was for local friends only, so I did not want to intrude."

"Will you come to the cemetery?" I asked.

"But of course," he replied, "and to the house afterwards, and tomorrow if I may?" I nodded in a daze and he smiled, patted my hand and then melted away into the crowd.

How good of him to come but then of course he had to as he was here to make his own investigation he said.

Then I heard Simon say, "Well I think it is time for us to go, it's getting close to 10 am." He didn't want to follow the hearse through the villages to the cemetery. He could never can stand that procession of cars we see at home going as it arrives so slowly with people looking so upset. "I will ask Toni to go a little quicker which will give us time there before everyone else who is following."

We walked down the steps and over to the car which Toni now had waiting at the bottom of the steps. Carefully walking around the dogs who seemed to be following, I was thankful to be once more in the cool of the car.

People stood back as we slowly drove over to the Vicarage and then down the drive past the tennis court to the gate. Here we paused for a moment and then out and across the road by the school fence.

That was one thing that I had to be so careful with when driving in Samoa as it was left hand drive, just like in the States or Europe, I must always remember to drive on the other side of the road. We turned the corner and took the inner road this time instead of along the waterfront.

The breadfruit trees shaded the road, and people were walking slowly along keeping to the shade underneath the trees. We crossed the bridge below Mr White's house and then through the village.

The cemetery was at Fungali Utu and a little higher than the waterfront area.

One of the few times we had driven this way, was to attend the Craft Group held on a Friday morning at one of the expat's houses. Mary the vicar's wife at one of the churches usually held the meeting in her big old colonial house. It had a huge enclosed verandah and was spacious enough to take the fourteen or fifteen women who attended.

It was always pleasant to sit and think about the many people who must have lived in the house over the years. Probably built at the turn of the century when Samoa was a German Dependency, like so many of the houses that still stand today, to prove that even with woodworm and hurricanes, they were built to stand the test of time. Most were painted white with a red roof, and had a central part of the house which was the living area. Along with a large kitchen to the rear and bedrooms opening out onto a large verandah.

All too soon we were passing Mary's house, she would still be following behind us somewhere. We turned into the gates and stopped under the shade of a large Flame Tree.

Toni came around and opened the door and Simon took

my arm as we walked between the graves over to where a group of Samoan men were standing near a newly dug plot.

Here were fine mats laid neatly on the ground, waiting for the pallbearers to carry the coffin from the hearse which was due to pull up to park a little way off. Simon spoke a few words to the men and then suggested we also walk over to some trees and wait for the arrival of Father Tala.

Then people started to arrive, as the temperature was becoming quite hot, many women held umbrellas to give them some shade. It was a colourful scene with brightly coloured umbrellas, and women in large hats, more like a garden party, Leticia would have approved.

Then Father Tala announced, "With the heat I think we better start the committal if you don't mind?"

"Of course," Simon agreed, "the quicker the better in this humidity."

So with a nod the pallbearers once more took the coffin from the hearse and walked over to the open grave.

Here they set the coffin down on the fine mat, and Pae who came from somewhere gently put her mat on top. Goodness I thought surely that is not going to be buried as well. A lovely bunch of local flowers were placed on top and then with Father Tala standing close by he put his hand to his side, a sign for us to move to his side. Thus the service began with the deep voice of Father Tala sounding rather loud in the silence. Simon had asked for the committal to be brief, so that nobody found the heat in the noon day sun too much.

What was the saying about, 'Only Mad Dogs and Englishmen go out in the Noon Day Sun?' I must not let my mind wander, but the Frangipani trees were just coming into bud, it was really like a park if one did not look at the graves. Some of the flowers had already dropped to the ground.

Suddenly the pallbearers came forward again and the coffin was lifted onto the slings that were placed across the grave, and on a given signal I knew it would be lowered into the ground.

Then two of Leticia's friends came forward with large island baskets full of Frangipani flowers and proceeded to take them around to the mourners. Each person took a flower which they held until the coffin was lowered into the ground. Then they walked forward and threw a flower each on top of the coffin.

Simon was holding my arm tighter now, so tight it almost hurt. I looked up and there in the background of the mourners in front of me was a slightly familiar face. Who could it be with those blue penetrating eyes, and grey hair but quite a young man, well maybe late thirties or early forties.

I gasped, and Simon thought it was a sign of me going to let go. He said quite sternly, "Hold in there, it is nearly over, do not let Leticia down now whatever you do."

"No, it's not that Simon. It is that man, Alberto over there by the trees, what is he doing here?"

At that moment the coffin started to sink into the ground and I was abruptly pulled back, thinking, 'Leticia I am so sorry that we did not have time to say goodbye. We will meet again you and I!'

Then we both walked forward and placed our flowers into the grave on top of that beautiful fine mat of Pae's. That was the respect that Pae and her family held for Leticia that was the highest tribute that could have been made to her.

People followed with their flowers and then moved

back under the trees, for the final words from Father Tala.

Should we stay or go forward again, or should I leave Simon to do that?

As I stood there undecided David was suddenly at my side.

"Let him go alone. I want to talk to you urgently now."

Thankful to have the decision taken out of my hands, I turned to him.

"What is the matter you looked up a moment ago as if you had seen a ghost, who was it?" David asked.

"Alberto," I said quietly, "He was standing right in my vision behind the coffin under the shadow of those trees."

"Was it the grey haired man?"

"Yes, with glasses on top of his head," I said.

"I'm so sorry, but I must leave you, I'll explain later." With that he was gone as suddenly as he had come.

By this time Simon was back in front of me again, "I think we will walk back to the trees by the car, and say our farewells to anybody who is leaving now and not coming back to the house."

It was cooler under the trees and people shook his hand or gave me a slight hug and then moved to the road. A few minutes later we too followed them to the car.

Once in the car Simon said. "I did not want to be there when the concrete mixer arrived. As it was, it was hard explaining we did not want the mixer close to the grave, which is the usual practice. The first time I went to a funeral here, it really upset me to hear the mixer being turned during the service. It is time they thought of the relations and waited until everyone has left the cemetery, a few more minutes would not make any difference."

We drove in silence through the village once more, and

then headed down hill to the offices of the United Nations, crossed the highway and through Pae's village. Once onto the waterfront it was good to see the sea once again and the waves breaking out on the reef. It was a favourite place for me to walk early in the morning, and fewer dogs in this area so it always felt safer. The dogs here were always a problem and often people walked with a stick or a fistful of stones. But here there were few dogs and most of them would soon run off quickly if you spoke to them.

In no time we were turning into the gates of the residency.

The Staff from the office had set up a long table under the trees as a bar. Already some of the men were carrying out chilli bins full of cold beer. It is the only way to keep drinks cold in the Tropics. I wonder what they used before chilli bins were invented.

The girls from the office had made themselves useful in the kitchen most of the morning, and there were tables with sandwiches and a large urn of tea and hot water for coffee were also laid out.

Simon went over to the drinks' table straight away and talked to the staff then to the office girls at the long table on the other side.

He also went to the umu which the men in the village had put down during the night in the village. There was now large coconut baskets full of food being carried in and placed in the other corner of the garden.

The umu always interested me since the day that I had insisted that I wanted to watch the gathering, preparation and cooking of the food traditionally, that they always cooked on a Sunday morning.

Grandfather, as we called him in the village, for years

had been coming to the Residency each Sunday morning asking if he may take two breadfruit from our tree for the umu. In return he would deliver an umu to start cooking at 9:30 am just before we left for Church. In return Mata had been instructed to give him a tin of pisupa or corned beef as we call it, in return.

So I would imagine that he had been in charge of this large umu.

The collecting of the breadfruit, coconuts and leaves of the taro which took place on Saturday. Then early Sunday morning he and his wife would sit down and the lengthy preparation would take place. Finally everything would be tightly packed into banana leaves then put into a basket especially woven from coconut palms, and lowered onto the hot stones which had been laid in the bottom of the umu hole.

All this was covered with more banana leaves and finally a sack and then sand or soil was carefully layered onto it. This was left for at least three hours and then the hole would be opened, and the food carefully lifted out. In most cases woman were not present when the food was removed, but nobody could tell me the reason why.

I was pleased to go into the house for a few minutes and have a quiet brandy before the guests arrived. It would be difficult to make conversation with people that I hardly knew, who would all want speak to me about Leticia.

The first person to come into the house announced by Pae was David. He apologized for intruding but urgently said, "I must have another word with you about this Alberto. As soon as I left you I made my way over to the group you mentioned but I was only in time to see a grey haired man moving off in the direction of the cars. By the time I made my way to the gate a car was already leaving in the direction it was parked, so I had no time to speak to him. The alert has been put out for a blue Nissan and have spoken to Sergeant Tui about my fears that we must find him as soon as possible. It will be difficult to trace him if he does not keep to the main roads, and then with the terrible telephone connections here, by the time we have with the village constable on the alert it could take all day. Do you think he has anything to do with Leticia?"

"Let us put it this way, why is here on the island? Why didn't he ring Leticia or make contact with her as an old friend? There is something amiss." I added.

"Well you said that he wasn't actually a friend, but if he could come to the funeral which we were hoping he would do, why not come up to you and make himself known. Now I better let you receive your guests and don't worry you will hear back from me in person. When this is all over I would like to be asked around here for dinner, it looks to be a lovely place, and I would like to hear more about your life." And with that he was gone.

I must admit he was quite a dashing man for his age, well it was a long time since I had thought any man was dashing, I had better look out, that could be dangerous. There had not been a man in my life for years now, like I had thought previously, he was probably married anyway all nice men were.

It was a long afternoon and the staff were wonderful mixing with the locals and seeing everyone had something to eat and drink.

People came up to me introduced themselves, mentioned in what department of government they came from, or where they had met Leticia.

I was certain most came because of her not because they knew Simon. She had so many friends in the local community especially the people in the village.

I became quite tired and looked around to find Aunty Mary and asked if she would come and sit with me on the patio. She was only too pleased to have a rest. Her 86 years did not show, she always looked so dainty and well dressed.

She held my hand and said, "We are all going to miss her, we had such lovely drives to Falefa but she always insisted I eat my breakfast first. Do you know I have porridge every morning thanks to Leticia?"

"So do." I replied, "Especially this morning."

Then we sat in silence unless someone came up to us. Thankfully the afternoon drifted by and people gradually took their leave.

Aunty Mary invited me along to Aggie Grey's Hotel for my favourite Tiffin, cucumber sandwiches served with tea at 4 pm.

I didn't really need the tiffin but thought just to be away for an hour would be good, as I knew Simon wanted to return to the office just to tend to any faxes.

So we asked one of the bridge girls if they would give us a lift.

We were soon driving along the waterfront, over the bridge and stopped in front of Aggie's. We walked into the lounge and decided to sit in the rear lounge as it was always cooler. There was talk of building a new frontage to Aggie's and we hoped that it would not take the character of the place away.

We sat down in the cool and ordered tea, and sandwiches.

"Good of you to ask me Aunty Mary."

"Not at all, we are both feeling sad today and me

especially as I have lost such a good young friend, also an excellent bridge partner."

We sat onto the end of the afternoon, and suddenly there was Simon. "I thought this is where you two would be, I have come to take Catherine home if she is ready?"

"Of course Simon how kind."

I stood and then lent over Aunty Mary and gave her a hug, "If I have time, I hope you will let me take you to Falefa while I am here."

"I would love that," cried Aunty Mary excitedly.

We walked out of Aggie's and there was Toni waiting for us. We stepped into the car, "Where to Mr. Simon?"

"Home if you think everyone has tidied up."

"Yes, everything is back to normal." He replied.

We didn't talk on the way back. And the road was busy with people walking home after work.

We were soon at the village and turned in through the gates.

"Lots of mail this afternoon," commented Simon, "I will leave it on the hall table for you to look at. You may like to answer some of it, if not I will take it back to the office and ask Ruth or Sally to answer it for us. The airmail will come tomorrow but I think it's too early for people to have written after just reading the notice in the newspapers."

We walked into the house, and I decided to have a rest before dinner and a pre drink. "See you at seven in the lounge," and with that he walked off. It was good to take my shoes off, and climb onto the bed. I put my lavalava on and dispensed with that ghastly frock into the wardrobe.

Pae had to wake me up at 6:45 pm as I had fallen soundly to sleep.

We had a drink in the lounge, and Simon put some tapes on thank goodness as neither of us wanted to talk.

Mata came in to say dinner was served and two very lonely people wandered into the dining room. Although I was not hungry the smell of one of Mata's great chicken casseroles was too good to miss. So we both enjoyed a good hearty meal. We returned to the lounge and Simon excused himself as he wanted to make some telephone calls in his study.

I sat there reflecting over the day. It really had not been as bad as I had feared. Everybody had been so kind, the worst moment was when I saw Alberto. Why was he here?

The music was a good choice, 'Moonlight Sonata,' 'Cornish Rhapsody,' and 'Warsaw Concerto' were all my favourites.

Not that I could play any of them but it didn't stop me enjoying them. Mother had been a wonderful pianist and probably would have studied in London if she hadn't married.

Simon returned and said he would turn in, and I agreed it was a good idea.

"See you in the morning then Catherine. Thank you for your support today. I think Leticia would have been proud of us both, and especially the staff." With that he vanished.

I stood up at the same time, knocked on the kitchen door, and said goodnight to Mata asking her if she would also lock up and tell Toni we didn't need him again until the morning. "Just ask him to lock the gates on his way out."

I walked slowly down to my room, running a deep bath filling it to the top and popping some 'Radox' bath salts in it. Sinking gratefully into the lovely warm water and relaxing. After some time I nodded and nearly went to sleep. Hurriedly I got out dried, and walked back into the room and sat on the cane lounge to cool down.

The cool thermos was by my bed, and I was soon tucked under the cool percale sheets. I turned off the light, and said "Sweet Dreams Leticia wherever you are my dear."

I started counting sheep backwards, from 689 and fell asleep in no time.

Chapter 6

The Next Day

The house woke late the day after the funeral. Maybe because Simon had suggested that everyone need not start until 7 am which still gave him time to be at the office by 8 am.

I woke with the usual light tap on the door and Pae walked in with the morning tea tray.

I sat up and welcomed her and the tray with tea as it was just what I needed to start the day.

"Good morning Miss Catherine, it is a lovely day outside and I am sorry to say but Sergeant Tui has rung to say he would like to speak to both you and Mr. Simon as soon as possible."

"So I think it is not a morning for staying in bed, but do not hurry as Mata has not started breakfast yet, so you have plenty of time to have a quick shower and breakfast before he arrives."

"Thank you Pae, tell Mr. Simon I will be ready in time."

No time to lie back with my tea, look at a book and relax in my favourite blue room. Such a pity. I gave myself just five minutes to enjoy my two cups of tea. Strange some people like a morning coffee but having suffered from migraines for most of my life, coffee was a definite no-no for me. The tea was hot as always and the tray looked so inviting I wished I could stay in bed a little longer.

Maybe better to be up otherwise I would lie here and my mind would wander to the good times, before coming back to the present I would only cry again.

So jumping out of bed after I had finished my tea, and off to have a shower.

It was good and hot, I washed my hair, and then let the cold water cool me down. Long ago I learnt to cool off with cold water otherwise you would be hot and sticky in no time.

Out of the shower and after rustling around in the bathroom drawers, I found the blow dryer and back into the bedroom to sit under the fan and dry my hair off. What a pity I could not wear my lavalava to breakfast as I was hot now. Just sit awhile and maybe I would cool down. Take a deep breath and think what to wear for the day. That was an easy decision, one of my many long shift frocks as I had no intention of going to town.

I was sure Pae and Mata would have enough food in the house for the day, or we could send Toni into the supermarket to pick up any immediate needs.

Reminding myself, 'Now just take your time you know better than to rush down the passage and arrive as if you needed another shower.' The turquoise shift would be alright for today, I would be ready in case we had any unexpected guests, may as well start the day prepared.

That is what our Mother always used to say, dress for the day then you will never be caught out. Leticia and I use to think what she was really saying was never be caught in a dressing gown with your hair in curlers.

Leticia and I never had to worry about either, as we never had time for a dressing gown and luckily our hair was naturally curly.

In no time I was down the passage dressed for the day and ready for a good breakfast. There had been plenty of food yesterday, but somehow looking after others, I didn't ever sit down and finish eating anything. So one of Mata's best scrambled eggs would be just the thing, after half a pawpaw. I had no sooner sat down than Simon came in looking immaculate as always, but his eyes showed his tiredness.

"Good morning, I'm sorry, I wonder why we English say that when most times it is not good, either due to the weather, or not a good night's sleep."

He walked round behind me and lightly touched my shoulders, and said, "It is such a comfort to have you here, Catherine, we need to say so little, but we both know what we are thinking don't we… it is a time when we must both keep each other going. They say time heals all, but at the moment we have a long road ahead of us and it will take a lot of effort to bridge that gap until the sun shines again for both of us. So just be patient and we hope for the silver lining that people say is over the horizon."

Goodness I felt just terrible and as usual could think of nothing to say that would be suitable. Sometimes it's better just to nod and wait until something came into my head.

Simon helped himself at the sideboard and sat down.

Pae came in shortly after that with a pot of hot tea, and asked if Simon would like his usual fruit, tea or toast, but Mata was making scrambled eggs for me and maybe he would like some also?

"Yes," he replied, "I may as well start the day with a good healthy breakfast, at least that may keep me going until lunchtime, and then maybe take the afternoon off. Thought I would like to go to the cemetery and then maybe over the hill to Tafatafa and have a swim, a change may do me good. Of course you may like to join me Catherine."

I could hear in his voice he wanted to be alone and that was a good thing, to go over the hill, it was a different world over there.

"No Simon I would like sometime to myself and where better for me than to sit in the morning room which I love and feel close to Leticia there. It was her favourite room and I feel that she is still with us in there."

"Good idea, we will have a day left to our memories, and then we must start afresh tomorrow and take up life again, and live each day as it comes." Simon states, "Remember those words, I am but waiting for you, for an interval, somewhere very near, just around the corner. All is well."

"Now let us enjoy these excellent scrambled eggs and then we will be ready when Sergeant Tui arrives. I wonder if he has any news, or he is just coming to keep us in touch in person, instead of by telephone."

"We must not have any false hopes, everything takes time, especially in the tropics as you know. He will be doing his very best. By the way have you heard from your friend David, he seems to be with us one minute and then disappears before you can have a word with him."

"Would you like to ask him to dinner, then we can make an effort to speak to someone we don't know, sometimes that is easier as he never met Leticia so we can talk of something else altogether without anybody being uncomfortable."

"What a good idea Simon. Do you wish me to ring the NZ High Commission, will they know where he is? Or perhaps ring Aggie's first?" I ask.

"Yes, you ring," Simon said with a twinkle in his eye. "He is your friend after all."

"Hardly a friend, but yes I liked him, he made me feel so comfortable and I would like to see him again, thank you."

We looked at our watches and thought we must eat up as it was nearly 8 o'clock.

Pae must have thought the same thing, as she entered the dining room with, "Just a few minutes till eight, but we will hear the car, so don't hurry I will go out to meet the Sergeant when I hear the car."

We finished our tea, and I hurried down the passage to wash my teeth and heard the car pull up outside.

By the time I returned to the patio, Simon was greeting the Sergeant and they were standing waiting for me.

"Good morning Sergeant Tui," I said brightly.

"And a good morning to you Miss Catherine. Maybe we could sit here it is such a relaxing place to sit and view the lovely garden."

So we sat and waited for him to start the conversation.

"Before I start you should know there is little news and so I don't want to set your hopes up. We have looked for this Alberto, through all the arrivals and departures over the last week, double checking all the nationalities coming into and leaving the country."

"We have checked on all hotels, guesthouses, and private homes of anybody without a work permit to be here.

As well as all the tour groups in and out of the country."

"We have even looked at all the yachts entering and leaving the harbour in the last week checking their previous port of call, and their next port of call. But unfortunately have found nothing."

Taking a deep breath before continuing, "This in itself is suspicious, as we cannot trace the men seen by Jack in the Deep. Where they are staying is also a mystery."

"Of course we do not know their names, people can come in with several passports, but all must have that little slip of paper giving them just one month in the country, before re-applying to immigration as you are aware."

"We have only one lead, that they could have come in from Pago Pago on the boat, people take little notice of passengers who travel during the night."

"We believe these men are possibly Italian, and if so are a little different to look at from the Samoans in the dark. Large build, dark hair and maybe a beard."

"There is only one doubt not covered, and that is the yacht seen in the harbour at Savaii. Unfortunately it was not reported immediately, and it was gone before we could send someone over to check on it."

"It also seems that someone hired a yacht down in Apia Harbour for a small trip to Salealonga. The man gave no name, told the Captain, he had missed the plane, had some urgent business on Savaii that day, something to do with aid for the hospital. He made such a good case, even said he had a return air flight late that afternoon from Salealonga back to Apia in time to catch a plane out that night for the States."

"That part is not true as he certainly didn't return to the mainland and could only have left Savaii by yacht, and I am afraid that is what must have happened."

"We now have contacted Interpol, who are involved and there will be an official notice out for the yacht, so far no name, if they are seen by any other yachts, so this will also put them on alert."

"So we have asked all yachts to get in touch with us as to their name, whereabouts, and next port. We have told them that we had a Mayday call and are unable to pin point the yacht, so could everyone please contact us."

"We are just waiting to hear from the last two or three yachts, that we have a record of. Now I am afraid we must just wait."

"Miss Catherine we would ask you to help us in any way possible. I think your Mr. Alberto will be travelling on another passport, he may even have two or three passports, one New Zealand, one Italian and goodness knows maybe a third."

"You say he was from Italy originally, any idea of the town city or area? I realize this is a long time ago, but he may have mentioned somewhere in Italy he loved, or had relations?" Sergeant Tui finishes.

"Sorry I have thought and thought, but we were young, and we didn't like him much, so we tried to have as little contact with him as possible."

"I know his father either worked at William Cable at the bottom of the Ngaio Gorge, or the Petone Workshops in Wellington as it was called. I think one built trains, and the other boats, but you could find that out. They would have applied for citizenship. So maybe you could find a lead there in Wellington in the mid to late 1950's?"

"Sorry not to be of much help. I will spend the afternoon trying to remember the slightest thing, and will write everything down as I go from the moment we met him. I hope that will help?" I offered.

"Well that is the best we can do for today. I would ask you Mr. Simon to please think again if she ever spoke of this man or anybody else that she knew in her teens, maybe a school friend, or a friend's brother?" Sergeant Tui asks.

"I believe it was quite a closed circle in the Wellington schools in those days, and pupils from each school played sport against one another, and met socially, there could be a clue there."

"Now I must be back at the station, in case anything comes in and we can check on it instantly."

"I will ask our counterparts in Wellington to start checking this information, we may get a good lead there."

"Interpol is a great help as they know where to check in Australia for instance. A lot of Italians live in Melbourne and a lot of them are involved with the wharf. In fact they seem to run the wharves. Somebody will talk, they always do if there is a reward."

"It seems there were a few Italians on your flight Miss Catherine and we are not sure if they are still here. They are not listed in any hotel but they also may have flown out the morning of the funeral to Savaii. It is hard to tell where people seem to disappear to on such a small island. Of course there are several flights to Pago Pago and onward flights out of there both north and south. We are going around the village once again just to make sure that everyone is aware that it is important to tell us of any stranger's movements in and around the Deep in the last few days."

"We are also putting some men in plain clothes around the villages to watch out for any strangers coming and going, especially around this property. We have to be careful there is not some overseas organisation that are not happy with Britain at the moment in some other part of the world."

"So if you will excuse me I shall be off now and let you leave for work Mr. Simon."

With that he put his hat on again and walked down to the car and drove off through the gates heading for town.

Simon stood up and came round to me, gave me a hug and walked off inside to find Toni to drive him to work. I went back inside and back to my bedroom, I thought maybe it is best to have a little lie down and then really work on some doubts that I had brewing in my mind.

It was cool in the room and I sat on one of the large patterned cane chairs and tried to relax.

Suddenly it felt as if Leticia was calling me, I got up and walked down the passage and stopped before her portrait, crying out loud, pleading, "Leticia! Help us, we need you to tell us what happened. For goodness sake guide me."

I felt a light touch on my shoulders but turning around there was nobody there. A shiver ran down my spine, thinking to myself, 'Goodness I really do need a rest!' Returning back down the passage to my room, I decided to rest on the bed.

It was so peaceful and the fans on the ceiling turning slowly over my head must have lulled me enough to fall asleep.

I woke to find Pae in the room, "Sorry to wake you Miss Catherine, but Mr. David Harris is on the telephone and he would really like to speak to you."

So I hurriedly walked down the passage to the telephone in the morning room. "David, how good of you to call.

Have you any news?"

"Not really, well nothing that you do not already know, but I thought you might like a change from the house, and perhaps come out and have lunch with me at Aggie's?"

"What a kind thought, that would be lovely, what time would you like me to meet you there?"

"What about a 12.30 luncheon? Would you like to bring Simon also?"

"No, not really thank you, he is at the office at the moment, and this afternoon he would like to visit the cemetery, then he may venture over the hill to Tafatafa just to be on his own. Well not actually on his own. Toni will drive him over, it should be very quiet on the beach today."

"Good, well then I will see you at 12.30 pm and we can have a chat, if you would like me to go with you to the cemetery we could do that also, that's obviously just up to you."

Then he was gone.

I felt better than I had felt for hours, and asked Mata if she could make me some tea and maybe bring some of her cake to me in the morning room, if Pae was busy.

'Now what would I wear for lunch?' That was the next thing on my mind. 'Nothing too bright, but not that awful frock from yesterday.'

I looked in the wardrobe and decided on one of my many lavalava's that settled I went back into the morning room.

Goodness I wished it was time to meet David already, I must not become too excited, as that would be a bad sign, especially if he was just being a good friend.

I started to read a book and in no time it was time to change and ask Toni if he would take me into town. Of course he would not be here but at the office, so I would ring for a taxi.

In no time the taxi arrived and I was laughing in the back seat, the taxi was so old I could see the road between the floor boards. The driver had the music on so loudly I could hardly think. We were soon pulling up outside Aggie's and there was David at the entrance waiting for me. He walked over opened the door, took by arm, and at the same time paid the driver.

It was nice to be taken care of as we walked together into the reception area.

There was something special about Aggie's and I often wondered if the Americans during the Second World War felt the same thing.

Aggie Grey with the help of her sister Aunty Mary had set it up initially as a club then a hotel for the American GI's on R and R. They were the first people to make the traditional American hamburgers, and sell alcohol to guests bypassing a nationwide liquor-ban, and this set them on the road to make a small fortune.

Auntie Mary said Aggie were on one of the first ships to the States where Aggie had invested in property. A woman after my own heart. You can buy and sell shares, but in bad times you can never find anything more stable than property.

Sometimes if you were lucky late in the afternoon you could see these two old ladies sitting outside the building behind the craft shop next door. Later they would go for a drive in their distinctive American car.

Auntie Mary lived at Aggie's now, her room was upstairs over the reception area. These rooms had been used by the pilots on the original flying boats that used to service the island shortly after the war.

Downstairs in the bar there were photographs of some of the early flying boats. The bar down there was not my favourite place as there was no sea breeze.

I much preferred the little front bar which had windows on two sides. It was here that David guided me and we sat down on one of those huge cane chairs.

Nothing much changed at Aggie's, the barman had been there ever since my first visit. In fact he always knew that I liked a Brandy which seemed to fit the climate.

David bought the drinks back to the table and sat opposite me.

"You will of course want to know if I have found out anything about Alberto. We are not sure as we have no photograph of him to show people while we make our inquiries. But we have spoken to a fisherman at the wharf where the boats leave for Manono. He said that he had been asked if there was a larger boat that would take a passenger to Pago Pago."

"He did not take the passenger himself, and the fisherman has not returned to the little wharf yet. But we are keeping an eye out for him. They do not have radio contact with the fisherman, so we will have to wait."

"We have also alerted American Samoa but many fishing boats come and go there. In fact there are just so many working fishing boats as you know, due to the tuna processing factory."

"It is important if you can think of anything that may help me.

I know this is a difficult time, but maybe your sister kept a diary? She would of course have a social diary, but that is not what I am looking for. In fact, would you have a diary of any sort? Especially about your visits to her over the years since her marriage."

"Why yes David, I do keep a sort of diary. Not in detail mostly dates and impressions of places and people I meet along the way when travelling. Do you really think that could help?"

"I would have to ask Simon about a diary if Leticia kept one. But you know women they usually keep those sort of things hidden. Especially if it is of a personal nature."

"We have good and bad days, and some people put that sort of thing down. But I have never had time or interest in recording that sort of thing, and Leticia probably didn't either."

"It will mean going through her personal possessions, and maybe Simon is not ready for that. Neither am I for that matter, but of course if it is necessary, we must do this."

"I have been thinking and I'm not quite sure how to ask this, especially as we have only just met..." A long silence then David reached out and took my hand. "It is a terrible thing to say, but David do you really think there is something sinister behind her death? It was not just by chance that she drowned. I don't mean that she was just in the wrong place at the wrong time so to say. I have felt that she has been uneasy over the last few years. There is nothing that I could put my finger on, but sometimes she was sort of looking over her shoulder, as if she was expecting somebody to come up behind her."

"It's silly really there is no reason for me to say it, but just a feeling I had. In fact I spoke to her several times about it. In a joking manner I would sometimes tease her, "Are you looking for Mr. Right?" It's an old joke we have played on each other since we were teenagers."

David looked puzzled and thought for a few seconds. "Yes Catherine, that is exactly what I think, but we will not trouble Simon about it just yet. We must have more proof before we worry him. Maybe Leticia was having an affair, sorry to put it so bluntly, but do you think it is possible?"

"Maybe this Alberto had come back into her life, someone from her school days. Sorry to ask these intrusive questions, but do you think she and Simon were happy? There have been no children have there?"

"I am sure everything was like any other marriage, ups and downs. All the travelling, being nice to perfect bores, attending functions when you are tired, seeing the same old boring diplomats several times a week, making the same comments, talking about nothing in particular. Really I do not know how either of them kept it up."

"There were no children unfortunately as Leticia had TB when she was first married. Picked it up somewhere, in fact she was quite unwell for a whole year, while they tried a new drug on her. She was in hospital for three months, and was told the possibility of children would be nil."

"This of course did not worry her as she does not readily believe what Doctors say anyway. Well not exactly, they have been proved wrong before but this time sadly they were right."

"They did think of adoption, but at the time Simon wanted to wait. There was some law in England at the time if you wanted to inherit a title, you could not be adopted."

"I remember a case where there were four adopted children, and the title had to go to a distant nephew. Well by the time they realized that it made no difference, as his brother had three sons by this time, it was too late for them.”

“Strange how the English have some old laws, a bit like us showing them up with New Zealand women having the first vote in the world.”

“Sorry for asking but you realize I have to have a broad a picture as I possibly can,” David apologises.

“Do you have a photograph of Leticia I can have. Simon has of course already given us a passport photograph, but would like to see her as she really was.”

“You often have a better idea of someone you have never met by a photograph, sort of brings out their personality a little. I realize all this is so difficult on you, drink up and I will buy you another. Sorry shouldn’t put it that way or you will think there is never such a thing as a free lunch as the saying goes.”

Taking a breath before plunging in, David asks, “I just want to say when this is all over I would like to see you on a personal basis once we return to New Zealand, that is of course if you want to. You see I have been divorced for some years now. It’s the best decision I ever made. We had not been getting on for years, I was always away on some case or another, sometimes for weeks and weeks.”

“Well you know sometimes murder cases are never put to rest until we find the suspect and have them in prison. I was married more to the job really. She of course became bored and turned to someone else, I don’t blame her really, as it wasn’t all her fault. It was just a matter of circumstances at the time.”

“But this is the first time I have met someone who I would like to get to know a little better. How does that sound?”

It was what I had been hoping for all along, and I felt a

warm glow inside or maybe it was the double brandy I had just finished rather quickly.

"That would be very nice, David, it is lovely to have someone to take me out to dinner sometimes, and perhaps a day out with a picnic, I am great on ham and egg pies. Not much of a cook I am afraid, but that is one thing that I can make."

"We must go into lunch or we will never get to the table, must be the heat certainly not the amount of drinks I have had," said David. So we walked down the steps, past the fale's with the famous names of film stars who had stayed at Aggie's over the years. I wonder if I became rich and famous they would name a fale after me?" I giggled and David asked what is funny. I told him and he laughed out loud.

Some people sitting outside one of the fale's looked up and yelled out, "Great place for a holiday isn't it, staying long?"

"Unfortunately not long enough," he answered.

The same maître d' greeted us in the large fale near the swimming pool, and showed us to a table for two looking out on the pool.

"Wish I could still wear a bikini like that blonde, she will keep you entertained all through the meal David," I tested.

He laughed, "Not at all, I am more interested in who is sitting opposite me."

The menu arrived, thank goodness to hide my burning cheeks, goodness I was behaving like a silly teenager on her first date.

"Just a salad for me," I ordered.

"No you are to have more than that, any fish chowder I

hear you are famous for it."

"But of course," said the waiter, "Would you prefer to eat it before the salad?"

"Yes please, we will have both, that is two fish chowders, followed by a ham salad, and a bottle of dry white wine. You do have that don't you?" David asks.

"Of course," the waiter replies.

"Chilled please, and an extra glass of ice blocks for the lady."

I sat back and looked at him thoughtfully.

"Penny for your thoughts?" queried David.

"You seem to remember the little things, you already know I drink brandy and water, and I like dry white wine, with a glass of ice blocks. I will have to be very careful or there will be no secrets left."

"I will have great pleasure in learning more in time, the unknown is always more of a challenge," David agrees.

We sat in silence for a while, both with our own thoughts, and then the wine waiter appeared as quietly as they always do at Aggie's and showed David the bottle. He poured mine first, and said, "The lady tastes the wine. She must have what she likes."

It was cold and I liked it very much and before long we were drinking our second glass.

The chowder arrived, and the salad to follow, it was all perfect and I was sorry when it was time for him to go back to work.

"Oh I nearly forgot," I said. "Simon and myself would like you to come for a meal tomorrow, lunch if you like, but dinner if you are free as we can take longer, and hear about your interesting career."

"I had hoped you would invite me. Yes, of course for

dinner, what time?"

"Say 6.30? Just as the sun goes down, drinks on the patio we prefer and then dinner inside."

He took me to the door, beckoned a taxi from the other side of the road, where the drivers sat and waited for a fare in their own special fale.

One turned sharply and came across to the pavement.

I was just about to hop in, when David swivelled me around and gave me a gentle kiss on the cheek, "See you tomorrow, if not before."

I was gone and looking back I saw him hail another taxi to go the other way into town.

***

After the drinks at lunch, I would definitely have a rest this afternoon, or casually read another chapter in the new paperback I had found in the morning room.

Settling down on my bed to read, but as usual my mind was still working overtime with thoughts racing.

'Leticia there has to be a reason for your death, if I go on thinking like this I will have a migraine.' Thankfully I drifted to sleep in the afternoon heat, but only for a short while.

I woke with a start, and realized that I had not turned on the overhead fan, and yes, I had a headache from the intense heat.

My usual way of trying to get rid of it was to pull my hair, and sip on a long drink of cold water.

If this did not do the trick it would mean a migraine pill. It was then that I realized in my hurry that I had not put them in my luggage. Well the next best thing would be some paracetamol and I didn't have those either, so I had better have a look in Leticia's bathroom and see if I could find one.

I hadn't been in her room, but was sure Simon would not mind. In fact sometime we would both have to look through her things. It was something that I had not thought about until David mentioned it over lunch, and I didn't much like the idea of going through her clothes.

Some people preferred to leave them in the cupboard for months, just having the idea that they were away on holiday, and they would return sometime soon.

I walked down the passage, opened the door of their wing and walked in. Everything was as usual, Pae would see to that.

I crossed the room and into the bathroom. Opened the cupboard and looked for the packet of tablets. There were none there so I thought maybe in one of the other cupboards.

Still no luck, returning to the bedroom I decided to look in her top drawer, maybe some were in there. Still nothing, then I had a brainwave, 'of course she would need to keep the medication cool, it would be in the top shelf of the refrigerator!' Most labels said keep under 25 degrees and it was a lot more than that here in Samoa. I turned and went off down the hall to the kitchen.

Here Mata was preparing the evening meal, "Something light for you and Mr. Simon tonight Miss Catherine," she said. "But something to keep your appetite, maybe one of Mr. Simon's favourite tasty beef casseroles."

"What a good idea Mata, Simon will be hungry when he returns from Tafatafa. I hope the tide is right for him to have a good swim." Dreaming to myself, 'Maybe tomorrow

I could suggest to David he might like to go over the hill together and have a swim.'

Thoughts of his investigation return, David seemed to have plenty to keep him busy, but he had found no trace of Alberto, and this was the only lead we seemed to have. Maybe Alberto had just come to the island for a holiday, and was too embarrassed to make contact with Leticia? Surely she had nothing to do with him, she always seemed uneasy when his name ever came up. But then again we had not discussed him for years. I always thought he was just someone out of the past, there were so many people like that in her life, today fast friends while on the same post, and then both drifting off in different directions.

Perhaps if I went for a walk down to the Deep my headache would go. I could just sit under the trees where it was always in shade. I found Pae and told her where I was going.

She looked uncomfortable, "Would you like me to come with you Miss Catherine. Do you think it will be safe?"

"Of course," I dismissed, then asked, "Why wouldn't it be Pae?"

"Well you know these Palagi have been seen down there, you will not stay will you if Jack is not there? You will not go into the water will you?" Pae fretfully asks.

"Of course not, Pae. Why don't you come with me?"

"Yes Miss Catherine I would be much happier about that."

So we walked across the road and along to the Deep.

We opened the gate and walked down the path, to find Jack sweeping. He looked up and was taken aback for a moment. "Good to see you Miss Catherine, especially a good idea to have Pae with you."

"We are all so nervous after the accident. We have been out to the fale several times especially when we see tourists out there, just to see they are safe."

"Some of them are so untidy, leaving things out there. In fact even when I went out to look for Miss Catherine, there were plastic bags out there."

"I suppose people take them out with their snorkels in them, and then just leave them behind, and then they blow into the sea. People should be made to reuse them, like we do in the supermarket. One of them had blood on it, somebody must have cut themselves on the coral out there."

Suddenly I felt a cold chill down my spine, it felt that someone had lightly touched by shoulder. I turned quickly to look, but nobody was there, just a rustle in the trees.

"I think we will sit at the far end of the beach, Pae do you really want to stay?"

"Of course," Pae replied. So we went and sat on a bench under the trees. Pae looked at me, "What is the matter Miss Catherine you are very white?"

"Pae I had a strange feeling back there, just while we were speaking to Jack."

"Maybe it was Miss Leticia trying to tell you something. Do you remember the first time you stayed at Vaiala you woke in the night and thought someone was in the room with you?" Pae asks.

"Oh yes and you told me later the story about the house girl who hung herself on the back porch in 1961. It must have been her that I felt in the room. I even thought I could hear her breathing. That is when you told me about her," I replied. "Do you really think it was Miss Leticia trying to tell me something? Toni mentioned plastic bags out on the fale. We must remember that, maybe it is important."

"Okay Miss Catherine," Pae replied.

We sat for an hour not speaking, and when finally my head had cleared, we walked slowly back to Vaiala.

I had a shower, changed and waited in the morning room for Simon to return.

He came in just before 6 pm and apologised for being out so late. He had a good swim and had stayed on to snorkel for a while, and even Toni went in with him.

"Everyone is taking great care of us, I almost feel like a child again," said Simon. "But they are doing it in the nicest way."

I told him about Pae coming to the Deep with me, and he smiled, nothing will happen to us it is almost like a bodyguard.

We had our usual pre dinner drinks, a lovely meal with wine, and then both of us felt suddenly very tired.

So I excused myself and returned to my room. I read the paperback for a while and was soon drifting off to sleep with some final thoughts. Two days since Leticia has left us, and already it was starting to feel a little easier as the days flew by. Simon had not mentioned having visited the cemetery, but tomorrow was another day, and I would definitely visit her tomorrow. Maybe David would come with me…

Chapter 7

Picnic With David

I was awake bright and early the following morning. Soon out of bed and strolled out onto the patio to have my early morning cup of tea. Such a lovely day, the flowers in the tubs on the patio had just been watered, everything looked so fresh.

Maybe I would ask Pae to pick some flowers and we would take them out to the cemetery after breakfast before it was too hot.

As I sat there, it was difficult to believe that Leticia would not come bouncing through the door in her usual jovial way, dressed in one of her lavalava's she often wore around the house, and join me. No, she would not be joining me anymore but I still had the feeling she was close by maybe just around the corner as she would say, waiting for us if anything ever happened to her.

Was she preparing us for her departure, surely she would not have known what was going to happen to her? But the more that I thought about it, I had the feeling she was warning us sometimes. Just strange comments she made, but now they seemed to have more warning to them.

Simon came through the door, "You are an early bird," he said.

"By the way did you manage to invite David to come around for a meal tonight?"

"Oh sorry, I already have asked him at lunch yesterday and he said he would be delighted, in fact he said he had been hoping for an invitation, I hope that is alright. Do you want to ask someone else as well? He may want to ask us some more questions. He keeps saying, 'Think back to anything that might give him a clue to what Leticia was doing, or saying over the last few months.' But I am a blank, think I have worn my brain out."

I look at Simon, "I hope you can settle into work again, you will want to be free when your family arrive. I think it would be better if I leave just before they arrive, so they can have you all to themselves."

"You do not have to go, you know that Catherine, but I realize that you have a life of your own. I hate to ask you but do you think you and Pae could tidy up her wardrobe, you know what I mean? I don't want anybody here wearing her clothes, and I don't suppose you want any of them? I'm not quite sure what to do with them. Any suggestions?"

"Why don't you put them into a suitcase for a while, there is no hurry to remove them. Some people like to just leave them there for a month or two, but it is all up to you," I replied.

"Yes, that is a good idea, I just feel I am not doing anything to help with this investigation, it is so frustrating."

"Simon this is a difficult thing to ask, but you know it is only for the best in the end. Do you think Leticia was having an affair? Oh now I have said it, I feel terrible, please forgive me, but it may help, there was something about her friendship with Alberto that always made me feel uneasy," I apologised.

"I have been going back over the years, she disliked him when we were young, but she may have been a little in awe of him. He was so much more adult than any of us. This could only be expected, he had lived through the war in Italy, and that experience would remain with you for always. I believe they were very hungry quite often, and he would have had to fend for himself and to help feed his family. He would have been five or six years old when War was declared. We did meet an aunt of his while in Naples. It was a very poor part of town, and she had very little. He probably was bought up in a similar home. Then he came out to New Zealand with his mother. His father came ahead to find work and somewhere to live."

"We lost contact with him, but Leticia said he turned up again on the Rangitane ship they travelled to England on. I feel it all started there, but cannot say what or why. She never wrote about him and I think they lost contact once they reached England. But there is just that feeling I have that she was seeing him, but she never said anything. She knew how we felt about him, not because he was Italian but he was so different from us. Goodness I am just going from one thing to another. You are probably embarrassed by my question."

"Poor Catherine, I have wondered the same question, and I admit there were times when I was sure she was seeing someone. Maybe not an affair but she definitely disappeared and nobody in the house would know where she was," Simon relayed. "It was a worry, as we have had some unusual postings, and it was a rule of the house, that we always told the staff, or each other where and when we had an appointment. But she broke this rule so often, and then would be so upset when I asked her about it. She would just say she hadn't realized the time when out shopping or sightseeing."

"She was always so interested in everything that was going on around her. The culture of the country, trying to make friends with the local scene."

"Her camera was a great joy to her also, she loved to take photographs. The ones she liked best were of the local people of the country. She would tell me about how long it takes to befriend people and make them feel comfortable before you take their photograph."

"She hated to see people just walk up to people in the street and take their photograph without asking permission. In some countries they feel you are taking their away their spirit and it is an insult to photograph them. Some tourists have even had their cameras damaged as a result of these photographs, and it jolly well serves them right in my opinion."

"Simon maybe we could look at her diary, she may have had more than one engagement book also. If this pains you I will look at them, if you would just let me read everything. David and Sergeant Tui seem to be having a problem with finding Alberto and anything may give them a lead. Of course it would be easy if we could only speak to this man, but he seems to have vanished."

"If he is off the island, and as it seems, he did not take the usual exit out. Although somebody must have seen him with his distinctive grey hair."

"Well that's if he still had grey hair when he left," Simon replies.

"What do you mean Simon?"

"Just what I said, lots of men in the islands dye their hair, have you not wondered why older men have such dark hair?"

"Well I suppose if we woman can colour our hair so can they."

"So they could be overlooking a man with black hair, Alberto would look very similar to the rest of the population. Maybe you could suggest it to David."

"Oh I don't think so, David has been in his business far too long not to look at a disguise, false passports and the like, but we will discuss it with him this evening."

Just then the telephone rang. Pae came out, "Mr David Harris for you Simon." Simon went inside to take the call.

A few minutes later he returned with a slight smile. "David has some news. He wouldn't tell me over the telephone. But it seems he has a lead from someone, who may have some vital information. He has only just found this person on a yacht in the harbour. He says he will tell us more, when he can be sure it will be of help 'beyond any reasonable doubt.' Whatever that means?"

We both suddenly felt hungry and wandered into the dining room.

It was a good breakfast, and maybe the news had given us a ray of hope. Which was just what we needed after hearing nothing for the last day.

Simon took off to work and I asked Toni before he left if he would take Pae and myself up to the cemetery before it was too hot. Pae came out with a basket and walked out into the garden to pick some flowers. They would wilt of course but we could put them in a jar of water before we left.

So putting on my brightest lavalava I walked back out to the patio to wait for Toni to return. He turned into the drive a few minutes later, and Pae came out with the flowers wrapped in some recycled florist's paper.

Nothing was ever thrown out in the islands, as sometimes it was very difficult to buy even the most simple of items. We walked over to the car and I suggested that we both ride in the back together.

Pae was so thoughtful and didn't speak but looked out the window. There were lots of people walking through the village, probably going to the post office at Four Corners, or to the United Nations Office.

"Would you like to check your post box Pae?" I asked.

"No thanks Miss Catherine, later will do," as we drove up the road towards the cemetery.

The Frangipani trees were in bud along the road and they looked as if spring was definitely here.

As we neared the cemetery I suddenly felt, 'Am I really going to visit Leticia? Is this the way Simon felt yesterday?'

We stopped outside the fence, and Pae looked at me, asking, "Would you prefer to go in alone Miss Catherine?"

"No, I would like your moral support please Pae, and Toni if you would like to come with us, please do. Otherwise you may feel happier to stand under a tree, no need to sit in the car."

Pae and I walked in together, she leading the way, she then turned and taking my arm we walked the last few steps together.

The grave was covered with flowers, mostly the paper ones that the local people seem to prefer. Poor Leticia would not like these, but then the thought was there.

Suddenly I wished we had taken her back to New

Zealand, why had I given in to Simon's wishes? Too late now, but when we both left Samoa we would be leaving her behind also. I must not think about that now, I had come to tell Leticia that we were thinking of her, and would find who had taken her life.

I looked down at the flowers, and wondered where we would place ours.

Pae suddenly said, "What beautiful carnations, they must have been imported from New Zealand."

"Of course why did I not think of this, Pae would you look please and see if there is a card?"

"No card Miss Catherine, but the florist in town will tell you who sent them, if you telephone them."

"Yes I must do that, they will have cost a fortune, I would like to write to whoever sent them. Maybe an order from Teleflora in England or New Zealand. I will do that first thing when we reach Vaiala," I decided.

I stood bowed my head, and tried to say the Lord's Prayer. That always settled me down when I was at a loss for words. Leticia had loved the 23rd Psalm, in fact she had learnt it by heart very early when we had gone to Sunday school. She won a prize that year, and our grandmother was so proud of her.

Later however it had become so popular that every service included it, and then it was put to words, and it no longer held that special place in her heart.

I stood there thinking of our Sunday school days, and realized Pae was holding my arm tighter.

"Please Miss Catherine you must keep out of the sun I do not want you to faint, it is my fault we should have bought an umbrella, we will next time."

Of course the sun was quite hot, and I did indeed feel a

little faint, so was happy to be led back to the shade of the tree where Toni was standing.

"I will just stand here for a little longer Pae I feel close to her here, you and Toni can go back and get into the car if you like."

They both walked back down the path, and I bowed my head. I felt more overcome than I did at the funeral service. It had all been so quick and there had been so many people around me. Suddenly I felt a familiar sensation, there was just her and me. Just like when we were young.

If we were naughty we would both go off up into the orchard of the house next door. The grass was always long there and we could hide and nobody would see us, unless they walked right up to our hiding place. We had so many good times together, in fact we did not need other friends as we were only eighteen months apart, almost like terrible twins.

Of course since she had married Simon and was always off travelling the world we did not see so much of one another. But their house was always open to Stephen and myself, and we had visited them in every country they had gone to.

She was always delighted to have us to stay, and would take us around the country they were based in, as much as possible.

Sometimes we would be away for maybe ten days to two weeks if there was an important site she wished us to visit. In each country, we would not always take the car from the Residency, but sometimes took a local tour, or went by train or bus.

Maybe if I thought hard, I may remember one of these trips, and if there had been any unrest with her at the time.

It was time that I stopped thinking of myself, and return to the car, and not keep Toni and Pae waiting, while I was daydreaming back in the past.

"Sorry to be so long, we better go home, and Toni take the car back to the office in case Mr. Simon wants it."

So we drove back to the house and Pae stopped on the way to check her mail box, and I suggested that we stop at the bakery and buy some donuts.

"Don't let Mata see them or she will think you don't like her cooking. I would not hurt Mata, but there was something about a locally made donut, maybe it was so crisp from deep frying."

It was good to arrive back at the house, I always felt at peace as we turned into the drive.

We walked inside and Mata came out of the kitchen. Why did I feel so guilty with the donuts just like a child who had been caught with her hand in the cookie jar?

Mata mentioned, "Mr David Harris has rung while you were out, he said he would ring again. What about a cup of tea out on the patio, or if that is too hot, there is cold coconut milk in the refrigerator or some orange juice, out of a packet of course."

"Tea would be lovely thank you Mata," and I hurried down the passage to my room with the donuts hidden behind my back.

It had been so hot in the cemetery, better to change again that would make me feel cooler.

I returned to the patio, wondering what David had to say, when the telephone rang again and it was him.

"Good morning Catherine, firstly I would like to see you of course before this evening, but secondly I would like to take you over the hill for a swim if you would like.

What about it?"

Secretly excited about this proposition I replied, "Sounds great, you realize it will take us half an hour to drive over to the beach, is that alright?"

"Of course I need a break and a swim at the beach of your choice of course. I believe there is good snorkelling over there. I will order a taxi from the hotel, should I fix a price first?" David asked.

"Oh don't worry about a taxi, the Subaru is here and I have a local license, so you say the time and I will pick you up."

"How about half an hour, and can we eat over there?"

"Well there is a place of sorts, but think they only serve lunch during the weekend. I will ask Mata to pack us a light lunch.

Right see you in half an hour, outside the entrance."

I was all a flutter, oh what to wear, but I must speak to Mata first. I walked into the kitchen. "Tea nearly ready Miss Catherine."

"Don't worry Mata I have been invited to go over the hill, could you please make a small picnic lunch? I'm sorry to ask you without warning. But some sandwiches with anything you have in the fridge for a filling would be great."

"Oh Miss Catherine, are you sure? Just give me ten minutes."

I went to change, pack my bathing suit, towel, lavalava, sun lotion, hat, glasses, goodness I couldn't think straight, I was just like a teenager on her first date.

A skirt and blouse would be better for driving, and in case we had to get out into a village for any reason.

Mata had the picnic chilli bin ready in the hall and a

smaller one with cold drinks. She looked at me and smiled. "I put in a bottle of wine, also, you may feel like that."

I hugged her, I felt so happy to be off on my first date. I walked out to the garage backed the station wagon out and came around to the kitchen door. Mata put everything in the boot, and I placed my gear on the back seat.

"You have forgotten a rug, Miss Catherine, shall I put several more towels in?"

"No just a coconut mat would be fine, do we have a spare one?"

"Of course Miss Leticia always took a local mat. I will be back in a minute."

I looked at my watch, I would be late but no matter. I drove out of the gates and along the waterfront. I looked at the wharf and saw there was a container ship in, the harbour was dotted with yachts it was such a pretty scene.

Over the bridge I drove and there was David under the tree at the entrance to Aggie's. I pulled up, he opened the back door, and he put his bag in with a snorkel sticking out. He climbed in and gave me a peck on the cheek.

"Oh David! The doorman is looking at you," I said a little embarrassed.

"Let him, he has seen that sort of thing before, of that I am sure."

We drove along the waterfront, and turned at the first corner and drove up the road towards the hill. I always disliked this part of the road with the over filled buses which came tearing down the hill at great speed. There was little room for the traffic going up the hill, you had to keep well over to the side.

Then there was the added problem of the deep gutter on the side of the road and you would not want to have a flat tyre in that.

I was concentrating so much that I forgot to ask David what news he had.

As we came to the gates of Robert Louis Stevenson's home I suddenly thought David may like to see the house. "Would you like to see the house Robert Louis built? I am sure the guard on the gate will let us in when he sees the car number plate."

David amazed me by saying, "I have already walked to the top of the hill to see his grave, Mount Vaea I believe. I will never forget the epitaph it has a wonderful meaning to it. But yes another time I would like to visit the house if I may, but not today."

Then to my amazement he started to repeat the words on Robert Louis' tomb stone, 'Under a wide and starry sky…'

I felt sad again for Robert Louis who never returned to his beloved Scotland but was buried here in Samoa and now our beloved Leticia was here also.

David realized I was upset and touched my arm, "Sorry, I shouldn't have told you."

"No not at all I must face facts and at least I can do that in front of a friend, I must face the future, it is just taking a little time for me to come to grips with it."

We drove on up the hill past some of the bigger homes on the island. Most of them we could not see through the trees and gardens.

The New Zealand High Commission house I pointed out, but the new Australian High Commission was built off a side road to the right so we could not see that. Leticia and I had gone there many times to play bridge and the view was wonderful, we were so high that Mt. Vaia was way below us. The verandah was a wonderful place to sit and have a game of bridge, and many BBQ's were held out here.

I pulled in where there was a small garden open to the public, and stopped the engine. "Would you like to see the flowering plants of the island, and perhaps you could tell me about your first call this morning?"

"Of course let us go for a walk."

We walked through the gate and started down the steep path and came to a seat just built with the view in front of us. We sat down and I turned to look at him. He took my hand in his and said, "I do not want to put your hopes up and this is worse than I had expected. But the person I have interviewed is a seasoned yachtie and there is no reason not to believe what he thinks he saw. As you are aware I have not been idle and followed every lead, and even made inquiries in the most unlikely places. But have been down to the wharf and talked to people who work there. Then I thought I would go out to every yacht and see if they had seen this mystery yacht we have been trying to trace that was seen anchored at the end of the airstrip on Savaii."

"Yachties talk to one another in each port, and listen in on their short wave radio to the usual chatter that goes on out at sea."

"There was a yacht that had been here before Leticia had died, and they had been over to Savaii, but returned here to take on more stores before heading south again."

"The yacht is skippered by an American who spends most of his winters down here in the Pacific. He was sailing into the harbour quite close to Pilot Point, the head land as you know that goes out beyond the wharf. His crew were bringing the yacht in, and he was out on the deck with his binoculars around his neck."

"He was looking at Jack's fale thinking he would like to go for a swim later in the day. There were a group of people standing there, and the woman seemed to be having some fun with two companions."

"At least that is what he thought at first, then he saw them put something he thought was a towel over her head. She didn't like it and so she sat down on the fale floor and they bent over her probably to say they were sorry."

"A few minutes later they picked her up and threw her into the Deep. Then they jumped in after her. He didn't think any more about it. You know how people react around a swimming pool, there is always lots of laughter if someone will not jump in for a swim. Usually someone comes up behind them and pushes them into the pool. Then they all jump in and have a swim or carry on with their pranks."

"It wasn't until I told him that Leticia had been out that afternoon swimming from the fale, and had drowned that he thought more seriously about what he had seen."

"He had not continued to watch as he was distracted by the entry into the harbour, and then when they came past the point the fale of course was out of view."

"He feels utterly terrible as he now thinks he may have witnessed a woman in distress, but being so far out at the time it just looked like a group of people enjoying themselves."

"He is quite happy to remain here for a few more days, to see if he can be of any further help. If you would like to meet him and his fellow crew, I am sure they would be only too happy. But I wanted to talk to you and Simon first."

"It was only this morning that I met them, and I don't want to put your hopes up too much. It would be impossible at that distance to identify anybody. But with Jack's help, we may have the beginnings of a case."

"But we really need to find Alberto, and the other men he was with down at the Deep."

I took a deep breath and started to cry. "Do you think there would have been much pain, did she suffer for long?" I asked sobbing.

Taking hold of my hand to comfort me, he replied, "No I feel it all happened so quickly that she would hardly have known what was happening, and then it would have been all over, and this is what you must think."

We stood up and he looked into my eyes, "I will do everything in my power to find these people, you must believe me. It is more than a case now, I have become involved with a member of the family."

I smiled we were so lucky that it was him that had been sent to Samoa to look at the case.

"Now," he said, "we are off to enjoy that wonderful snorkelling I have heard about, and see what is in that chilli bin. I do have a local license as well would you like me to drive?" David offered.

"Yes, I would like that," so we walked back to the car, and continued our climb to the top of the hill.

I pointed out the shop that sold liqueurs, "They are quite good, but you can try one tonight when you come to dinner."

It was quite cold on the top and I suggested that he looked for the sign to the waterfall, if there was enough water it was really quite a sight. He pulled in again and we walked to the edge of the track, but today there was little water falling over the top of it, and not worth a photograph.

We continued down the hill and were soon at the turnoff.

Turning left, I looked at the speedometer it is exactly two miles to the turnoff to the left. Sure enough we found the dirt track and left the main road. It was very uneven and so we took it carefully, you really needed a four wheel drive.

"Are we ever going to reach the end?" he asked.

"Oh yes, just be patient it is worth it."

Around the next corner and we were there. We parked the car under a tree, and decided to swim before lunch.

I think David was a little disappointed at the black sand beach.

But the perfect cove looked inviting.

"It is a difficult walk through the sand, but well worth it, the far end of the bay is best."

So we walked along the wet sand to the extreme end.

"If we swim out to the side of the bay the coral is best."

We put our goggles on and wet our masks, then sat down and pulled on our flippers. We were now ready to enter the water… It was always cold when you first enter the water especially with the rolling surf which we always found at Asanga Beach.

We slowly swum out over the wonderful coral branches which must have been ten feet to the bottom of the lagoon.

The sun above caught the white branches and made everything look unreal. I motioned to David to keep well up near the surface, knowing how dangerous it was to have coral cut on your legs.

When we were younger there was always a bottle of Jensen's violet kept in the bathroom cupboard. It had been instilled in us, to never take a cut lightly and to cover it as soon as we came home. Leticia spent most of her holidays with large purple marks on her legs. But better to be careful than end up in hospital.

We had heard of tourists who did not realize that live coral continues to grow, and with a small piece in your leg this can be almost fatal.

He nodded in agreement and we continued to swim further out into the bay stopping every now and then to admire some of the small electric blue fish that were swimming in and out of the coral branches.

Over the many years that I have snorkelled in many different Pacific islands, my memory always returns to this beach which is the best I have ever seen.

Of course with the many scuba divers who are able to go beyond the reef there are sure to be good areas all around the Pacific. But scuba diving is something I have always been a little afraid of.

The thought of having a tank on my back, and forever keeping an eye on the time you are under water worries me. Also the many films we see today, often show a shark that seems to swim far too close to the divers.

Time flew by very quickly and coming to the surface I realized we were now far out and nearing the headland. This often brings difficulties as there could be a swell taking us across the bay to the other headland and the snorkelling was not as good there.

I signalled again to David that we should turn for home and he waved in agreement, and immediately I felt safer.

Although Leticia and myself had had no fear of the ocean and were both strong swimmers, the recent event never seemed far away with no use being in trouble in this isolated area.

David was a strong swimmer, so I had no worries of having to save him, it would have to be him that came to my rescue if need be.

It was so good to feel so free and buoyant in the very salty sea, we hardly needed to float it was so relaxing, just what we needed to enjoy the outdoors, after the horrific several days that I had had since arriving in Samoa.

It was still a cloudless day as we returned to the shore, and I was looking forward to our picnic lunch. Funny how a swim makes one so hungry. The picnic basket would be excellent if Mata had anything to do with it.

As we approached the beach my heart sank, remembering the awful time that the family had been here many years ago.

There was a large swell that day and it had been difficult to enter the water as the waves were very large.

As each wave receded it made a backwash and then suddenly dipped away into deep water.

We had swum out a little into the bay, but feeling the tide was stronger than my swimming had decided to return to shore.

Coming in on the waves had been fun, when suddenly to my horror I realized that it was more difficult to swim through the waves that were crashing onto the shore.

When I went to stand the following wave caught me from behind and knocked me over, and under. Then before I could come up to the surface, the next wave caught me and kept me down at the bottom of the sea.

Then it started rolling me over and over like a top, and I then I realized it was up to me to somehow reach the surface before I needed to take another breath. As my feet finally touched the sand, the receding water was tearing at the sand around my feet and in a moment would take me back out beyond the waves.

With a great effort the water finally released me and I staggered ashore. Instead of the family rushing to help me, they stood back and laughed. They probably thought it was all a dramatic act, instead between crying and taking large gulps of air I lay down on the beach.

It was then that they realized that there had been a problem and that a little comfort was what was needed.

But today it was calm on the edge of the sea, and there was no problem in coming ashore, and taking off my flippers we walked up the beach to the shade of a tree.

David took his towel to dry himself off and graciously waved me to sit down. Then he asked me if we should have a drink before lunch.

It all seemed so natural for him to take the lead, and although it was my chilli bin and picnic he took the man's place and I liked that.

He opened the chilled bottle and was soon toasting us. He looked very serious as we clinked glasses, and I felt a warm feeling that had not happened for such a long time.

I must not let him see that I was so overcome, and jokingly said, "Now what have you selected for us to eat?"

"No idea it will just have to be pot luck," he joked, "But I promised you there will be many more outings like this in the future if you are agreeable."

"That sounds fun, and yes it would be great to have another picnic while you are here," I replied.

"That is not exactly what I meant, and I hope that we will continue to see one another when this whole case is finished. Otherwise I will have to delay any findings we make, just to keep you here on the island."

I knew what he was trying to say, and tears came to my eyes, hoping that he would think it was the thought of Leticia that was making me cry. But it was not, it was the thought of finding someone again to fill that void that had been in my life for so long.

He immediately lent across and touched my cheek, "Sorry that was mean, but what I really meant is that this is the beginning of a long lasting friendship I hope."

"Yes I know what you mean, it is just that I am so happy."

"Well, let us have some lunch I don't know about you, but food is the next best thing that is important at the moment."

And so we relaxed and started opening the plastic containers eagerly to see what was in store for us.

The picnic went well and unfortunately it was soon time to think of returning over the hill to Apia. I think we both hated the thought of leaving such a special place, but the shadows were taking the sun from the beach, as it lost its sunlight early.

We were packed up in short order, and walked back along the beach. The sand was deep and we took each step mindfully one at a time, while our feet sank deep into the warm sand.

By the time we reached the far headland the tide had definitely gone out, and quite a lot of the coral was now exposed.

My wish each time I left the beach, was that it would always remain like this, with no accommodation ever being built here.

There were so many lovely spots in the world that had

started off just like this. A lovely lonely beach with no facilities, and then someone built a shelter and next there were buildings.

It reminded me of a trip to Mykonos in the Greek Isles. I had been taken by some friends that I had met on the island. This mother and daughter had sailed on the same ferry boat as me. We found we were staying at the same place, and had struck up a friendship as one does when on holiday.

One day the suggestion was made for us to take a local bus to the other end of the island. We went as far as the last bus stop and the driver showed us a track down to a beach.

We had a lovely day here where a fisherman had a small cabin where he served freshly caught fish. It was a simple meal and we had the beach to ourselves.

Some thirty years later, Stephen and myself had gone to Mykonos and I took him on a similar bus to visit my little beach. But by this time the bus was full of tourists who all seemed to be heading for the same place.

We walked down a concrete path this time, to a crowded beach.

There must have been nearly a hundred people lying in the sun. The edge of the beach was lined with restaurants, the whole place had changed. The disappointment was so great, we returned up the path and caught the next bus back to town.

With so many people in Europe looking for a summer holiday close to home, these islands are now visited daily by huge cruise ships from Athens.

On reaching the car we were soon packed and veering up the bumpy track heading towards the main road. The huge trees reminded me of some of the Kauri trees on the west coast of Northland in the far north of New Zealand. These trees must have been over a hundred years old and have weathered many a cyclone.

Further up the hilly road, many of these beautiful trees had been stripped in a previous cyclone, and were now large stark bare sentinels of another age.

The people in the villages along the road were out walking. This seemed to be the hour when children were sent to the local shop to buy the ingredients for dinner. Most of the houses had no refrigerators, and relied on locally caught fish, otherwise it would be a tin of corned beef.

Again with no electricity, it meant that firewood had to be collected each day, so that a fire could be lit for cooking.

Slowly with a little more money, a few people acquired kerosene cookers. This consisted of two elements and made life much easier for the cook in the house.

I much preferred the umu which was the Sunday meal cooked in the ground. It took a lot more time to prepare this type of meal, and took most of the previous day, to collect wood, and coconuts from the heavy forest. However it was well worth the wait and all the preparation that went into cooking it.

As we turned the final corner and started on the mountain road David laughed and said, "I wonder who designed this road. It just goes straight uphill, and must be difficult for the buses to make such a steep climb."

"I had often thought the same thing, it would be so much easier if it was a zig zag road. Just as well the modern car does not overheat as it climbs up the hill."

We were silent as we drove home, not wanting to break the contented feeling we both had started at the beach. It was too late to visit Vailima as we descended and I was pleased as it would be an excuse for another outing. As if David had read my thoughts, he said, "Next time we have a date, why not come up here and walk up the hill to visit Robert Louis Stevenson's grave?"

"Yes I would like that, but it has to be early in the morning, what about 6:30 am?"

"Well that is certainly early but if you say so, I am guided by your thoughts of a cool walk."

"Why don't you stop outside Aggie's and I will ask Toni to pick you up later?"

"No need for that, a walk will do me the world of good, so I will walk along to you, did you say 6:30 or 7 pm tonight?"

"Whatever is convenient to you, we always sit out on the patio before dinner, so even if Simon is held up at the office, I just sit out there and enjoy the last rays of the sun in the garden."

We pulled up outside Aggie's and I took the driver's seat and drove home.

Oh dear Leticia I am so happy, and it is all due to you dear. What a terrible thought, here I was so happy, and it was only bought about by Leticia's death. Don't think too badly of me but it is a long time since I have had such a happy day.

If only this was the beginning of many more, and I hoped that David was thinking the same thing. The children in the village gave me a wave as the car slowed down to enter the gates of Vaiala. I had just made it through the village before curfew.

Curfew was very important to everyone in the village, it usually only lasted 45 minutes, it was a time for prayer before a meal, and to mark the end of the working day. All traffic must cease in the village, but respect was made for Simon's cars, but we tried not to break the curfew.

In fact Simon often stayed at the office another 45 minutes if he was running late, just so Toni would not have to drive through the village. The people of the village were most protective and it would be very difficult for someone to enter the village after dark without being challenged.

Of course you could always come in by sea, but that was most dangerous, and even more so for a boat to try to go out through the reef.

It was not difficult to walk around the sea wall from the port at low tide if you knew your way. But again you would have to climb over many rocks, if you did not walk in through the Queen's Representative's old home. There was a family living there and they were paid to watch the grounds and they had ten dogs, it was not a welcoming sight for ten dogs to come growling and leaping over one another, trying to climb over rocks.

So once through the gates there was a feeling of peace and security and the lights on the verandah were always a welcome sight.

Why does one always feel it is good to be home before dark, maybe it is something instilled in us when young? The dark means the unknown, the reason being we cannot see. Therefore we feel quite unsafe as we do not know what is out there if we cannot see. How lucky we are to live on a safe island, let us hope it will always remain this way. The Pacific Islands remained safe, but there were the rumblings of trouble in the Melanesian islands, and the islands north of Australia. Let us hope everyone would settle down with their new independence on these islands.

Chapter 8

Dinner with David

I just had time to park the car and run into the house before the curfew in the village rang. I took my shoes off at the door and hurried down the passage with the picnic basket into the kitchen.

Mata was busy over the stove and looked up smiling, I think for the first time since the funeral.

"Oh good you are back we were a little worried as it was nearly curfew, and we did not want you to have to wait at Aggie's until the curfew was lifted. But Pae said you were in good hands with Mr. David, and he would look after you. Is that right?" Mata asked with a twinkle in her eye.

"Well yes, that is right," and hoped that I did not blush, "It was wonderful to have somebody to look after me again, if only for a day and to take me for a picnic."

"Mata thank you, everything was perfect in the basket, and the ice cold wine was just right. I have had a lovely afternoon at Tafatafa, the tide was in and we snorkelled a little at Asanga, and went out to the edge of the bay, the coral branches are still just as I remember them. What is for dinner Mata? And what is for sweet?" I asked.

"Just you wait and see. I used to say that to Miss Letitica. You are just the same, always wanting to know what we are having for a meal, and Miss Leticia would see the menu every morning and still she would ask. You just wait and see. You will like it," Mata smiled.

I went laughing down the passage, everything was just the same, strange how life continues just the same, except that Leticia was not here to laugh with any more. But it felt that she was just around the corner as she always said she would be, maybe in the next room but had just slipped out for a moment. Saying those words to myself regularly, I felt it made a difference to the grieving process I was going through.

I walked into my room and threw my belongings on the bed, except for my bathing costume and towel which I hung out on the verandah.

Hopping quickly out of my clothes and into the shower, to wash my hair and rid myself of the sea salt. It had been a very salty swim today, and although I loved the salt on my body, it would scratch later on and be most uncomfortable if it became humid.

I lay on my bed for a rest and drifted off to sleep, only to be woken by Pae gently calling my name. "Time to dress Miss Catherine, if you are to be ready for Mr. David. Mr. Simon is already home and out on the verandah with a sundowner if you wish to join him, he said."

I jumped off the bed and headed towards the wardrobe and looked at the few dresses I had. Usually I would go into Leticia and borrow one of hers, she had lots of lavalava's, but it did not seem right to do that now.

Maybe that should be one of my first constructive things I could do tomorrow if Simon wanted me to.

Pae stood there, "I know what you are thinking, may I suggest Miss Leticia had three new frocks delivered the other day, none of which she has worn. All were to be a surprise for Mr. Simon, so he will have not seen them. Shall I bring them to you and you may like to wear one of them?"

"Do you really think that would be alright, Pae, are you sure Mr Simon has not seen them?" I asked.

"No, I went with her to the dressmaker in the village, she is the Pastor's wife, and the material came up from New Zealand a month ago."

She hurried out of the room and returned in no time with a plastic bag. It was fun taking the frocks out and she put them against her. One pink, one blue, and one floral.

The blue I liked instantly, it looked like a design I had seen in Cairo. Straight, with a split on the side and the neck, outlined with braid the same colour and a pattern down the front.

Just right for tonight, it would make me feel good, and I wanted to look my best for David. Really I was behaving like a skittish young girl. I threw it on and instantly felt good, in fact really great, and with some perfume and a little jewellery my black pearls of course I would be ready for an evening out. Then I panicked and felt overdressed. But it was too late Pae said she could hear the taxi arriving, so I rushed down the passage to greet David at the door.

"Gracious he said, and stood back and looked at me as if for the first time. You look like a model! That colour does suit you, may I have the pleasure of introducing myself," he kidded.

We both laughed and he took my hand and kissed it, and then feeling a little self-conscious we walked down the hall and out onto the rear patio where Simon was waiting for us.

"I must say you make a very handsome couple, sorry don't want to embarrass you David but it is so good to see Catherine looking so formal and happy to boot!"

We all laughed and sat down and waited for Simon to offer us a drink. "I think I would like a stiff brandy please, with ginger ale and ice, instead of a wine if I may, I think we are all going to need it by the end of the evening," David boldly asked.

"I know you have something to say David, and it is up to you whether you tell us now or after our meal," Simon stated.

"Well of course we all want to hear what the news is if any, but we do not want to spoil a good meal, as Mata will not be pleased with us," I interrupted.

"So let us enjoy a drink or two and then go into dinner," Simon decided.

"Good idea Simon," agreed David. "There is no concrete evidence at this stage, and it is really one of you that we think holds some vital information. However you will not be aware yet that you hold the vital link at this stage. Something you think quite unimportant, something that did not have any meaning at the time, but will probably just come to you without any warning."

"I have found over the years that if you try too hard to remember it will stay locked up inside your brain. So try not to worry, and I know it sounds difficult, do not go searching over the years in your mind too much."

"Think of the good times you have had in your different

postings and touch lightly, you know on the people you met, the people you liked, and the people you did not like, or did not feel comfortable with, people who visited the house."

"But more particularly people you met maybe again and again but in entirely different postings, countries, whether on business or on holiday."

"We are looking for a connection however unimportant, people or friends of Leticia's or for that matter people or a person that Leticia did not seem happy on meeting. I don't mean someone she met for the first time, we always meet people that we do not wish to continue a friendship with, but someone that made her uneasy. Catherine you must try to remember any letters or conversations when you had not seen her for some time or any change in her usual happy self? It will be difficult for you both, but I would like to have a look through all her personal possessions at some stage. That means her clothes, diary, engagement book, if I may with your permission, is right now okay?"

"I have a man outside who could do it with me, or if you prefer one of you but I definitely would like one of you in the room at the time."

David looked down, I could see he was definitely uncomfortable. He was becoming involved as a friend but was here of course to investigate Leticia's death.

Simon stood and took over, "Of course David you must do your job, and the quicker the better. Catherine dear, would you show David our room, and I will have another drink, there are one or two calls, that I should have made at the office, and I will tell Mata to hold dinner, would half an hour be alright David, or a little longer?"

"That would be just fine, Simon. Catherine, would you

show me the way please?"

We stood up and walked back into the house and walked down the passage. David took my hand as we entered the bedroom.

The room looked light and cool, the fans were rotating slowly and the sheer curtains on the windows were blowing gently in the breeze.

"Where do you wish to start David?"

"Maybe the bathroom, you sit there and I will have a look."

David went into the bathroom and I heard him opening cupboards and drawers, and he came out with several bottles.

"I wonder Catherine if you would ask Pae to go out to the car tell her there is a detective in the car so she isn't surprised. Ask her to show him in, via the bedroom door here that leads onto the patio."

"I do not wish to disturb Simon more than necessary, and to see a policeman going into his wife's bedroom is quite unnecessary."

So off I went down the passage, Simon was in his study so was not aware of me speaking with Pae who was clearing the drinks off the patio.

I returned to the bedroom and by this time David had the drawers in the dressing table out and had Leticia's personal books spread out on the bed. The little birthday book I had recently given her was there, her large engagement book, and a small blank diary I had also given her. "Have you seen any of these books before?" asked David.

"Oh yes I have given her two of them, she was always mislaying her birthday book, which she took seriously, and liked to keep in contact with her friends at least once a year, on their birthdays, and again at Christmas."

"The floral covered diary, was one she always carried with her, you know with passport numbers, visa card and bank account numbers, and when insurance, and rates were due. She would go nowhere without it. She always carried it with her passport. That is how important it was to her."

"Her address book always went in the same folder, so she could contact anybody she knew when in a foreign country or back at home."

"Excellent," said David. "I will take these with me tonight, and do my homework, and then will go over them with you and Simon tomorrow."

There was a light tap on the door, and David opened it for the detective. He came swiftly inside, acknowledged me, and waited for David to speak. "Nga, I want you to take these bottles, and have them analysed. Also would you go over the bathroom cupboards, and see if there is anything I have missed, and if so remove them also."

David then opened the wardrobe and removed the clothes, one by one looking for pockets in the garments. These he put back and by the time he had finished, it looked just as it had been when he opened it.

Next he took the shoes out one by one and looked at these, he removed one pair with heels, and put these with the books.

Then he walked over to Simon's wardrobe and looked in there.

Nga came out of the bathroom with the black bag, pointed to the books and shoes, but David said "No I will take care of those for tonight except for the shoes you can take those."

He opened the door again and Nga slipped out with the

bag. "Well we seem to have everything for now, but is it not strange, that except for a few pieces of jewellery in the dressing table that Leticia wore so little jewellery would that be correct?"

"No Leticia did not like jewellery really, she had her favourite pieces and those she mostly wore all the time. Of course in England and New Zealand she had some family jewellery that she did not travel with it. She always said such a nuisance and to only take what you can wear."

"Well we must not keep Simon waiting any longer our half hour is up. Shall we go? Thank you for being here it could not have been easy. I would prefer we do not mention Nga we want to cause as little pain for Simon at the moment don't you think?"

I agreed as I was happy to a part of this investigation, and Simon could be relieved of this.

.

I stood for a moment and hesitated, then waited for some sign, did I expect Leticia to give me a sign, suddenly a door banged in the house, a sudden gust of wind, I thought, but everything was still. I looked at David and nodded and went ahead down the passage feeling confident that this was a sign from my sister, that all was well.

Simon came out of the study at the same time as we came down the hallway and said, "Well I hope all went well and we can now enjoy Mata's dinner and a good bottle of wine."

David offered me his arm like a true gentleman, smiling I accepted and he led me into the dining room as if nothing had happened.

As usual the table was set perfectly with two brass candles already glowing, Leticia always insisted on candles as it made it so much easier, if there was a power cut in the middle as so often happened. She jokingly had mentioned that it was also much kinder to a woman's skin and made a dinner party more intimate and so candles were on the table even if they were not used.

Although Pae came and went with the food, and Simon kept filling our glasses, the evening without Leticia was not the same. Her conversation always included her guests as she said, 'Just ask a man about his work, if you can't bring him into the conversation, then sit back and meditate, and say how interesting every now and then, and the evening would just fly by if you were bored.'

But this was not the case, we all were lost in our own thoughts, and I felt sorry for Simon, but also David who was trying his best to talk of other topics other than the obvious one of Leticia's death.

Maybe it had not been a good idea to have this dinner until he had completed his investigation, or was he using this time to sum both Simon and myself up in an informal manner?

Finally dinner was over and we retired to the Morning Room, it seemed we kept going there, instead of the living room which was too large for the three of us.

We sat drinking our coffee, and then David said, "If you don't mind I have some things to do before I retire, so I will say goodnight now, and keep you both posted tomorrow with any new events."

Simon stood and shook hands, and I led David down the passage to the front door.

He gave me a light kiss on the cheek, and said, "Please forgive me for asking so much of you in the bedroom, but it is all for the best I can assure you. I have become involved with the family now, and it is more important than ever for me to find what really happened to Leticia and how and why."

Then he was gone, and I was left standing there watching his car depart, feeling very much alone.

I slowly returned to the Morning Room to witness Simon slumped in his chair, at first I thought he was asleep, but he looked up looking completely lost and bewildered.

"Oh Catherine, reality is setting in, Leticia is gone, truly gone, not for a holiday, not to another room, not down at Aggie's playing bridge, but gone, gone and we will never see her again well not in this world. She was such a bright light, I felt sometimes she was in a shadow like behind a cloud. But she would always come back from the shadows, but this time the light has gone out forever and it is dark and lonely."

There was a long pause each of us deep with our thoughts, it was true what he was saying, all through dinner my memories travelled back to meal times we shared. It was always a happy time with everyone contributing with conversation about their day.

Not like when we were both young and our father who had lived in England for many years really could not stand our voices. Probably he had the worries of the day on his mind, and two young girls chattering at the table must have been difficult. Not so much difficult but we realized later that it was our accent. Well we spoke just like all our friends, a true New Zealand accent. He despised our nasal twang he detected in our Kiwi accent as he put it.

It was not until we returned from England that we realized how our accent had changed, it had evolved. He seemed delighted with our rather BBC voices, although he didn't actually say so.

Leticia had for fun with our first Christmas in London decided to make a record of our first six months there. I went with her to a recording studio where we were told she could talk for thirty minutes.

So she prepared a written script and we returned to cut the record. It was one of those large records, and she sat in a studio reading her notes.

With a nod from the announcer she stopped, and the record was turned over. It was quite a descriptive record of her feelings and thoughts of her arrival and our living conditions in London.

Having a parent who had arrived in England in the early 1920's and lived and studied in London for some twelve years it must have been so interesting. Especially to hear his daughter some thirty years later finding her feet in the same big city.

Father had of course had to work his way to the UK by being a steward on a ship, and paid a peppercorn passage of one shilling. He told us stories of running a bath for his passengers each evening. But always managed to have the cook keep him the best outside carving of a roast at dinner time. He had to wait on tables as well and so his passage must have been so unlike ours as fully paid passengers on the pride of the New Zealand shipping line.

He had to study at the London University and later worked for an Import Export firm in the City. Unfortunately he must have been short of funds or savings as he never mentioned travelling to Europe.

But his knowledge of buildings and architectural wonders in Western Europe and even the Middle East was amazing, and his letters were always full of places we must visit, and what we must look for in small corners, nooks and crannies of cathedrals and buildings.

One of his favourites was St. Paul's Cathedral by Christopher Wren. Maybe he had worked close by, and of course while we were in London the cathedral stood proud and strong with the ruins of the war time blitz all around.

It was a wonder that it was never hit. That must have annoyed the German bombers who tried night after night to bomb this sentinel which stood for so much to the Londoners. Only one corner was hit but the dome stood proud through the blitz.

Oh dear here was I, deep in my own little world and poor Simon was needing my attention and support.

"Simon we must remember what David told us to do. He wants us to remember everything we can, and I suggest that you go back to the beginning. That means from the time you met Leticia in England, then to the time in New Zealand before and after you married, and then your life together with your postings around the world."

"I know you would have kept a diary for work? Did you ever keep a day to day account of your life and thoughts?"

"Somewhere in there may be a clue and no matter how hard it is for you to think about, remember it may clear up the reason why Leticia has been taken from us."

"I am going to do the same thing, a sort of going down memory lane to the good and bad times we had together, not sure whether to go back as far as I can remember in our childhood, but I am sure the key is not there."

"I just have the strangest feeling that it all begins with Alberto, he was the first stranger to come between us. Not like other friends we made at school, at the Bay or the tennis club when we joined. Not even at school dances which we attended in the holidays."

"Alberto although a similar age, made us aware that he was a man of the world in form three, he took out girls in the sixth form, so he must have had something, other than begin very tall, and heavy set and with the dark complexion of an Italian. So I will start there, and you start from your first encounter. Maybe you took her away into a different world, of diplomats and government officials."

"She would have definitely met those type of people in London with you, whereas I only mixed with girls in the flat, so a few Australians, Canadians, New Zealanders, and Englishmen who thought it smart to go out with a Colonial. Under the mistaken idea that we were all sheep farmers' daughters with masses of sheep, acres of land, and fathers living it high on wool cheques."

Simon looked at me with those penetrating blue eyes of his, trying to fathom if there was something there that lay hidden. But I looked directly back at him, there was nothing to hide, just suspicions. Suspicions yes, but what foundations? There was nothing concrete, but I knew we had the key between us, and who was going to be the first to unlock that vital memory?

It was so peaceful in the room, the room that Leticia liked best, she had furnished it as a haven and it was, almost an English haven we could have been in their English Country House at Hinton St George, except it was never this hot there.

Suddenly Simon asked, "Do you want a nightcap, or shall I ask Pae for a cup of tea?"

"No not really, but a cup of tea would be nice, you know I never say no to a cup of tea. Even in the Tropics."

He rang the little brass bell that Aunt May had given

them, and could be heard as far as the kitchen.

I think Pae has guessed already as she appeared with a tray already set, with an English tea set, and a small plate of shortbread.

We all laughed, "Pae you read our thoughts. You could not have made the tea so quickly."

"Will you be mother, Miss Catherine, or me?"

"I will pour Pae, you should be tired, so don't wait to take the tray away, we will wash up," said Simon kindly. He like all of us had a soft spot for Pae. She was so kind, efficient and forever thinking of others.

"Well then a goodnight to you both. Toni will take me home if that is alright, and I will see you both for breakfast, unless you want me earlier."

"Good night Pae and thank you for all your support over the last few days, I hope that things will settle down a little now. Maybe you would like some time off?" Simon asked.

"Oh no thank you, I will be here just as long as you need me, until they find out about Miss Leticia, she would want me here to look after you two."

With that she was off out of the room, and we heard the kitchen door close gently down the passage. I poured the tea and handed it to Simon, his hand was shaking when he took the saucer.

"Sorry, it's just this set was one of Leticia's favourites, maybe I should put it away in case a piece is broken."

"Certainly not," I snapped too quickly. "Oh sorry Simon, but I am sure she would like us to use it and think of her, whereas if you put it away in a cupboard it will be forgotten about. Things like to be used and it is so pretty and makes the tea taste better if drunk out of Bone China."

He laughed, it was refreshing to hear him laugh. "You are a bossy person Catherine, aren't you? Of course we will use it. We cannot put most of the house away in cupboards, just because Leticia used it. Otherwise we will have no sheets, towels, crockery, glassware, silver or anything to eat with."

We sipped our tea, and took a piece of shortbread which was delicious. Some distant cousin had once given us a lesson on making shortbread, we would roll it out into a long thin piece, just like making bread rolls. Then cut it thinly into 24 pieces, and put them on a tray and cook for thirty minutes. We watched to see they did not burn and they always came out just the right size which would later melt in your mouth.

Goodness if I could remember making shortbread why couldn't I remember the one clue that David had asked for? What did he say just wind your mind back and then suddenly you will be there.

Maybe it would be better to try hypnosis except where did you find a reliable person here that would be able to do that? You always saw these well-known names overseas, unless you went to a Doctor with some training.

"What are you thinking about Catherine? You look so serious," asked Simon.

"Oh just trying to think back, all I can think of at the moment is how we used to make shortbread, but that isn't really what David has in mind."

"Yes I know what you mean, I was thinking of the first time I was allowed to go out for tiffin. My mother took me to Raffles as I had just turned five, and she thought it would be a treat for me to have high tea. I think it really was an excuse for her to go to Raffles as she had never been there, and it was not all that pleasant when we sat down."

"In fact the waiter made her feel so uncomfortable that we went elsewhere, and it was some years until my mother took me again and we had sandwiches, scones, and cakes on a silver three tiered cake stand."

"We didn't have shortbread except at home, and of course when we visited Scotland to catch up with the relations. It was such a wonderful life although when you are small you do not appreciate it, we just take it all for granted."

"But suddenly it was all over, and we were hurried to a ship bound for England. We should have left months earlier, but mother did not want to leave Papa and we never thought that the Japanese would come from the north through the rubber plantations, all the Colony's guns pointed out to sea."

"We had a lovely garden in Orchard Street, and of course in those days, it was mostly private homes. Life was conducted in a strict orderly pattern and it was strange to not go back there until after the war. So much had changed I think it is called progress," Simon reminisces.

"If you don't mind I think I will turn in now, it has been a long day, not that one complains but the trip over the island, and the swim in the sea snorkelling was more exhausting than I thought."

"David I see you and him as an item already Catherine, he seems such a nice sensible person. I know they say time heals, I am too new to grief to be able to give advice, but we are all entitled to some happiness. You have been on your own for some time now, perhaps too long and if the right man comes along, stand back and look hard at him, don't rush, but also do not turn him away too quickly. It takes time to let a friendship blossom, but if it feels right just go with it, let it happen. Enough said, now off to bed and sleep tight!"

I walked over to him and touched his shoulder as I left the room.

I walked down the passage to the kitchen to take a cold bottle of water out of the refrigerator. There was no thermos in the usual place, probably Pae had thoughtfully already put one by my bed.

The kitchen looked and felt refreshingly cool all painted in white with small delicate pieces of blue china laid neatly on the shelves. Some small café curtains with blue ducks were blowing gently in the breeze, a new addition to the kitchen since I had visited last.

Leticia always made the most of wherever she lived, no matter how long or shorter time she made the house feel like a touch of home. She had found it important to take the little things with her, and of course they were allowed a container of personal items to go along with them to each posting.

Sometimes in more difficult posts, she preferred to take very little with her. She would buy a few things in a market, but felt that if there was trouble and they had to leave in a hurry, as had happened in Iran she did not want to leave anything behind that she would regret.

Vietnam had been unforeseen, and she found leaving the local staff one of the hardest things she had done in her life. They had worked so well for them, and then had to be left to goodness know what.

She said it was just a matter of picking up a small overnight bag, with papers and driving to the airport along back roads, wondering if the taxi knew where he was going.

The Diplomatic Car they felt was too obvious and we had taken a taxi instead as the Viet Cong had eyes everywhere.

When Simon arrived at the airport, the girl behind the desk asked where would you like to fly to today.

"I don't mind," answered Simon. "Just give me two seats on the next plane out of here." He must have been worried, as he was usually so well organized, and knew just where and when he was flying. But on this occasion he just wanted them both out of the country as quickly as possible.

For Leticia it was the first time that she had not felt in control. Although we had travelled together to some strange places before she was married, and even later when they were based in other countries, it always seemed a game to us to travel as two tourists.

We would try and melt into the local scene and go on local buses, trains, ferry boats, and occasionally we would be the only tourists staying in a small village.

But Leticia had a way with her, she always said. "In trouble just smile, sometimes it will just break the ice. I don't think she was ever frightened, except maybe on the border of West and East Germany.

Somehow the Russians were always portrayed as the bad guys in films, and in books. So you would picture yourself ending up in Siberia and never heard of again. She had always wanted to catch the Trans-Siberian Express from Vladivostok and cross USSR.

The problem seemed to be to get to Vladivostok to start the journey, or if it ended there, how did you move further south.

The overland journey from London to India was another must on her bucket list, but here again we heard so many stories, of trucks breaking down in the wilderness, and being the subject of bandits, it was alright for the men but goodness knows what would happen to the females on the trip. Once in a harem nobody would ever find you, and how would you find your way back to the real world?

There had been articles in the London papers while we were there, telling stories of colonials answering advertisements to be nannies to rich sheiks in the ever growing oil areas of Saudi Arabia. Even nurses being interviewed in London and asked to travel with the family to their palaces there, all seemed in order on the surface. But as time went by families worried when there was no mail or communication from their daughters.

One managed to escape to a local embassy and told how her passport was taken on arrival in the household, that she had to work seven days a week, and she was treated with no more respect than a maid. Even less as they thought her stupid to have come with them in the first place.

Even in those days Leticia mixed with some of the expats who arrived to study music, singing, and dancing in London. She also joined the Victoria League and went away in the weekends to marvellous homes in the country.

At that stage I was away working in the English countryside myself as I had found London too cold and miserable in the winter.

But Leticia was always writing of these wonderful houses, and the people she met there. A completely different world she would say, servants, wonderful dinners in the evenings, everyone dressed for dinner, and she was a novelty as she came from the colonies and so nobody enquired into who her relations were, as she didn't have any in England. Or so we thought at the time.

She also joined another more exclusive club that our father had belonged to when he was in London. It was run by two elderly titled ladies. They would hold afternoon tea every day, and you were welcome to just ring the bell. The butler would ask your name and go off to see if you were acceptable. Of course after a few visits you would be welcomed and shown straight into the drawing room.

Here one of the elderly ladies would ask you to join her for afternoon tea. Then as others arrived you would be introduced. Finally at the end of the afternoon you would be asked if you would like tickets for a coming concert at the Albert Hall.

The ticket was an entry into one of the boxes, it seemed some of their friends had permanent boxes, and when not in use, kindly gave the tickets of these elderly ladies to give out to members.

On one occasion at the famous Tea Dance held every Sunday afternoon, Leticia wrote to tell me that by chance she had run into three people she had casually known in Wellington.

These three young men had won a scholarship to study art, and were staying at London House. Their friend was also staying at London House, but was working for the New Zealand High Commission.

The three teamed up and one or other would take her to a concert. She thoroughly enjoyed their company but was never invited to one of the exclusive dinner parties held in Kensington.

The young diplomat was most sort after, especially as an extra man to make up numbers at the last minute. He jokingly said, well it really was a free meal. All he had to do was to put on his dinner jacket, and be at a given address at the given time.

Usually he would be rung late in the afternoon by a desperate hostess and asked, if he would care to join her party.

He knew that it would be to fill that spare chair at the dinner table, but why worry. He would be met at the door by the butler, introduced to his hostess. She may ask him several questions about his position in London and then introduce him to the other guests on their arrival. He was always asked to arrive some fifteen minutes earlier so she could pretend she already knew him.

He met some interesting people mostly to do with the theatre. The dinner would be served early, and then the guests would leave to see some show or concert. He was not usually invited to go on with them, but he was content to talk to the guests, in return for an excellent meal with drinks, and then wish all a goodnight pleading a heavy work load.

While she was enjoying living the winter in London, I had chosen to go to the country to become a companion to a rather lonely titled Lady.

She lived not too far from Paddington Station in a lovely part called Marlow where there is a famous public house. She lived on Winters Hill which was a few miles from Marlow, and quite close to railway station at Cookham.

It was my position to drive her husband to the station on Monday morning where he took a train to Paddington and then onto the Embankment where he worked. After a few weeks he found it easier to stay at his club in Pall Mall than come back in the dark at night. It also meant that we did not have to wait for dinner, or that I would have to drive down to the station to collect him.

It was a quiet time for Lady Patricia and myself, with a married couple who were cook and maid. They had a small apartment at the top of the house, while Lady Patricia and myself slept on the first floor. When I was originally interviewed I was shown a room on the third floor, but upon my arrival I was shown one of the guest rooms. Maybe my interview had gone better than expected.

Lady Patricia was not her real name, as she had come from Poland, one of the countries behind the Iron Curtain. She had been studying in London in the late 1930's just before the war, had never returned to her own country, and met her husband at a concert where she was one of the young pianists.

They had married, but there were no children. He was a Scientist and led a very private life. She on the other hand had real interests, one working with the film people who worked at RAK Rank Studios at Bray, and the other was the collecting of Antiques.

We spent many hours driving through the countryside stopping at small antique shops. It was another world to learn the history of some of these valuable pieces, which she educated me thoroughly on.

When the snow set in, we spent a lot of time indoors, watching TV which was quite new to me. The programmes were most interesting but we mostly watched BBC. Simon Templar was my favourite.

Some nights I would be asked to go down to the cellar for a bottle of Dom Perignon, or for lunch a bottle of Nuits Saint Georges, which were a new taste for me.

We were both so different she was always looking for and easily found excitement whereas I just hoped it would come along.

There were times when it was difficult to go along with her as one was never sure quite what would happen. If there were two of us of course it was safer, but one would always wonder what would happen if she was on her own with no transport to get home again.

Everything was an adventure to her, and she did not think of the end result, and in most cases she would fly through a situation without realizing it had the potential of becoming a nasty situation, a lot like Leticia.

I always remembered the time Leticia and I were travelling together in Tangier. We had taken the little ferry boat across the Straits and made light of the film we had seen, with Alec Guinness in it taking the part of the Captain of the ferry boat. He had one wife on the Gibraltar side and one in Tangier. He would always go down to the cabin at the half way point and turn the photograph over of the wife that was waiting for him.

Sometimes I thought of Leticia like this, one side which I saw and the other side her friends saw.

We met a bunch of Australian ranch holders from Queensland, a group of four who said they were going to drive across North Africa to Cairo in an old land rover. They took the two of us under their wing, and suggested that we all visited the local Casbah for the evening.

We set out from the hotel and walked up the narrow alley ways to the top of the hill where the Casbah was situated. We sat down and were served cups of tea by some Eunuchs, the first we had ever encountered. The evening wore on and both Leticia and I became quite uncomfortable. The boys seemed to be enjoying themselves and refused to leave.

After repeated pleas from Leticia she excused herself

to go to the Ladies Room and never returned. It took a while for us to realize that she was not in the building. Finally when it dawned on us, we all hurried out and asked if anyone had seen her leave.

"Oh yes," was the answer. "The young lady said she did not need a taxi she would walk home" and that is exactly what she did.

She walked down the narrow dark alleys back to the hotel, which was quite a distance. Not to mention the many twists and turns that the narrow alleys took along the way.

We repeatedly stopped and asked the people sitting in their doorways if they had seen her, and each one of them pointed downhill.

Sometime later we arrived back at the hotel and the four Australians gave her the biggest ticking off she had ever had. They had been so worried that she would have been lost, and goodness knows if we would have seen her again.

This was the type of risk she would take, unthinking most of the time, she just wanted to go back to the hotel, and nobody offered to go with her so she just wandered off on her own. I lay in bed thinking back to these times we had spent together but this was not want David wanted, but maybe I would still break the puzzle for him.

The wind had come up, and I could not make out if it was rain on the roof, or just the wind in the palm trees. It did not matter how long I stayed in the islands I could never tell the difference. I snuggled down beneath the sheet, and tried to count backwards, an old trick someone had taught me.

The trouble was I had become quite good at doing this, and could count almost as quickly backwards as forwards.

Maybe someone would ask me to do this on a guessing game worth a trip around the world. Well you could always live in hope, and that is the way I finally drifted off to sleep. Counting, and wondering if it was raining outside and how safe I felt where I was.

Chapter 9

Savaii

The next day dawned one of those perfect days on the island. Even before I was awake and had time to draw the curtains I could hear the telephone ringing somewhere in the house.

A few moments later Pae knocked on the door, and called out, "Are you awake Miss Catherine? Mr David would like to speak to you, or should I ask him to call you back?"

"Oh no Pae I am awake now, and will take his call."

Nervous excitement filled my stomach as I leapt out of bed and walked quickly to take the call, "Good morning David, you are an early bird, or have I overslept?"

"No Catherine, there has been a new event, and I wondered if you would like a day on Savaii? If so could you be at the Fulialonga Airport strip in 45 minutes. I have reserved a seat for you if you can come along. I just thought as you know the island so well you may be of help? There is a local Detective going alone, and don't think he knows the island that well. Well how about it?"

"Yes of course, I will be there, I will just dress and have a quick cup of tea. The airport it is so close to here as you know, I will see you there."

I jumped out of bed, hurried into the bathroom, had quick wash and hurriedly dressing, ran down the passage to the kitchen.

Marta looked up, "You are always in a hurry, where to this time.

Miss Catherine?"

"I'm just off to Savaii with Mr. David and must be at the airport in 45 minutes, is Toni around? If he could please take me or if not please call a taxi. Oh and can I have a cup of tea and toast please?"

"Certainly Miss Catherine, just you get ready. Toni is outside and I will call him as soon as I make you some nice hot toast."

Everything was happening so quickly, I wonder why the hurry to Savaii. Never mind must collect my camera, and my bag with costume and bathing towel, glasses, sun cream and a hat. By that time my toast would be ready.

I felt a thrill at seeing David again, but thought I must not interfere with his work. It was beginning to be hard to make the division, as we were seeing each other every day, and I was feeling a warmth towards him that I had not felt for several years.

If he would only make a move, but then men were slow, and he knew that there had been nobody in my life, since my husband had died. At least he had some respect for me, not like the dreadful men that had turned up at the house with a month of the funeral.

I had always heard that a widow was so vulnerable, and neighbours, and other friend's husbands would probably call on the pretext to see if there were any odd jobs needed. Offers to mow the lawn, cut the hedge, and they once an obvious invitation if I wished to invite them inside.

It made me quite sick, to think these people had played golf with my husband, eaten at our table, and been one of the crowd.

But this was not the case with David, who had met me by chance, a horrid chance, but if Leticia had not drowned neither of us would be here now.

Maybe it would all end too soon, and both of us would go our separate ways, but I hoped this was not the case.

Day dreaming again was not going to help me, reach the airport in time, especially if I wanted that cup of tea before leaving.

Goodness knows when we would eat again. Perhaps we would go to the Vaisala Hotel as there was nowhere other than that to find food on the island, except at the port at this end, and I was sure we were not going to the east end of the island.

I hurried back to the dining room and there was the table set for me.

I said down and started on my toast, and poured my tea,

Looking at my watch I realized that there was little time, but Toni would have me there in no time, ten minutes at the most.

I gulped my tea down, and took two pieces of toast in my hand, went through the house to collect my bag, and out to the front where Toni was waiting for me.

"Morning Miss Catherine, and lovely one for a flight to Savaii. We better be off, I don't want to break any rules with you in the car, Mr Simon would not be pleased if we are stopped. Little chance of that, but he likes to abide by the rules, and does not expect any allowances made for us speeding."

"Of course not Toni, yes I am all ready, so off we go."

I sat back in the car, and we were off along the waterfront in no time. No need to worry along here, there were no houses, we turned through the village, turned left at 4 corners and along through the village. We were soon along the water's edge and turned inland, across the funny little bridge and up the hill, and in minutes we were at the airport.

I looked for David, and as he was not there, I went over to the man with the Bathroom scales. It always amused me that the kitchen scales were used to weigh the passengers and their luggage.,

At that moment David arrived with a stranger I had not seen before.

"May I introduce Tim Sinclair, he is a colleague from Wellington."

Tim did not look a bit like a detective whatever that should be.

"Glad to meet you, may I call you Catherine, David never stops talking about you. May I say how sorry I am to be here at such a sad time, my condolences for your loss. I hope there may be some assistance to solving this case."

Next moment we were all laughing as we each stepped on the scales to be recorded for weight, before walking out to the plane.

***

We took the flight in the small plane looking down over the ocean to Savaii and then to Salealonga to land.

Here there was a van awaiting our arrival to drive us to Vaisala along the coast, a two hour drive. We did not stop at the blowholes but continued along the coast until reaching the hotel where we had a quick lunch on the deck. Then back in the van along the causeway to the small lagoon where the yachts would moor and the local fishing boats anchored. There was only one yacht anchored there, so we pulled up as close as possible on shore.

David jumped out, "Stay in the van with the aircon on and I will catch their attention."

Soon a small dinghy rowed ashore with two people on board. David had a talk with them with a lot of pointing towards the now empty bay.

He returned with the news, "The yacht in question has now gone and the crew said they were heading to Pago Pago where one of the crew was catching a plane to New Zealand he thought. We are too late, the bird has flown. I think it may have been Alberto but we cannot be sure until we are in touch with Pago Pago police. He will be in American Territory by now where the law is different. But Interpol is everywhere if we need to bring them back here. I suggest we go and book in at the Vaisala for the night as we have missed the plane to Fungalea for today. I will use their phone and ring Pago Pago airport and see if a person of Alberto's description has flown out."

It seemed a good idea and a cool swim was in order, a cold wine and dinner before an early night. But first a call to Simon keeping him up to date.

We had a lovely evening and I appreciated the early night. We took two rooms on the top deck overlooking the beautiful turquoise water.

Next morning David was up swimming in the lagoon

before me, and over breakfast he said there was no news yet from Pago Pago, so we ordered a van to drive us back to the airport which was another two hours along the coast, where we arrived just in time to fly in the little plane back to Fungalea and back to Vaiala.

We arrived home to find Simon already there and we brought him up to date, and then David revealed his suspicions that Alberto may actually be the notorious Mr Casino, the infamous worldwide drug trafficker. Although how Leticia was involved was a mystery to him.

Then David rang the Pago Pago police, only to hear the bad news that Alberto had flown out that morning to Los Angeles along with two other people. The yacht had departed they thought to Tonga. This made sense as it is the usual route for yachts if it was on its way to New Zealand.

It felt all so disappointing. How would David ever be able to ask Alberto all the questions in the hopes he could maybe clear up why he was in Samoa and why he never contacted Leticia when he obviously knew she was there?

It seemed best for David to fly to LA as soon as possible and hope that Alberto had been traced by Interpol. So Simon arranged for him to fly on the next flight to LA via Hawaii which was the fastest route to LA from Samoa. It was sad to see him leave as I felt for the first time that there was a real connection with a decent male after so many years since Stephen's death.

Of course he would be in touch by telephone from the New Zealand Embassy in Los Angeles with any developments in tracing Alberto.

I would just have to be patient and use my time constructively trying to remember anything that may help with the connection between Leticia and Alberto. Maybe I should meet up with the bridge girls and that would take my mind off the problem of trying so hard to remember a vital clue. So I rang Aggies and asked when the group met. By chance it was that afternoon so off I went to Aggies catching the little bus that stopped outside the house and would drive me there.

The bus pulled up under the old tree at the door and after a short drive I was soon on the verandah to the side of the main entrance of Aggies, meeting the bridge group. Everyone was very friendly and we were soon playing. What a delightful mixture of girls, all expats with husbands working on contracts except for one local girl Mellie, who turned out to be the best player by far.

Time flew by and it was time for 'tiffin' the English name for afternoon tea. There was the usual chatter until Greta a Dutch girl mentioned a spate of burglaries that were taking place around Apia targeting expat houses.

She interesting enough mentioned that in her house like many others, she had a set of drawers in the bedroom where if you pulled the bottom drawer out it had a decent enough space for hiding passports, money and jewellery. A cold shiver chilled through me and I nearly dropped my cup. Mellie looked concerned and held my hand and whispered, "Are you alright? Maybe it is the heat, the fans above are slow today."

"Yes," I replied. "This side room has no sea breeze thank you."

"I will drive you home after the game if you like, I was a close friend of Leticia's and played bridge with her too."

Mellie kindly drove me home saying how sorry she was, also mentioning she knew something was worrying Leticia, but that she would close up when asked if she could help.

Mellie dropped me off and we arranged to go swimming next day in the pool at Aggies and have lunch. I couldn't walk into the house quickly enough. Pae asked if I wanted tea but I excused myself and hurried down the passage into Leticia's room before Simon would be home.

Hurrying to her bedroom drawers I pulled out the bottom one and there was the space beneath it that Greta had mentioned. There lay a small red book neatly concealed in a colourful sponge bag. I hastily pushed the drawer back into place and scurried back to my bedroom with the sponge bag.

I sat on the bed and with trembling fingers nervously opened the sponge bag again. Inside, next to the red book were not one but two passports, the old New Zealand blue one and a new black one. Why would she have these hidden? Besides she always travelled with her red diplomatic passport like Simon. It gave her easy access wherever they went plus their luggage would not be examined so thoroughly if they used the diplomatic bag for papers.

I opened the old blue passport, still in her maiden name, and found its pages filled with stamps of her travels before she was married. The second was her New Zealand passport made out in her married name again full of stamps with Visas for mostly Italy as they had to be renewed yearly.

By this stage I felt in need of a large brandy to give me some Dutch courage before I peered into the red book. Should I wait for Simon before reading it? Maybe not, it might reveal too much and wound him deeply in his grief.

I took a deep breath and slowly opened the red book to find a large letter addressed to me which I put to one side, before I quickly turned the books' pages and discovered it was not a diary as such, but just years, towns, and countries and some brief notes and names. Nothing much was written in full, but I could make out some of it, like times and tourist destinations.

I spotted a shiny white sheet of photo paper on an angle slightly protruding from the back of the book. Flicking through quickly, a number of photos spilled out onto the floor. Kneeling to pick them up, I saw featuring in all of them Alberto of all people, along with other men. One of whom I recognised as the man on the flight over to Samoa who had dropped his book in the aisle. My hands started shaking as I for the first time realised the hold that Alberto had over my sister.

If anyone casually came across this and tried to decipher the contents, it would appear initially as a tourist itinerary but I did not think so. I wish David was here, he would be able to make out what it all meant. The year all the entries had been made were not mentioned. However, this could be worked out when reconciled with the dates in the passports. Just then I heard Simon returning and panicked wondering what should I do?

I decided to jump into a cold shower to help me calm down and then wander out for the usual drink which I was badly in need of.

We met on the verandah, our usual drinking place. Simon had had a tiring day with people wanting passports and he needed to relax completely. I felt it was not a good time to produce my latest findings, maybe after breakfast in the morning. Now for a very large brandy or two. I caught him up on my day by relaying I had played some bad bridge and needed a strong brandy which he poured. After idle small talk, I tried to relax but I couldn't. Should

I tell David first what I had found?

Then making my decision and taking a deep breath, "I'm so sorry Simon, but I have made some important findings today and there is something I have just discovered. At bridge one of the girls reminded me of a hiding place we had forgotten to check, so I searched under Leticia's set of drawers and there was a drawer containing a diary we have not seen before. It is full of dates and places of her travels before and since you met her."

I hurried back to my room and produced the book, photos and passports.

Simon looked through the material, "This is a terrible shock to us both but I have had my suspicions for years and you may have had them also."

He continued looking at the diary and read some of it out loud shaking his head. It read:

1985   Samoa Alberto here, I wish I could end it all
1984   Samoa
1983   Thailand Bangkok Cover nearly blown with Catherine here. I must travel to Chiang Mai for collection
1982   Thailand Bangkok, Collection and pickup Antonio
1981   Sweden Stockholm, House outside city with park Karen
1980   Sweden Stockholm, Holiday house, perfect for drop off Lars
1979   Egypt Cairo, Eman
1978   Egypt Cairo, Zamalek
1977   Greece Athens, Easy travel to Alexandria for shipment
1976   Greece Athens, Good centre Natalie
1975   Turkey Samos good connection with Turkey

1974   Turkey Access to Malta
1973   Austria Elfie
1972   Austria
1971   Italy Rome, Natalie
1970   Italy
1969   Spain Madrid, Ava
1968   Spain Madrid
1967   Jordan Amman, Thomas
1966   Jordan Sayonara
1965   Canada Tony
1964   Canada
1963   Wellington Homewood
1962   Wellington
1961   Wellington
1960   Australia Melbourne, South Yarra
1959   Wellington Lowry Bay and Whakapapa ski hut
1958   London Germany, Denmark, Sweden, John
1957   London France, Spain, Italy, Austria

Simon looked up his face ashen, "It all makes sense now. All the spur of the moment decisions that Leticia made having to go off to see something that had to be done now. A photo she must take, the light would be perfect. Never waited for a driver she would just take a taxi and return tired and drawn out and that large camera bag so heavy with photo lens she said."

"We must contact David at once, I believe this is the lead he has wanted. Let us hope he can find Alberto and bring him back in handcuffs to face justice. He is probably wanted in many countries. He is certainly the international criminal we have been seeking, known as Mr. Casino."

"Why didn't she tell us at the beginning and we could

have put a stop to it. I am sure she was not on drugs she didn't need the money and was not interested in all this cat and mouse carry on. Alberto may have threatened her with her life. Or maybe even one of us," ponders Simon.

"Leticia would have done almost anything to keep you safe."

"Maybe he threatened your life too, but how do you feel Catherine knowing now that your sister had this hidden secret and has lived a double life for all these years?" asks Simon.

"She is at peace now that is all that matters and we must see that Alberto is brought to justice. Should we send what we have found to David immediately?" queries Catherine.

"Of course I will return to the office now and meet my secretary there and telex this through. You may come if you wish instead of sitting here and going over it again in your mind. I will have Toni bring the car around now. Tell Pae to hold dinner we will eat later if she would just leave something we can serve up ourselves. I'll meet you out front in ten minutes."

We drove to the office in silence, lost in our own thoughts. Ruth the secretary had already opened the security gates and we drove straight into the consulate office. We climbed the stairs unlocked the next security door and entered the main office. Ruth took the passports and sent the details and the pages of the diary. Nothing was said between us all and we returned downstairs to the car. On the way down Ruth squeezed my hand as much to say it will be alright from here on.

Next morning David rang before breakfast to say he had received everything and with the latest good news.

Alberto had been detained with two companions. One

of which gave evidence in the hopes his prison term would be avoided or cut short. They would be returning to Samoa on the returning flight as soon as possible. However, he thought it best for Simon's career if he left for England immediately on urgent business accompanied by me so that we would not have to go through the trial and media attention.

Therefore, arrangements were made for the next flight out of Western Samoa that afternoon for us both to fly to London via Los Angeles. It was best not to fly via New Zealand and risk arriving to the breaking news.

Simon broke the news of our departure to Mata, Pae and Toni while I hurriedly packed my belongings. Then while Pae and I helped Simon pack his bags, Mata made us one of her finest cooked breakfasts, which we hungrily devoured.

Toni had loaded our bags into the DC 1 diplomatic car and was all ready for our departure.

"Now Pae, you must be strong for us and hold the fort for Mr Simon," I advised her as we hugged farewell.

Mata was in tears, "Oh Mr Simon, when will you be back?"

"I'm not sure just yet Mata, now a word to you all, mind you don't talk with any of the news media reporters, just say 'Mr Simon has to attend a family matter in Great Britain and will answer all questions on his return. Come now Toni, we will be late for our plane." Simon instructed.

It was sad to suddenly leave our friends behind in Samoa, but I knew I would return and they would understand why we departed so quickly.

Following David's instructions we flew out, stopping over in Los Angeles and arriving back in the UK.

It was on the trans-Atlantic flight that I recalled our time in Bangkok and then remembered to read my sister's letter she left for me in the drawer.

Chapter 10

Recollections of Bangkok

I dozed in and out on the flight back to the UK remembering our horrific time in Bangkok and comparing it with our happy times in Scotland with our cousin.

Smeaton was the ancestral family home in Scotland, only a thirty minute drive from Edinburgh airport. It was here that the family would visit each time they were in England. It was by chance that the family connection had been found in the seventies.

As happens with most families who left the United Kingdom over one hundred years ago, contact with family has often been lost. We were no different. If it had not been for a chance advertisement in the Samoan Times we would never have found some distant Scottish cousins living just out of Edinburgh.

Annette McLeod had come out to Western Samoa to visit some friends and pay respect to her descendants who had died and were buried on the island. While there she decided to see if there were by any chance living relations of her father's cousins still residing in Western Samoa.

Leticia while reading the daily newspaper came across the advertisement and excitedly rang the telephone number in the paper immediately.

Yes, she thought that there was a connection, and Annette came around straight away. Leticia of course did not carry the family tree with her, but she had enough details to prove that they were in fact cousins.

That was enough proof for Annette and so the next time Leticia and Simon were in England staying in Simon's Hinton St George, they took a break and drove up to Scotland to see the relations. Everyone fitted in so well that a trip to Smeaton was to become a regular sojourn every time they were in Britain. Other members of the family were always welcome, so a steady stream of New Zealand relations arrived at Smeaton over the next few years.

It was on one of these occasions that the whole extended family sat around the great long table in the Smeaton dining room. There was much laughter, and I will always remember the impeccably laid out table setting with family silver and sparkling crystal glasses.

It was the first time that I saw Sterling Silver Grape scissors being used to cut the grapes that had been freshly picked and bought in from the homestead's glasshouse.

We used to take tea in the glasshouse every afternoon while there, as it was warmer in there and the plants that could not be grown out of doors, made us feel more at home.

The garden was set out within an enclosed brick wall for shelter and it was always fun to walk down the paths and be so completely hidden from the house.

The guests always slept in the older part of the house.

When Annette and Hamish bought the property they had skilfully added a new addition with large windows facing onto the pretty garden. The new addition comprised of a living area with a beautiful old grand piano, dining room and kitchen.

The family lived upstairs and the older wing was left for visitors. When the children were younger this was their domain with a school room, playroom, and small kitchen and bathroom downstairs. All self-contained.

Upstairs there was another playroom and off this were three bedrooms. The main bedroom was my favourite with floral bedspreads and curtains. A lovely old dressing table with water colours that had been painted by some relation long since gone.

It was to this bedroom that Leticia had come when she returned from Bangkok. Leticia and I had always wanted to see the real Thailand, so while Simon was posted there we decided to take a three week holiday and go north.

As a last minute diplomatic issue came up Simon was not able to come with us.

It was a great experience as we had heard of the Golden Triangle where the drugs came from, but at this time of the year the poppies would all be in flower. It was a wonderful sight to see, and we were quite safe there as it was before the harvest time when they were all busy.

One morning we braved the awful traffic to the airport. It was a drive that nobody ever wished to make. Long streams of cars and trucks with lots of heavy pollution. It meant you had to give yourself a good hour just to make the journey.

The suggestion had been made that we should drive all the way, but it seemed easier to fly from Bangkok to

Chiang Mai direct and save the long drive overland.

Simon's last words of warning, "Now you girls be on alert all the time, never let your overnight bags out of your sight. Don't even put them in the luggage hold. Take them on as carryon luggage. DO NOT carry anything for another passenger."

We thought this all a bit of a laugh, but at the time Leticia just shrugged her shoulders, "Oh Simon you are so stuffy who would want to ask us? We are not stupid, and you've been reading too much in books and taking it all far too seriously."

It was a foggy morning and we set off in great spirits, one shoulder bag each and my camera as usual. I never went anywhere without my camera, and preferred to take photographs of people we met along the way, than of too many nature scenes.

We were soon through the check in and waiting in the departure lounge. Here we noticed another couple who looked smartly dressed, and I hoped they were on our tour.

Oh yes Simon wanted to make sure nothing happened to us, so he booked us at the last minute on a tour, which was to start at the airport in Chiang Mai on arrival.

The flight was not too long and the hostesses were some of the most beautiful girls I had ever seen. The service was excellent and put us in high spirits for what was to come.

In no time we were descending down and were soon off the plane and into the waiting hall. A girl came from nowhere and asked if we were Leticia and Catherine, and please to follow her. It was here we met Orlando and his daughter Sophia. It turned out they were from South America, and he dealt in Antiques from around the world. He was in Bangkok on business, and having come with his daughter thought they would take a holiday and see the North.

We were soon in a Kombi Microbus driving to our extravagant hotel. Goodness it was so large, with lovely tiled floors and ornate chandeliers. We were shown to our room and told to meet down in the entrance hall in one hour for our first sightseeing trip of the day.

We laughed as we sat on the beds, and argued who would sleep nearest the window. It was all so modern, even with a fridge containing cold drinks, and a jug to make a cup of tea.

We didn't dare lie down or we would have gone to sleep, as it was much hotter up here, and the air conditioning didn't seem to cool the room. We would fix that and leave it on while we were out.

We met in the hall and soon our guide Nid and the driver were driving us through the town to look at some of the local craft in the market. There were many stalls and Leticia had her eye out for some bedspreads, and maybe some cushion covers.

I had no definite plans to buy anything but was tempted to buy a sun frock as I could see it was going to be hot. Also a large hat each was going to be a necessity and a 'Coolie' hat would be just the thing if it was small enough to stay on my head.

Orlando and Sophie of course were looking for any small figures and bells for sale that interested them. They kept asking Nid where they could buy some really old figures but she said they were rare now, and were usually handed down from one family to the next.

We had a good afternoon, however Leticia seemed to be constantly looking over her shoulder all the time. In the end I jokingly said, "Looking for Mr Right are you?"

She snapped back which was not like her, "What do you mean by that?"

"Oh take a joke! You seem to be looking behind you all the time, why not in front the people are so interesting."

She apologized and became intent on finding the bedspreads she wanted.

We returned to the hotel at sundown and strolled into the bar with Orlando and Sophia for a well-earned cold drink. Nid came in and asked us, "How about an early start next morning?" as she wanted to take us to some temples of great interest. And maybe if we had time to visit some of the Hill People who had a small village where we may find the bedspreads Leticia wanted.

We had fun in the van and decided who would sit where, but of course Nid and the driver always sat in front. We asked so many questions she laughed and said she could not answer them all, but would find out tomorrow.

We visited the Buddhist Temple and had to climb a multitude of steps, and when reaching the terrace at the top there were many monks in their Saffron gowns coming and going. The bells were all beautiful and when rung they were very melodious but we were told it took many years of training to strike them at just the right moment. The view stretched for miles and as it started to warm up we decided to sit in one of the smaller temples.

We realized how little we knew of their religion, but were told young boys go into a monastery for several years when they leave school. Everyone was so polite and left us sitting quietly at the rear of the temple.

I noticed Leticia seemed distant. It was as if she was waiting for someone all the time. She kept turning around looking at any new comers who entered the temple. I did not ask why after yesterday's outburst and pretended I had not noticed.

Then it was time to leave again and we followed Nid back down the steps again pleased to see the bright orange Kombi van waiting for us.

Nid mentioned she was not happy about eating at wayside stalls, and had had the hotel prepare a picnic lunch for us and would do so each day. Being very considerate she hoped we didn't mind. Of course not, she was very thoughtful, and none of us wanted to be sick on the tour.

She even had a large chilli bin with cold drinks for us, sealed bottles of course, we were just to ask for one as we travelled along.

We were out in the countryside again, and then turned inland onto an unsealed road. She explained we were going into the Village which although small would give us an idea how the Hill People still lived.

We pulled up in the centre of the village and out came the children and surrounded us. It seemed they did this every time and Nid had a bag of sweets ready for them. She divided the sweets up and gave us a handful each. Just give the children one at a time she suggested. Otherwise the older ones would take them all if you throw them onto the ground.

This we did and with great delight picked out the smallest children who seemed delighted not to be forgotten.

The village was very poor and most of the men were out in the fields, leaving the women and children back in the village.

I noticed an elderly couple sitting just inside their little hut, and asked if I could photograph them. Nid came over and we sat down with them on the doorstep. The man was smoking a pipe and he seemed excited that I wished to take his photograph.

A pleasant hour was spent here, and the women showed us some jewellery they had made. We each bought a bangle they would always be handy as a gift. The workmanship was lovely and must have taken many hours to make.

Then it was time to be off, and the monk in the village came over to bid us farewell, and whispered are there any sweets left I would love one.

Goodness we had not thought of sweets for the older members in the village, but we would not forget next time.

We drove back to the main road, and the driver pulled off near a small river. The picnic lunch was carried out and we were soon enjoying the food the hotel had prepared. A little further away were some roadside stalls, and Leticia asked the driver if he could stop there on the way out.

"Of course" exclaimed Nid. "Just ask if you see a photograph you wish to take, or anything else." So we stopped and here we saw the loveliest embroidery of all. After much bargaining Leticia bought two beautiful bedspreads which would end up in one of her guest rooms.

I fell in love with some delightful cushion covers all in dark blue with a small pattern of people and trees in the centre.

Orlando and Sophia not finding any antiques settled for some more jewellery, then we were on our way again.

It had been a long day and being quite some way from the hotel we turned for home looking forward to a nice hot bath.

Nid remarked, that although the traffic was light there seemed to be another Kombi van on the road not far behind us. We all turned and sure enough there was a white van tailing behind us, but then Thailand was full of white vans.

I turned to comment to Leticia but she had gone white, the colour of the van. "Are you feeling alright?" I hesitantly asked.

"Oh I found the last stop a bit much, suppose it was the excitement of buying the bedspreads, they were really expensive but I did want them."

No more was said until we reached the hotel.

Orlando said he was going back to the market which was only ten minutes away and would Leticia like to go with him.

I had already said it was a bath for me, and Sophia said she wanted to lie down until dinner.

Leticia thinking it was a good idea, as she had seen some little boxes she liked and would be pleased to have company. So off they took and I retired up the lift. Leticia arrived back some time later, delighted with her purchases and as they were already wrapped put them straight into her carryon bag.

We concluded the day with our usual meal and turned in early to be ready for a longer day tomorrow, as we were to go by boat down to a village and visit some caves along the way.

It was quite hot the next day and we were a little hesitant when we arrived at the river. It was as if the tide was out, as little water. However Nid assured us there was enough water for the boats to float down the river on.

We crossed in twos, and Nid stayed with us, while the driver was sent on to pick us up further downstream. We pulled into a landing and visited a cave. Another long climb and we were quite exhausted when we reached the top. Again I wish that we had studied the culture a little before we had set out on the trip.

We climbed down the steps again, and were helped back into the long boats. It was very hot by now, so Leticia lay down in the bottom of the boat and we opened a large umbrella and covered her with it.

Soon I followed suit and asked the boatman to put my umbrella over me.

Umbrellas are one of the most versatile necessities to carry when travelling. We obviously use them for the rain but on many an occasion I used mine while on tour to keep the sun off me. The other must is a lavalava as it is great to sleep in, wear over a bathing costume, or cover ones' arms when out in the midday sun. They are known as sarongs in Thailand.

We were soon woken as the boat bumped into the jetty. We had arrived at our destination. Once again we were helped ashore and were met shyly by a small group of children. One came up to me and held my hand, and beckoned me to follow her.

We followed her into the centre of the village, where yes there were some tables set up under a tree, with their local handicraft. We always felt we should purchase something, and jewellery seemed the most obvious. But this time they also had some tie-dyed sarongs so we purchased one each.

We were asked if we would like something to drink, but declined and asked to see their temple. The little girl gladly walked ahead to show us.

A Buddhist monk appeared and bowed and graciously guided us inside.

Leticia seemed distressed again saying, "The little girl is so sweet maybe only nine or ten, I hope her parents do not sell her to work in Bangkok. I wish I could save all little girls in Thailand who think they are going to school, or work in Bangkok. It just doesn't happen as they usually end up working in a brothel. It was as if the sun had gone behind a cloud, the mood changed and it worried me so much that it spoilt the whole day for me.

Soon we returned to the boats, and for the first time was pleased to settle back into the little narrow wooden boat. We had expected to float down a river lined on each bank with trees.

Brochures had mentioned the forests of the north, but when we enquired from Nid where have the forests gone. She nodded sadly and said they had been cut down, as Thailand needed the timber.

We therefore floated down the river with bare hillsides so stark in the hot sun. "They should be replanted," Leticia pointed out. "We cut pine trees in New Zealand in the centre of the island, but the contract always says whatever is cut has to be replanted. It takes about 30 years for the trees to grow there, I wonder how long it takes here in Thailand."

Nid looked so sad we decided to drop the matter. Instead we asked how long it would be until we reached the village which was connected by road, where the Kombi would be waiting to pick us up.

"Not too far," she replied, "and we will have lunch once we move away into the countryside. That is what you all prefer isn't it?

I must say we were all hungry by now and looked forward to getting another packed lunch from the hotel.

Around the next bend and we could see quite a large village this time, and a long high terrace of steps. In no time we were climbing along the steps and helped out of the boats once again.

The steps were enormous, and we had trouble trying to climb up them. You needed to take two steps across the terrace, and pull yourself up onto the next step.

A lot of people seemed to stand around watching, but no gentlemen were here to give us a helping hand. They must have done this most days when tourists arrived by boat at the steps.

We were back in the Kombi all exhausted and on the drive opened the chilli bin to have a well-deserved drink. Then out of the village into the countryside.

The first spot the driver found we stopped and had lunch. Nid explained to us the programme for the following day. We would make an early start and drive to the Golden Triangle and then return to the main road, and turn off as we would spend the night sleeping in a hill village. This village was known for its wonderful working elephants and we were all looking forward to this.

We drove back to the hotel and prepared to depart the next morning. Nid excused herself and said she was going to meet some friends to have a meal with them and would see us in the morning.

Next day she arrived late, and we had already had breakfast, so she hurried us into the van. We drove for a long time, all of us quite excited at going to this new famous area.

However, it was such a disappointment, we stopped at a tea house on a hill overlooking the Mekong River and she explained we were looking at Laos. But it was unsafe to actually enter Laos from this area.

We asked about the drug trade, but she either thought better not to talk about it, or actually did not know much about it.

So we returned to the van and were looking forward to our lunch. We seemed to drive a distance and arrived in quite a big town. Nid said, she thought we would like to see the frontier post into Burma. This had not been mentioned before, so we walked with her to the border.

She told us a lot of local people used this frontier to enter Burma once a year to go to the large sale of gems. It seemed it was an international market of precious gems, and jewellers from around the world attended the sale once a year.

We walked along the road, and she hesitated outside a restaurant before going in and asked us to follow her. She suggested we find a table in the shade, and sit down and then looking very subdued apologized to us.

"I am very sorry but last night I forgot to order our picnic hamper, and this morning when I arrived they said it was too late to make one up. So I have ordered a selection of dishes for us, and I am sure you will enjoy the local food."

The dishes soon arrived and as all of us were very hungry we soon loaded up our plates, with mostly a mixture of vegetables and what Nid said was chicken.

Looking back we should have only touched the rice but it is easy to look back on a mistake and think the opportunity was there not to proceed. But how many of us ignore our intuition and continue on when faced with a decision to avoid embarrassing others?

So we ate everything in front of us and then returned to the van, for our trip to the elephant village.

Everyone in the van were sleepy and I must have dropped off to sleep, to be woken by a nudge on my right arm from Leticia.

"What is it?" Thinking she had seen a photograph I would want.

"I feel terrible, I think you had better ask Nid to stop the truck.

NOW." So I tapped Nid on the shoulder. "Please stop Leticia is going to be sick."

She spoke to the driver and he pulled in and ran around to slide the door open. Leticia was out in a flash and was very sick on the side of the road.

I wet a small face flannel we always carried with some water from the bottle and gave it to her.

We waited for a few minutes before she climbed back into the van apologizing, "So sorry everybody, must have been the lunch."

We drove for a few more minutes more until she asked, "Nid you must find me a toilet quickly?"

Nid once more asked the driver to pull in at the next little house.

Nid jumped out rushed to the house, and spoke to the owners and returned to take Leticia by the arm to the rear of the house, with me following close behind.

She opened the door to the outhouse, and in side on the mud floor was what we called a long drop. By this time Leticia was shaking heavily so I lead her over to it, and told her to sit down.

This she did. I then left saying call if you want me.

"Don't leave me Catherine I feel faint and my legs feel funny."

We stayed here for at least ten minutes until she said she thought she was strong enough to return to the van.

The family all came out, and I thanked them for

their help, even though nobody understood me, but Nid explained, and I asked for their address. The eldest boy who was attending school wrote it down for me, they would definitely receive a gift of thanks from us.

We returned to the van, but by this time Leticia said she could hardly stand, so was helped into the van, and insisted on lying down on the bottom of the van between two seats.

Orlando and Sophia were most concerned, and suggested we didn't go into the village where we were to ride the elephants, but return to the hotel at Chiang Mai.

I was too worried to argue and gratefully accepted. Nid said she would ring through to book us in as they would have a Doctor there.

On the edge of the town she stopped at a relations' house and rang through to the hotel and asked for a Doctor to meet us. By the time Leticia seemed to be floating she said, and this worried us all.

We pulled up outside the grand entrance of the hotel, and Orlando and the driver each took one of Leticia's arms to support her and almost dragged Leticia inside. She seemed to have lost the use of her legs.

I noticed the opens mouths of the tourists and locals standing in the lounge, and the lights from the chandeliers were too bright.

Leticia was up the lift and into a room in no time with Nid and myself following. They lay her on the bed, and the Doctor entered almost immediately with his large black medical case.

Taking a blood pressure cuff from his case, he expertly wrapped it around Leticia's upper arm, then he put his stethoscope to her wrist looking very concerned. Speaking out loud, he said "The lady has very low blood pressure."

I do not remember how long we sat there while he examined her, "I will give her some pills, but the best place for her would be back in Bangkok when she feels better."

"But to tell you the truth you must realize she is very ill so we will sit with her for a while. If she improves a little, then I can go." So we worriedly waited in silence.

Leticia told me afterwards, she thought she was floating up towards the ceiling, looking down on her body. This was the first time I had ever spoken to someone who had actually admitted to floating above their bodies. But having read about Near Death Experiences, I accepted that she probably did.

She was also concerned as we had asked what the little chapels were on the roadside, and found they were for the dead. We had seen so many over the last few days, she must have thought about them in her subconscious.

Sometime when it was dark, the Doctor said he thought she was a little better, and why did I not ask for room service. This seemed a good idea so ordered for two. But when it arrived this time only ate the rice, and asked for a strong brandy if they had such a thing.

Later the Doctor left but gave me a severe warning that if I was concerned for any reason, I should contact the desk immediately and he would come.

It was a hellish night for me, I dozed off and on and Leticia seemed to be asleep each time I awoke and whispered to her.

Finally morning came, and I rang for hot tea.

She woke and said she felt terrible, and was frightened, as was I but I didn't let on. She wanted the Doctor back, and within fifteen minutes he was there.

He examined her again and looked puzzled, "I do not

like her heart beat, the quicker she goes to Bangkok the better, it must be some sort of food poisoning and we do not have the facilities to find out exactly what here. If we take samples and send them to Bangkok they would only go on the same flight as you, so it's better for you to fly with her as soon as possible.

"What a responsibility, Doctor, I will phone her husband and tell him the problem and he can make arrangements for her to see a Doctor in Bangkok if you think she is fit to travel."

With that Leticia opened her eyes, and pleaded to fly south.

She told me afterwards, she felt she was dying and wanted to be back with Simon if that was going to happen.

I asked the Doctor if he could give her something to make her comfortable for the flight, and he looked long and hard at me and answered, "Yes of course I will."

With that he opened his medical bag and took out three lots of pills.

These he carefully separated into three different small plastic bags, and labelled them 1, 2 and 3.

Giving me instructions, "The first is to be taken one hour before the patient leaves here, that will hopefully give her legs some strength.

"The second is once she reaches the airport here, as they will not want a sick patient on board. Do not mention she is ill.

"The third is if she is in great pain during the flight, I hope you do not have to use it, as she may pass out. Please only use this one in an extreme emergency."

Thanking him, I took the pills, and asked for his bill. There seemed a long pause before he told me how much, it was very little I argued it was too little but he said, he had not made her better, and wished he could have helped more.

With that he left, and a few minutes later there was another knock at the door.

Orlando and his daughter entered. He looked so concerned, and asked if he could see Leticia privately. This seemed strange but I felt he had helped so much it was rude to say no. He came into the bedroom and was shocked to see such a lifeless figure lying on the bed. He spoke to her but she did not answer, and that was when he insisted that he would watch her, while Sophie took me down to have some breakfast.

He promised he would not leave her side and persuaded me that by me being out of the room it would help me to have a break and prepare me for the journey ahead. It was also a good opportunity to make the booking for the change of flight at the desk, and speak to Simon out of her hearing.

So I gratefully stood up and headed for the door. Looking back I checked, "Are you quite sure you will ring the desk if there is any change in Leticia, any at all?"

"Quite sure," he said. "Just go with Sophie she will make sure you eat breakfast."

I had a small breakfast as had lost my appetite from all the worry, made several calls through to Simon personally, and asked for the flight to be changed, then hurried back upstairs.

By this time Leticia was sitting up with Orlando smiling next to her. "Is all is well?" He asked, "I hope you can fly soon."

"Yes thank you, we should be leaving here within two hours."

"Well in that case we will say farewell, we may have already left the hotel by the time you leave. Nid has arranged for us to view some antiques somewhere a little out of town," Orlando replied.

I thanked him for all his help and support and he left.

The trip to the airport, and the flight was not as bad as I expected. Leticia's determination ensured she could make the effort to walk when required.

It was such a relief to arrive back in Bangkok where Simon met us with a car, and in no time the three of us were heading into town to a Doctor.

His lame advice was that all we could do was wait and see. He took the necessary tests, and much to our frustration found nothing regardless of the fact that Leticia continued to feel awful. She mentioned she felt a pain in her chest with one in her side, and dizzy spells.

It was then Simon decided it would be better to take her out of the heat, and return to London, but better still he suggested Scotland.

Of course she could have gone to Hinton but Simon's parents were always making such a fuss about illness, she said she would be happier at Smeaton. Besides cousin Annette was a trained Doctor and could keep an eye on her.

Arrangements were made for us to fly to England, where I would spend a few days, and then I must return to New Zealand. I had a small job working as a feature writer and my employer had been very generous with allowing me time off, but would not keep my position forever. However, I did love Scotland but I knew Leticia would be in safe hands up with the rellies in Scotland and just relaxing, once she had seen the Harley Street Specialist.

She asked me to pack for her, not much to pack as at

this time of year only warmer clothes would be needed in Scotland. Besides this would be a good excuse to buy some new winter clothes, good quality Scottish made materials.

I'm not sure why I decided to unpack the carryon bag that Leticia had taken to Chiang Mai. The bedspreads had come in a separate bag and were now spread out on the beds in my room. I unpacked the carryon and took out her sponge bag, and a few clothes.

Then I remembered the boxes she had bought in the market, but the parcel was not there. Strange everything else she had bought was there, the small packages with the jewellery but not the boxes.

This worried me, so I went into Leticia's room and asked, "Dear sister, I have unpacked the carryon as I thought you may need it on the plane as hand luggage. But the boxes you bought with Orlando are not there."

She looked startled, nervously replying, "Oh I forgot about them completely, that is strange. Are you sure?"

"Of course I am sure, they are not there. Nobody could have taken them as we never left the bags unattended not even on the plane. They were with us in the van on the last day, as we were moving hotels that night. Nid suggested all the luggage stay in the van while we were in the village for the night."

"Did you leave the room at all when I was sick?" she asked.

"No I only went down to have breakfast, when Orlando kindly offered to sit with you."

Then she relaxed and said the strangest thing. "Don't worry it must have been Orlando."

"What do you mean Leticia? Orlando would not take some parcel out of your bag, surely?"

"Oh course he wouldn't, did I say that? How stupid, I must be still high as kite, it must be the medication." Her mood then suddenly changed and she became agitated, so I let the matter drop. She was not herself and Simon said to keep her as quiet and calm as possible.

Simon made the booking for the necessary flight, and thought a week would give her time to feel strong enough for the trip.

He tried for the most direct flight, or at least only one stopover with the shortest layover. At the same time he made an appointment with a Harley Street Specialist who was well known as the leading specialist and Doctor of Tropical Diseases. He felt sure he would be able to find out what the problem was.

***

A week later, back in the UK – London

In no time at all, it was a week later and we were off to London. A city that had always felt comfortable for me as I had lived and worked there.

We booked into the Bed and Breakfast in Grosvenor Street we had used many times before. Leticia was very tired so we had a light meal sent up to her room.

Next morning we walked to Harley Street which I thought would do both of us good. Leticia reminded me of how much she liked this particular area of London and hoped one day she would have a Mews Flat when they returned to the Home Office in London.

We arrived in plenty of time to see Mr Salisbury the Specialist who came out to greet her. Leticia was in his surgery sometime, before he called me into to have a quick chat. "You realize it is most difficult to find exactly what your sister has picked up in Thailand. Of course we have taken the usual tests, and these will be sent over to the laboratory at the London Clinic if that is in order."

"Of course Mr. Salisbury we are entirely in your hands. Should we wait in London for the results?"

"No that will not be necessary, are you going to take her down to Mr. Winchester's family at Hinton St. George?"

"No, we have decided she would feel more at home with her relations in Scotland. Her cousin Annette did four years of her training to be a Doctor before she married. We think she will be fine there, a complete rest, and we all love the family home of Smeaton very much."

"Do you think that is too far away? There are quite a few daily flights from Edinburgh to Heathrow, so she could be back here if you wanted to see her again."

"Not at all," the Specialist replied. "She should be where she feels most comfortable. The cooler weather will do her some good. In fact the sooner you fly there the better."

Satisfied with what the doctor had to say we headed back to the Bed and Breakfast, and rang to book on the early morning flight to Edinburgh. I checked in with our cousin Annette also checking it would be convenient, and to be no bother we would book a rental car, and drive straight out to Smeaton and be there for lunch.

So after another early night, with a quick meal at our local pub on the corner, we were well refreshed for our hire car when it arrived early the next morning. Considering it was so early we had an easy drive to Heathrow and we were there in plenty of time for the flight.

***

Back in Bonnie Scotland, at Smeaton after enjoying another good second breakfast on board the flight we were soon coming into land on the outskirts of Edinburgh.

I picked up the keys for the rental car and we were off on the old familiar road to East Lothian. The countryside looked so green after Thailand, and I think Leticia seemed automatically much more positive being back in familiar countryside.

We turned into the village of Preston, drove past the old watermill and turning right up over the hill heading towards the inviting gates of Smeaton.

The avenue of trees was always a joy, and we were glad that the park had recently been opened to the public. In fact every tree had been named and the old path around the lake had been cleared and we were able to catch a glimpse of a couple with their dog walking along it.

Suddenly we were upon the private area leading to the grand entrance to the house and pulled up outside the front door. "Home at last," Leticia exclaimed a lot more happily. "I feel better already."

Annette was out in no time to open the car door and greeted us warmly. She threw her arms around Leticia, "My poor cousins! What a terrible time you have had, but you are at Smeaton now and everything will be alright. Come in and have a cup of tea, Sally has made a batch of fresh scones which I know you two will love."

The living room looked just the same, tables covered with thick heavy books, and the French doors were swung open to reveal the sunny patio. We both took the two chairs closest the window and happily looked out over the familiar garden.

Nothing seemed to change here, it was always peaceful

and there was something about the air. Maybe although we could not see the sea, it must have been the wind from the North Sea that carried up the river Tyne.

Sally came through from the kitchen with the tray, and as soon as she placed the home made goodies down, we all ran over to her and there were hugs all round.

"What is this I hear about you Leticia not being well? We cannot have that! Some good homemade cooking will help fix that which ails you, of that I am sure. In no time you will be off again back to Simon in Bangkok. How is he, poor man being left out there with nobody to look after him, you should be ashamed of yourself," Sally mockingly scolds.

Leticia's face fell. "Oh Sally it was so awful out there I really thought I was going to die, and end up in one of those dreadful little roadside crematoriums. That horrid thought is all that kept me going, I wanted to come home either to Scotland or New Zealand. But everyone thought the Doctors here in the UK were the best with tropical diseases. You know we had a cousin of our fathers who was a Doctor of Tropical Diseases, Edinburgh trained and all. He lived in Singapore in the 1930's and was interned by the Japanese in Changi Prison. But as soon as the war was over he came out to Auckland for a few years until he was as good as he could be after such an awful time, and then returned to Singapore to practice again. Unfortunately he is long dead, or I would have gone there. Listen to me digressing!"

"Never mind," Annette says calmly. "We are not too bad here either. You know a lot of New Zealand Doctors come here to train for their FRCS." Seeing the blank look on my face, she adds, "That's the Royal College Surgical fellowship Catherine. Anyway we will make sure you are fine and dandy Leticia before we ever let you go."

"How long can you spend with us Catherine? We would like to show you that castle on the coast you have always wanted to see. If time allows we will go up to the Lodge on the Loch before we close it up for the winter. What do you say about that?"

Leticia looked as keen as mustard, however she was already starting to look a little tired.

"We will put her things in her favourite room upstairs, and she can have a lie down before lunch. Maybe one of the boys may come in from the farm and have lunch with us. They always like to keep an eye on their Colonial Cousins as they call you two."

We followed Annette down the passage and into the old wing, through the side door to the car. In no time the two carry bags were upstairs and we settled into our adjoining rooms. It was like being children again, and we sat on our beds and had a little giggle as we felt we were back at boarding school.

"See you at 12.30 Leticia," and I crept out, leaving her lying on her favourite chintz bedspread with the wind blowing the curtains across the dressing table. Thinking to myself this healthy Scottish air will do her the world of good.

Back in my room I hung up some of my clothes in the cupboard, grinning at the memory of Leticia and I finding the secret hiding place we discovered in there and speculating what it may have contained over the years. But first I thought a quick lie down would be good, at least I had delivered Leticia to Smeaton as promised and now I could think of returning to New Zealand.

It had been nearly six weeks since I left home and my wonderful feature writing job. I had managed to turn a writing hobby into a career.

Maybe I could have a few days here, but better not go up to the Loch or that would be at least another ten days, as much as I would like to.

Mr. Salisbury's report on Leticia's condition came through a few days later, it seemed that this one of those diseases which were difficult to name, and sometimes it was a matter of time sometimes years, before the body's system was able to rid itself of whatever it was. However as Leticia was feeling like her old self with no relapse of symptoms, he suggested that it would be fine for her to return to Bangkok in a few weeks' time.

So I made a booking to return to New Zealand and another for Leticia to join Simon for the last few months of his Diplomatic term in Thailand.

Chapter 11

Leticia's Letter

Iwoke up on the Trans-Atlantic plane, my poor neck was stiff from the unnatural angle I had dozed off in. I glanced at Simon, who was fast asleep in his seat, he had the foresight to use a pillow and looked quite comfortable.

With a start I remembered that I hadn't read Leticia's letter, so I frantically fished around in my handbag and found it tucked away with my passport. Taking a deep breath I plunged in:

Dear Catherine,

When you read this letter I will probably already be dead. It sounds terrible but time is running out for me.

Your darling younger sister is not all she seems, in fact she has another life just like 'Jekyll and Hyde' as you would say.

You often wondered about me travelling all the time. Well yes you could say being married to Simon has meant a lot of travel, but then there are the times that I have gone off by myself alone. Times when the family could not understand why I was always on the move, more like gypsy folk some would say. Well, it was not all of my own making.

Alberto has been the reason for my travels, no I am not in love with him and never have been.

He may, I think, have found you and me a challenge in the beginning, and probably wanted to be like us. However he moved onto other things, and this is where I was a help to him. I was not willing to go along with his plans in the beginning, however, he found a way and blackmailed me. It was not about the money or excitement, but he threatened me into becoming one of his couriers.

It started out all innocently at first, I was not even aware of what he was asking, I was more like an old friend helping him out. Then I made one big mistake.

It all started the first night on board the ship when I left for London, I was on my way down to dinner at the Officers' Table, when Alberto appeared from nowhere and grabbed me on the shoulder asking, "Fancy seeing you again after all these years. I think you have grown up at last, maybe we should have a game of deck tennis."

I must admit. I have never trusted him and when I saw him again after all those years, a cold shiver ran through me and I felt sick every time I saw him. You know being on the same ship for four weeks, it was not easy to avoid him.

The first night the Captain told us there are 67 males on board compared to over 250 females. I think he asked all the Officers on duty to dance with us. There seemed to be a lot of Engineers and Officers' parties and they were always on deck when off duty to join in with the deck games.

Everything went reasonably well until we arrived at Panama. A group of us had arranged to go ashore once the boat berthed and the Officers were off duty. Unfortunately the Captain decided he needed to keep back the Officer that was going to accompany me ashore.

So there I was standing on the deck wondering how I would catch up to the others, or worse still go ashore by myself. Being my first trip out of New Zealand this did not appeal to me. When along the deck sauntered Alberto.

"You look like a wallflower standing there, been stood up have you?"

"No, the Officer has to stay on the bridge while we are in port and the others have already taken a horse and gig and gone to some resort to swim."

"Well I had better take you for old times' sake," Alberto proudly said.

There was nothing else to do than smile and try and look as if that would be great. He took my arm and down the gang plank we went and along the wharf.

Plenty of people came up and offered to show us around and with great authority Alberto haggled with one or two and finally helped me up into a horse drawn gig. There weren't too many cars in Panama at that time, they were only available to the upper class and some senior government ministers back then.

I settled back and began to enjoy myself having never been in a gig before, it was very old fashioned, and the clip clop of the horse made me feel like a film star. We rode past the poorest houses on each side of a very poor street, with people old and young sitting on the doorsteps. We must have looked like millionaires to them.

Soon we were out into the countryside with an avenue of trees to shade us. In no time we arrived at the resort, but unfortunately our friends must have decided to go elsewhere. There was a lovely golden beach with huge beach umbrellas, and waiters walking back and forth with lovely long orange drinks on silver trays.

"Well," said Alberto, "we may as well have a drink here and a swim if you like, the sea looks like heaven after the ship's overcrowded pool."

I replied, "No thank you, but I would love to just sit under an umbrella and look at the beautifully dressed people."

The afternoon went well and a well-dressed man befriended us, or that is what I thought. He spoke to us for a few moments asked where we came from and insisted he bought us another Pimms.

Later he suggested that he was going our way back to the boat and would we join him for a meal near the ship. He said he was on his own as his wife was not well and was resting back in the hotel. Of course it seemed rude not to accept. So back to town we went and stopped off in a well-lit street. The restaurant was fabulous and he pointed out never to drink anything served in a glass. "Always ask for a bottle," he suggested, "and have it opened in front of you, Coke is the safest." So we all drank Coke. As we left the restaurant he asked me to help him choose a gift for his wife. So we went into several shops and looked at the beautiful jade jewellery on display.

I had my eye on a black skirt with insets of lace, great for the fancy dress we were having on board the next night.

After a lot of discussion he bought lovely green earrings, and a ring surrounded with silver, the jade had a face cut out on it, truly beautiful.

He then insisted we look at the perfume for his sister Claudia and again he explained he was out of his depth, we chose a perfume called 'Shocking' in a beautiful cherry red box. He bought a small bottle for me to say thank you for my help.

As we walked down the street back to the ship, he suddenly remembered his sister in London had her birthday in two weeks' time, and asked if I would mind taking it back for him.

"But I don't know where to deliver it."

"Don't worry," he said. "She will contact you."

"But I have no address as yet, my friend is meeting me at the station and we have a room in Earls Court."

"In that case I will give you her telephone number and she can arrange to meet you. She has a lovely flat near the London Clinic in a little mews you could probably stay with her until you settle in. I will send her a telegram. She may even be able to meet the boat at Southampton as she goes down there often to visit an aunt."

So all was arranged and I was suddenly in charge of a huge boxed bottle of 'Shocking.' It was a large box, and we were told in the shop it needed special packaging so that it would not break. Goodness how naïve can one be, but in those days nobody thought twice of carrying a parcel for a friend. Especially one who had been so kind to us both.

That was the beginning of the end, unbeknown to me I had become a courier and of course Alberto had arranged it all. Even to having the Officer detained on the ship that afternoon. He had pleaded with the Captain that I was an old friend and he wanted to take me ashore. He made it sound all so romantic that the Captain fell in with his plans.

Later I heard from my Godmother who was an old friend of the Captains, who rang her next time in Wellington to see if I had become engaged to Alberto whom he had met on the ship. Alberto would never have guessed the connection between the Captain and my Godmother, who had travelled to London years ago when the Captain was a very Junior Officer. They had been good friends for many years after. It is such a small world.

Of course Claudia was on the wharf to meet me, and driving me to London and to her Mews flat at the back of Harley Street. She was most kind, when I explained I had friends in Earls Court and wanted to move closer to them.

In fact she drove me and my luggage to Devonshire Mews off Harley Street and I was soon sharing a room with three others in a very old Victorian house with many others. Next I was busy finding work, and enjoying London. Off to the country in the weekends and going to concerts.

Then friends invited me to travel to Europe for three months in May. The cars were terrible in the second-hand market, so I asked our parents if they would help me with finance to buy a brand new car instead. When father found out it was duty free, he readily agreed, provided they could sell the car I already had in New Zealand.

So off I went shopping to Berkley Square. I really wanted a Morris Minor, but the salesman thought I was window shopping, so I took myself off to look at an Austin Ten, Ford Anglia and finally a Standard Ten. One was available immediately as it had been ordered by someone overseas, who had that morning cancelled the order. So lucky me I was able to purchase a brand new car for only 400 pounds.

It seemed most of my friends were also looking at cars, Margaret had already purchased an Austin Ten and had been driving it around London for six months. The trouble was we had to return them to New Zealand within 364 days or pay the tax.

Who worries about things like that with 364 days ahead of them? The first of May arrived and three of us were on our way to Dover to catch the ferry to Calais. Roof rack on top for our one large suitcase, boxes of tinned food, coffee and a large yellow tarpaulin to cover the top with a snake, a circle of expanding wire with many pieces all around to hook into the side of the racks.

Our trip was amazing and it was much unexpected to meet Alberto yet again this time in a Youth Hostel in Rome. By chance he was visiting his relations further south, and decided to do a few days of sightseeing in Rome.

He said he would not be returning to London for some time, and would I be good enough to take two Venetian Italian leather boxes back with me as Customs would wonder why a man wanted two jewellery boxes. At the last minute he said he could make a lot of money in London selling Italian leather boxes and why didn't I take some myself. They were only six shillings each so of course we bought six.

He was also helpful and said the car would not be safe on the street, and why not drive it into the hostel grounds at night, as nobody could drive it through the locked gate. Thanking him we moved the car and there it remained for our whole stay in Rome.

We left Alberto and travelled north and did not arrive back in England for another six weeks.

Once we arrived back in Earls Court, Alberto appeared and collected his boxes. He also suggested that the car should be washed and cleaned throughout, and he had a friend in Kensington who worked in a garage and would do it for nothing.

So off I drove and left it in Kensington for the day while I was at work and I picked it up later in the day looking bright and clean and smelling sweetly inside. The blue and white upholstery looked as good as new.

Little did I realize the car had been taken to pieces, so the illicit bags of drugs that had been hidden in the car while it was in the hostel grounds in Rome, could be secretly removed.

Obviously my travels were proving a great deal of help to Alberto and his friends. Being unaware of how I was being used, I continued on as I would leave London most weekends with friends and drive to the coast to stay overnight in a hostel or at camping grounds.

On one such trip, my two friends from Wellington bought along a third member Simon an English gentleman who was working in the Diplomatic Service in London. He seemed a quiet person to start with and readily agreed to stay with us wherever we choose to go. There was always a deep discussion each week as to which area we would explore all within an hour or two's radius of London.

I preferred towns near the coast, and preferably with a castle. This was not always possible as Luke and Stephen wanted to sketch and preferred the small villages which were easier to find inland such as Suffolk and the Cotswolds.

Also we were growing tired of the restrictions of YHA, such as having to be in by 9.30 pm each night and not arriving by car.

We went to no end of trouble on one trip to Devon and Cornwall, not to arrive by car after being caught the first night in a hostel. We had parked the car in a country lane and walked back to the hostel. Next morning a policeman arrived at the hostel at breakfast time and asked who owned UDUl33. Realizing the four of us could lose our YHA cards, I owned up and said it was mine. The other three people had just been given a lift to the hostel and we were not travelling together.

The problem was the car was left where cars were parked when there was a breakout from Dartmoor Prison and the police had been watching the prison all night. Then the number plate was checked and it showed the car was an export number and obviously the owner must be staying in the village. Where else but the YHA. The hostel mother was most kind, and said in the future park your car in a pub carpark and nobody will notice it. So we continued our four weeks' holiday with no further problem.

A few weeks later one of the group was unable to come so the boys bought along a new friend, it was Simon.

Like I said, he was quiet at first and we wondered if he would fit in with the rest of us. We had long ago given up staying in youth hostels and had found caravan parks as they gave us more freedom and we were able to go to pubs in the evening and not worry about a curfew.

One particular night we had returned a little worse for wear and once we had settled down to sleep, I had to get up and go out to the toilets. It was then we realized that someone had accidently knocked the knob off the gas cylinder under the stove and gas was leaking everywhere. It was not noticeable until you went outside. So we would not have woken in the morning.

We realized what a close call it was, and imagined the Wellington paper, the Dominion headline, 'Four young people gas themselves in a caravan in a deserted caravan park in southern England.' One being a young diplomat would have looked rather suspicious.

The next few weekends were fun, and I started to go out with Simon during the week. Well once a week to start with, as he worked late most nights, and was very popular with the hostesses around inner London as he would make up the extra man at the dinner table.

Well as you know we had only a short time together before it was time for you to arrive Catherine. You seemed to be so content with your stay in England so I was surprised when you decided to go and work in a Finishing School in Switzerland.

If we had travelled to and around the UK together then maybe that would have been different. But you were so intent on leaving before me, I think it must have been that Officer you met six months before you sailed on the Rangitane with him.

We were just as pleased though that you did not become engaged to him but you must have been upset when I finally arrived some months later. You really didn't give it enough time, as you never really loved London like I did.

We all thought it strange when you said you had applied for that position in Switzerland although we all knew how much you loved skiing. It must have been quite lonely for you over the winter months, and although you seemed happy when I visited you that summer, all the girls seemed such snobs to me.

Wasn't it strange that you went all that way to teach a girl who had come all the way from Wellington to attend the same school? It must have cost her parents a fortune to send her, when she could have had lessons from you practically only thirty minutes away.

So when you returned it was really only to spend a few weeks together before we left to come home.

You hardly had time to meet Simon as he was always so busy, and frankly I didn't think it was going to be a lasting relationship. But everything is always glamorous so far from home.

I really loved it when he took me down to meet his parents at Hinton St. George. I don't quite know what I had expected but the old manor house was just something else.

From the moment we drove up the drive and saw this gracious old stone house sitting there with a back drop of huge old trees I fell in love with it.

The entrance hall with the light shining through the tall paned windows was a beauty in itself. The house was huge and I must admit I would never want to sleep there on my own.

His parents were just like ours very gracious, but wondering why Simon came home with a colonial instead of some smart society girl from London.

They asked the most discreet questions which made Simon laugh. I think I told them straight away that our father was working in the Import Export trade with a Commerce degree from London University. In fact he had lived and worked in London in the 1920's.

Of course it was much later after getting to know them better that I said he had worked his passage to London as a bath steward. He had been paid the one shilling that showed that he was a paid crew member.

That weekend is a haze now with walking along a valley to a pub in the next village, having lunch outside under a big tree in the back garden and the smell of the countryside which you do miss in London.

The little Church was so old and the Rooster on the steeple was the crest for the Lord of the village. It wasn't until later that I realized that when Simon's grandfather died his father would inherit a title, and of course Simon after that.

Fancy I would become a Lady if I married Simon, it sounded rather grand Lady Leticia. But that was looking a long way ahead.

Maybe I would sail away with you and never hear from him again. We were so young, there was so much more of the world to see. Who wanted to settle down at twenty-two? It really did not enter my head in any serious way.

We returned to London and all too quickly it was time for me to pack. Your arrival and seeing my favourite places before we set off to the Brussels Fair.

Remember the night we took our luggage down to the ship?

What a performance of asking the steward to put it in our cabin.

"Can't do that Miss we don't sail for several days."

We had to explain that we would not be joining the ship until Marseilles and we could not take our trunks overland as we were only travelling with our backpacks. His face went so red, I thought he would have a fit.

He had to find an Officer to give him permission to accept our luggage so early. I think the problem was that we had just driven up to the wharf and it did not go through Customs.

Here again Alberto came into the picture, he must have known that all along and once again had asked me to take some presents in the trunk as he hoped to join the ship in Naples.

If only I had used my head and asked why he always wanted me to carry parcels.

So soon we were off on that great adventure to Brussels together and down to Marseilles to wait for the 'Strathmore'

But Alberto also caught me out in London, remember I tried to be a model, well I suppose most people think they have a chance at happiness and making it big.

So I went onto a modelling school, learnt how to walk and pose, I even had a small portfolio of photographs taken. I was quoted in a newspaper once when I was silly enough to say I had been out with a title. It was in an English pub on a fine summer weekend, once when I went with one of my flatmates, Marie. I cannot even remember the host's name, they had returned from Africa and wanted to host young colonials for the weekend. Here I met some young men about town and visited their home for the weekend, our host and hostess had arranged for them to take Marie and I to a pub on Sunday morning. Here we met an older set of people who told us about weekend house parties. It all sounded rather grand. You would be invited for the weekend, arriving late on a Friday night, and then a weekend of swimming in a heated pool, eating, and drinking for two days solid.

So when one of them called and asked me and Marie to join them we couldn't say no. We met at our Mews flat and they were quite impressed. They did not realize that there were five of us sharing the rent. Never mind we were off in this guy's Black Sunbeam car and very nice it was too.

We arrived after dark at the house, well it was more like a large country manor. Masses of tall chimneys, are all I can really remember about the outside. It was huge inside, with an enormous staircase like in the movie 'Gone with the Wind.' Old oil paintings of ancestors dotted all the way upstairs, and along the gallery to our rooms.

We decided to share a room as we had heard a little about these weekend house parties and what sort of naughty nonsense went on during the night. Someone once said a gong was sounded at 5 am so everyone could go back to their own bedrooms. I never heard a gong if there was one.

We had a great weekend and the older men all of fifty years of age and up, they were gracious and nobody made any advances to the two little colonials.

So when we were asked again of course we accepted. But the next time there were two really smart girls a little younger than us. One dark hair, and one blonde, they were beautiful to look at, especially in their two piece bathing costumes.

Also there were a couple of older male Continentals who could hardly speak English so we took little interest in them. They did not like to swim, and I don't blame them as they were very fat.

They took a liking to the two girls who I realize now had been especially invited for these two foreign men. They hardly mixed with us as we were busy with the younger set, and went riding on the estate, and swimming in the pool.

However it was definitely off limits to leave the property. I do not mean they would have stopped us, but they said the village people did not like the parties and they advised us it was better to keep to the grounds.

Well everything was there so why should we want to leave?

As Saturday drew to a close, we realized that most of the men must have been drinking as they seemed short of conversation and even looked glazed and sleepy.

Well Marie and I were quite naïve in hindsight and had never seen drugs or the effects of them at this stage, let alone met a prostitute. We also drank very little compared to them, the most we drank was the odd Pimm's.

We had a lovely dinner, but everybody said they had had a hard day and would retire early. Of course as guests we did also.

We did hear a lot of laughter late into the night but thought some of them must still be up and talking perhaps in their rooms.

Sunday was another day of riding and swimming and lunch before we headed back to town. We had had a lovely time and when asked if we would like to come again we said but of course. Any time just give us a ring. Well what a surprise when a few days later one of the M.P.'s at the house party rang me at the flat and asked me to have lunch, said he had something interesting to suggest if I still wanted to model.

So we met at a little pub quite close to where I was working. He was a perfect gentleman, you know grey distinguished hair, with that tremendous BBC speaking voice known as Received Pronunciation. He said he was in touch with a modelling agency who could be looking for someone like me, and would I send in my photographs.

I didn't have any so he suggested a photographer, who I rang and made a booking for the next evening. Just bring along a bathing costume, a frock you like, and maybe some baby doll pyjamas if you have some.

Well Edward that was his name, insisted he came along with me, as he said some photographers were insistent on other photographs, and he wanted to make sure that no one took advantage of me. Quite old fashioned and I thought it sweet. So we met outside the photographers in Kensington High Street, and he went up to the little studio on the second floor. The photographs were taken without incident, and we left again shortly afterwards.

He suggested that we should have a meal, and as I was all dressed up, he would take me to a nightclub in Mayfair.

This was just too good to be true, and I readily accepted.

We had a lovely evening, drank wonderful wine, the whole place was all mirrors and lights with people dressed in the latest fashions. It was even mentioned that occasionally royalty came here, it was one of their favourite nightclubs and I could see why.

He took me home and gave me a chaste kiss outside the Mews flat and promised to see how the photographs turned out and he would collect them and pass them onto his contact.

It all seemed like a dream, and so when he asked me out the next time, he suggested that I may like to go to another house party, and this time he heard a whisper that royalty would be there. How could I resist?

So I was collected from the flat late on a Friday night and driven into the country again this time by a chauffeur. It was like being a princess and when we drew up at the mansion, there was Edward to meet me.

Our hostess greeted us and the maid took my bag and said, "Follow me and I will show you your room."

We went up the stairs and along a very long passage and at the far end the far door was opened and we were shown in.

Edward thanked her and put my bag next to his in the dressing room. I suddenly felt a cold shiver,

"But where is my room?" I stupidly asked.

"This is your room Leticia don't you want to share it with me?"

Well I didn't but how did I say this without causing offence and he had done so much for me?

He smiled and said, "Never mind we can work something out. Why don't you change as our hostess will expect us to go down for drinks in a few minutes?"

I didn't want to embarrass him and so I meekly did as he suggested.

Oh Catherine, I can't go on. He was so patient and kind and of course I fell in love with him. Who wouldn't? But by then it was too late, he was married of course. The usual story he didn't get on with his wife. He had a position in the government and could not divorce her.

This affair continued for the whole summer and then it was all too late for me to draw back. He was just special and I was silly enough to think he would make a change in his life for me.

The final weekend he asked me to bring Marie with me, she had been asking and asking to accompany me.

I think he wanted to break it up at this point and having Marie with me would be the perfect time so that I would have someone to lean on.

He told me after lunch the following day, and then sent us back to London with the chauffeur. I think I probably cried most of the way. Marie was great and said it was all for the best, he was a married man, with a career ahead of him, and would probably end up in the House of Lords.

But we didn't hear from them again.

Reading the paper some weeks later we realized why, we had been innocently staying at a weekend house party, with Russians from the Russian Embassy. There had been a leak to the newspapers and all the older men it seemed were from high places. There would be a Court case and probably if convicted they would go to prison including the two girls.

Marie and I were terrified that someone would come around to the flat so we decided to go to Ireland for a few weeks. All in a great hurry we changed our minds at the last minute and without telling anybody we headed to Cornwall instead. We watched the newspapers and then when nothing more was reported we headed back to London.

Unfortunately Alberto appeared at the flat, and said, "Naughty, naughty what have you been doing?"

How he found out I have no notion, but he hinted that I was now in his power, I thought he was just joking of course.

It was not until later, when I went out with Simon that Alberto snidely said well you certainly are meeting the right people, keep it up.

You can guess what happened next, he always hinted that if I did not do what he wanted, he would tell our parents that I was involved with the drug scene and worse than that but also I was mixed up with Russians spies.

I was so scared that I believed him, so that is how I became his courier. But it was not until after I married Simon that he showed more of his true colours. He even had the cheek to stand and watch us having our photographs taken in the Botanical gardens when we were married, back home in Wellington.

Remember me going over to the fence to see who was standing watching us. You said afterwards. Did you know those two people you look as white as your frock. It was him and some other Italian woman.

From the moment that I married Simon he had me carrying drugs whenever we travelled. Well not so much while Simon was in New Zealand, but the Pacific Islands were being used as a halfway house for transferring. That was perfect for Alberto as we went from island to island either on vacation or on business.

So of course it was even better when we were in the East, and finally Thailand was just perfect for him. The main drugs of course were coming from the Golden Triangle.

With me travelling on a Diplomatic passport hardly anyone ever took notice of a wife. I could even put things in the Diplomatic Bag until the sniffer dogs came on the scene. It was all much more difficult to carry drugs personally, and so my use was clearly nearly over, as container ships had come into their own. Sealed all the way from a Port to its destination, and hardly ever opened on the wharf.

Yachts were also of use, and there again I become friendly with many people with yachts. You always wondered why, as I did not like anything smaller than a cruise ship.

I knew my time was up in Thailand, somebody was following me all the time on that trip of ours. Then I was ill and terrified you would leave me for a moment as they would then have access to me. I even worried about the Doctor and was worse after he came to see me in the hotel.

I was so pleased when we finally flew back to London and more so to arrive at Smeaton. I felt so safe there. Anyhow I decided to jot this down in writing in case something ever happened to me.

So you would have a lead with Alberto if you could ever find him he travels a lot on different passports, never the same one. He is very clever and feels at home in Italy,

Australia especially Melbourne, there are a lot of Italians working for him from there.

New Zealand is a little slower, but he has a house on the point at Opua, in the Bay of Islands just where the ferry boat goes across to and from Russell.

With his grey hair he may be harder for you to trace as you would think of him with that dark black curly hair, from the Bay days but those piercing blue eyes are always the same.

If I could help you with contacts I would but he was always so clever that you never knew the next courier, just a password. This too also changed with each run so you never saw the same person twice. I tried to take photos of Alberto and his associates when I could.

He was just at home whether it was Hong Kong, Singapore, London or Paris but especially Rome or Southern Italy. He was always discreet, he never rang the Embassy or Residence but always somehow managed to leave messages with somebody who would call at the house for some other reason.

He would appear at a function if he was desperate but would never approach me directly and never in front of Simon. Poor Simon would never have been aware of him until the last posting in Samoa.

Maybe he thought I was having an affair, because I often went shopping or for a jog early in the morning and would meet Alberto for a discreet coffee, if I was to collect another assignment. This made me very nervous and probably it showed at lunchtime.

Of course he offered to pay me, but where do you put the cash. You have to open a bank account and then they want to have a home address and that would have been difficult.

But there is an account in Switzerland and you are welcome to it. The number of the account is in the back of my address book. Look carefully for a number which is preceded by the Swiss international phone number.

You will be able to remit money into your account, but better not to do so directly but through an offshore tax haven. Isle of Man or something like that.

There should be enough there for you to buy a lovely home, and you can say your sister left you the money in her will. People would accept that, and in fact it is partly true.

I want to say what a great sister you have been ever since I can remember. We had so much fun in our younger years, and just a few gaps once I married. But then you were able to visit us in nearly every posting, and you were always there when we went to New Zealand.

I was sorry when you were widowed so early, the first of the group. But maybe there is another somebody out there just keep looking. They appear just when you do not expect it, or so they say.

You would never let me help you financially but now you should be comfortable for the rest of your life, enjoy it.

I worked hard to make that money but that is not the reason that I took up being a courier. It was frightening and that is where those terrible headaches came from, the constant worry of those customs people at every airport, always looking for people like me.

I am pleased our parents are dead as they would be so upset about my life, and the only reason that I have written this is so Alberto does not keep getting away with it.

There are probably many others like me that keep carrying on as he has something over them also.

Interpol must know of him, but he never carries the drugs himself, he is much too clever for that. He uses the very young first time overseas travellers who are short of money, and old ladies, one of his best carriers is I believe in her early eighties.

Here is hoping that I will return to destroy this letter one day but that is only a wish.

Do not tell Simon if you think there is any way of avoiding it, he trusted me so much, with all the problems he had from time to time in his work. Even telling me about some of the drug smugglers that they were sure were working within the Foreign Office, he would be so upset to find out that it was his own wife.

Be happy!

Life is so short, and we never know when the time will come for us to leave all those that are near and dear to us.

At Smeaton you will find a journal hidden in our secret hiding place in our guest room with more information, I've tried to remember all the details from when I was first manipulated into this whole horrid mess. And the little address book with the Swiss account.

Your loving sister, Leticia.

Chapter 12

Smeaton

Soon after we touched down at Heathrow, Simon had to go into the Home Office in London to explain the situation before going onto Hinton St George and after contacting Annette, I left on the next direct flight for Edinburgh, my destination Smeaton and the family.

Smeaton, even the name sounds interesting and so it is. A beautiful estate in East Lothian in Scotland. From the moment one drives through the big gates and along the drive with large leafy trees at least one hundred years old lining both sides, eventually revealing the graceful stately home, a sense of awe overcomes you, and knowing the reception you are about to receive, makes you feel like you are coming home.

As you reach the highest level of the Estate, there is a view to the left of rolling green meadows, and a small glistening lake at the bottom of the valley. If that is not enough for the senses to take in, there is the overall feeling of peace after the congested motorway we have been travelling along since our arrival at Edinburgh airport.

It is always a surprise to finally find the village sign which can so easily be hidden if one is not looking out for it. The village of Preston remains unspoilt with the familiar chemist on the corner and the picturesque water mill.

Through the village to the other side there is the small, quaint sign announcing, 'Smeaton.'

I can hardly wait to catch my first glimpse of the house, well hidden behind the trees which form the home cottage garden.

Then suddenly there it appears the stately grand home with a car parked outside proclaiming someone must be in residence.

No sooner have I pulled up alongside the bright yellow car saying to myself, 'who on earth owns that? Has Hamish got a new toy?'

A sudden urge rises within me and I need to find Leticia's journal! I know there are more pieces of the puzzle to find here at Smeaton.

Then the front door opens wide and Annette walks out excitedly with her arms wide and I know I am at home at last. What a long way I have travelled over the last few days, to this sanctuary of peace, quiet and I hope safety. That is the one thing in the world that I need right now and I hope that nobody finds me until I am ready.

Annette chuckling and in her strong Scottish accent greets me with, "What a lovely surprise! We could not believe it when you telephoned to say that you were at Heathrow and waiting for the next flight to Edinburgh."

Wrapping her arms around me, we hug warmly, then Annette pulls back, "I'm so sorry we couldn't make it to Samoa Catherine. It must have been very difficult for both you and Simon. Letitia was a very special woman and we will miss her sincerely."

"Oh, thank you Annette."

"Well, come in dear Catherine, and we will have tea in the garden just the way you have always liked it."

"It will not be as warm as when you were here last, but it is always warm in the glasshouse, or would you prefer to sit in the drawing room? It is always warm there at this time of day when the last of the sun comes in there."

Taking my bag and typewriter out of the car I followed her into the hall which seemed so dark after the sunlight of the garden. The lovely dark Persian runner in the hall looked just the same, I had always loved the runner which seemed endless and it lay proudly on the longest passage to the second wing where I always slept.

"Would you like to freshen up and of course you will want to stay in your old room in the nursery wing, or would you prefer to be downstairs in the guestroom this time?" Annette inquired. "Both the rooms are ready as you know as we are never sure who will suddenly arrive with the family coming and going from all parts of the world."

"When we were first married it was a big occasion if someone came from London to stay, now it can be a friend from Hawaii or Samoa from the South Pacific. It would have taken weeks for them to travel to us by sea, and now a 24 hour flight is all it takes."

"My old room would be fine, it is small and cosy and I like being upstairs so I can peep out the window and look down on the garden. I hope this unexpected visit will not put Sally out and make a lot of extra work for her in the kitchen."

"Oh no, she would be hurt to hear you say that she always loved your visits as you ate everything and had no dislikes, well not that you ever told her."

"Freshen up and I'll see you out in the glasshouse, unfortunately there will be no grapes out there at this time of the year, but we will have strawberry jam on our scones which you love."

I walked on through the library expecting to see Hamish at any moment but maybe he was at one of his meetings in the city, he seemed to be on so many boards, the names of which I never remembered.

The French doors out onto the patio were firmly closed which was unusual as they were often wide open with the scent of the garden wafting through the house. But of course it was late autumn here, well actually it was so cold in the house it felt like a touch of winter.

Of course the family would not notice it, having lived here most of their lives, and Scotland was not known for its warm temperatures, except for the odd occasion in August.

I almost ran to my room, desperate to find Leticia's journal. Flinging open the door, I dropped my bag and threw my typewriter onto the bed, then rushed to the closet.

The closet door opened, I bent down and ran my hand along the wooden panel to locate the small handle. Carefully I pulled it open to reveal the secret hiding space that Leticia and I had discovered together on one trip to Smeaton.

Reaching inside I soon felt the leather cover of the journal, quickly pulling it out and opening it up to the first page to reveal more of my sister's words: *'Voyage Home'* – *Brussels Fair.*

Tears came to my eyes as I recalled our voyage home together on the Strathmore, I decided that I should take my time and read the journal a little later.

I stood and went to the bathroom to wash my face and freshen up, before descending the stairs, and out of the library, down the path through the hedges that gave privacy to the home garden and there was Annette sitting as usual in the glasshouse.

The glasshouse looked bare without the dark green leaves of the grape vine, just a few dead leaves still hanging in there. But it was warm and the tea tray looked most inviting, sitting on the old wrought iron table.

Everything was always just perfect here, and I hoped it would always remain so even when the next generation took over if they ever did. There had been talk of an offer from some American Botanist wanting to buy Smeaton. Mainly because of the wonderful collection of imported trees that Hamish and his father had planted many years ago. Now they had grown to maturity it was regarded as one of the best collections in the whole of Scotland.

Annette looked so at home sitting on one of the wrought iron chairs, with lovely plump cushions covered in a pretty Sanderson material. The Scottish knitwear she was wearing was put to the best advantage with a pale crushed strawberry pullover, and matching skirt printed in the same colour with a hint of blue.

"Ah, there you are Catherine. Do sit down and tell me all about it dear, if you wish and in your own time."

With that she took my hand in hers and those penetrating blue eyes looked deeply into mine and I felt uncomfortable about how much I could tell her and how much did I really know? What would she think of Leticia once the truth came out? Oh where would I begin?

"Annette dear, I'm not sure where to begin. Please understand that there is more to the story I am about to tell you than what will appear in the newspapers. I'm sorry to tell you this but we now know that poor Leticia was murdered."

The colour drained from her face, "Catherine, that is terrible news, who…"

"He has been arrested and will be standing trial soon, Simon and I were advised to leave Samoa to avoid getting swept up in the news media storm that will surely follow," I replied.

"Well, you are definitely in the right place my dear, Hamish and I won't allow any nonsense from the media, stay as long as you like to rest and recuperate." Annette invited.

"Thank you Annette, you don't know how much that means to me. Now where should I begin, Leticia wrote some of the background in this journal and I will know more once I've read it. Of course I'll have to contact David the Detective who is investigating the crime, I do hope I will be able to see him again soon."

Annette interrupted my train of thought handing me a cup of tea designed in her favourite flower pattern. "Help yourself to milk and sugar, I can never remember who takes what these days. And of course try the scones they were freshly baked for you so you must eat them up or Sally will be put out. Now what's this about wanting to see David again?"

Blushing a little, I coyly replied, "David and I have become rather fond of each other while he was investigating in Samoa, you must think I'm awful courting while my sister has been murdered."

Annette looked at me directly, "Catherine, it's about time you found another husband, you have been single for far too long. I hope I get to meet this new man of yours too. Of course I know you will want to go shopping, you always do, and we have a good excuse to spend some money getting you some flattering clothes to woo your new beau. Well tomorrow we will go to town to do some shopping and have a spot of lunch, what do you say?"

With that we both laughed and it seemed to break the ice and we both were able to sit without speaking and enjoy our tea and scones like the old friends that we were.

The sun was setting and soon the cool temperature would drive us out of the glasshouse, but I knew that Annette would like to show me around the garden so I thought it would be better coming from me. "Annette you must show me what you have been planting in that new garden you were digging in at the entrance, before we go back into the house if you have time."

"Of course! Sally has the meal prepared and all is in hand until we have had a drink, then I think some of the family may call in to see you and welcome you back. You know you are quite a celebrity in the family, they are always talking about their cousin who thinks nothing of catching a flight to Britain when she has been away too long."

"Let me help you with the tea tray and then we will find some old gumboots in the boot room if you think it will be muddy under the trees. Have you had much rain lately it always seems to be muddy away from the home garden?" I asked.

With that we strolled back to the house, Sally had put the lights on and had lit the fire, the house looked and felt warm and inviting. That still gave us time to have a quick walk before we retired inside for the evening so I could finally read Leticia's journal.

Chapter 13

Voyage Home

Isat in one of the old leather armchairs in the library with Leticia's journal. Taking a sip from a large brandy that Hamish had kindly poured for me, I carefully set the glass upon the antique side table. Hamish and Annette had kindly left me in peace for my next task.

Taking a deep breath I opened the journal to the first page again and this time started reading:

Brussels Fair.   Leticia

Having arranged to have the car shipped before we left, under the guidance of Simon who was sure that if I didn't leave the UK within the next few weeks, there would be tax trouble over the duty free status for the car.

This gave us just enough time for a brief holiday before catching the boat from Marseilles, after having visited the World Trade Fair in Brussels to see the futuristic Atomium built especially for the Worlds Expo.

Four of us from the flat set out to catch the ferry from Dover.

No longer having the car which was being shipped

from Liverpool stored somewhere in a warehouse in the Docklands area. This time we had to go by public transport and catch a ferry from Hull. We all decided on reaching the Continent we would hitch hike. Having never done this before it was all rather an adventure.

Now on the Continent, walking along the wharf at Zeebrugge, we were very pleased to be picked up soon after walking away from the ferry. Our first hitchhiker host spoke perfect English and suggested we see one of Belgium's best well known cathedrals, St. Michael and St. Gudula Cathedral in Brussels. As we were soon pulling up outside the cathedral, he laughed as another car pulled up alongside us. It was his brother he said who had been following us since he picked us up.

They were both returning from a seaside holiday home they shared, and his brother had noticed with amusement when he stopped and picked up four girls.

After visiting the cathedral they insisted on a drink and something to eat. Food was always of prime importance with our small budget, so we readily accepted.

Then it was decided we would split up, something we had been told never to do. Two would go in one car and the other two in the second car. Arrangements were made to go to a hostel near the main square. As there were so many tourists in Brussels it was suggested that if this hostel was full they knew of private accommodation that was not too expensive.

We arrived in the capital Brussels late in the afternoon and drove to the hostel. Unfortunately it was full so we followed their advice and booked into a private guest house nearby for almost the same price.

Then they insisted we all had another meal together,

and this seemed a great idea, so we all went to the large square where they found a great little restaurant where we could eat outside.

Arrangements were made for them to pick us up the next day and take us to the World Trade Fair. We were all thoroughly enjoying ourselves, and pleased we had decided to hitch hike.

It was becoming clear that the men had their eyes on two of the other girls, and said we did not mind if they wished to split up. We were quite happy to explore the Fair by day and if we found it safe, we would return in the evening.

We only had two days in Brussels and then we had a week to cross Belgium, and head to the south of France to Marseilles in time to catch the 'Strathmore' for our journey homeward.

All went well until the other two girls decided to return to London to work earlier than planned as their money was running out. Late in the afternoon of the third day we said our farewells, and headed out onto the main road to hitch hike.

We were lucky and were picked up by a young student who insisted on taking us home to his parents for the night.

I never was sure what his parents thought of him bringing two New Zealand girls home for the night. They had a lovely home in the Ardennes forest on the border of Germany. It was so nice we reluctantly left the next morning and were taken back to the main road.

Hitch hiking back then was relatively safe and we were astounded to see who the driver of the next car was to stop. It was Alberto! He said he was going to Italy. This was too far off our track, but he insisted when he heard we had not seen the famous Milan Cathedral and that we should go with him. He was so insistent and even offered to drive us to Marseilles if we would go via Milan. This seemed a wonderful opportunity and adventure we could not miss and soon after getting into the car he told us some of his travel tales since he had been in Wellington.

So instead of heading due south we headed southwest and drove through West Germany, via Austria and then into Italy to Garda the first of the picturesque Italian Lakes.

We had not seen any of the other Lakes either and it seemed a wonderful bonus to see Iseo, Como and Lugano.

We stayed in a small guesthouse and Alberto stayed further along the lake in a smart resort.

He would visit us each evening and take us out for a meal. He said he liked to practice his New Zealand English with all the funny Kiwisms and Kiwi slang which he had missed as was just unique to New Zealand.

With our holiday coming to an end, it was time we headed to Genoa, and then along the coast to Marseilles to wait for the ship.

Alberto was agreeable and so having visited the Cathedral we were soon travelling along a scenically boring road to the coast. Once we arrived at the coast it was lovely to see the sea again. The drive along the coast was beautiful and we stopped the night at one of the small villages on the Italian side.

Alberto apologized and said he could take us no further, as unexpected business had come up, and so we made our farewells and had one of the most difficult parts of our trip hitch hiking this last section.

We finally arrived in Marseilles and travelled further along the coast to a small naval base and then at the next bay we decided to stay there until the ship came in. We were both running short of money and we decided to live on pizzas for the next two nights.

We swum and lazed on the beach, and made our way to the wharf on the second afternoon to make sure the ship had arrived.

It had, so as soon as we showed our tickets we were able to go on board and find our cabin. It was good to feel we had no more worries until we reached Sydney where we were to stay with our parents' friends who ran a local newspaper.

They were to take us to another wharf so I could catch the Wanganella to Wellington and finally home, while Catherine stayed on to work as an intern.

We went down to dinner the first night, and found two old school friends on board. They laughed when they saw us and said, "We read the passenger list our first night out of Tilbury and there under Marseilles were you two. Well the surname was fancy enough and you catching the boat from this port how brave."

"Not at all," we said, "It was seventeen pounds less to pick the boat up from here and the savings would pay for us to travel to the World Trade Fair at Brussels and then hitch down to the boat."

The next few days were relaxing and then our next port of call was Naples. We had driven through there once on our way south on a previous holiday, but had never seen the city. There were tours once we reached shore, and we tried to decide if we wanted to go down the Amalfi Coast.

"Let us wait and see," was Catherine's idea. "Our money is not that great, maybe we could just see if there is any local transport we can take from the wharf to visit a village along the coast."

This seemed a good idea so when the ship berthed we made our way along the wharf and took a local bus into town to have a look around.

Imagine our surprise when who should we meet but Alberto.

"You turn up in the most amazing places don't you? You would think you were following us around."

"Well not really, but one of you girls mentioned ages ago you were booked on the 'Strathmore' going home. So I decided to come along on the ship also, as I have seen enough of the relations and need to go back to Australia and do some work."

"Now as I know this place, let me show you around for the time you are here. Would you not prefer to go down the Amalfi coast? It is rather wonderful."

It all seemed too easy so of course we both accepted. So for the day we took a local bus that followed the coast, and stopped high up on the cliff road.

Alberto lead the way, "Follow me, we will have to walk down the hill to the village I have in mind. They have some small blue grottos I would like to show you. This coast has lots of grottos but most of them only used by the locals. We may find a fisherman who would take us for a few lira."

In fact this is exactly what happened, the village was tiny just a tavern hugging the hill, and tall houses almost clinging to the cliff face. Alberto soon found a fisherman who would take us, and being such a calm day he rowed us around the edge of the cove and then suddenly turned towards the cliffs.

It was hard to see the opening but he told us to duck our heads and he found a rope on the side of the cliff, and pulled us gently into the grotto.

It was an amazing deep blue, and the water was so clear you could see all the way down below. We sat in silence looking at the small entrance behind us. He then turned on a torch and showed us the ceiling high above us. I even managed to take a photo which I was delighted with when returning home, it gave off this lovely dark blue colour.

We were pulled back out into the brilliant daylight and rowed along the coast around the headland and back into the village.

The fisherman pulled us ashore among all the other fishing boats, and bid us goodbye, "Arrivederci," he called and was gone.

We sat at one of the tables with a red patterned tablecloth and Alberto ordered some wine.

The waiter and owner was in his fishing clothes, with black fishing hat, it all seemed surreal, such a lovely spot, something like the paintings one could buy in a gallery.

We had a huge Italian salad with lots of oil which I had become accustomed to, and fish almost freshly caught straight from the sea.

All too soon Alberto said it was time to walk to the top of the hill and catch the returning bus to Naples. He had yet to collect his luggage from his aunt's and come with us down to the ship.

It was a stiff climb up a narrow lane to the main road, and here we sat under an olive tree and waited for the local bus.

The drive along the cliffs will be something I will never forget, how lovely to live on this coast, or better still have a friend with a house. Earlier in the year we had travelled along the same stretch of road, and had taken a boat out from Sorrento to Capri.

I had even had a swim in Gracie Fields' swimming pool. Gracie Fields had been a very famous British actress, comedian and singer who died back in the late seventies. Her pool was open to the public when she wasn't using it, so for sixty shillings, we had pretended we were from the rich and famous jet set. I must admit I had an eye out all the time in case she walked by. Such a distinctive character with her golden hair.

Along the coast were some wonderful cliffs which if I close my eyes I can still see today.

The bus took its time on the way back stopping many times, to pick up and drop off passengers. Alberto became concerned that we would have little time to see Naples.

Quite frankly it did not worry me, as Naples was a city that we had been told to be very careful of. Crime was bad and evidently the back streets were very dangerous.

On reaching the city Alberto suddenly asked the driver to stop. He did so, and Alberto again said, "Follow me, we will go to my aunts."

We followed him over the cobbled streets, and then turned into a very narrow lane. High above us there were rows of washing hanging, and laughter as one housewife would call from her balcony to her neighbour across the way.

He stopped outside a door and giving it a hard knock walked inside. An old lady all in black threw her arms around him.

"Alberto, Alberto," she exclaimed, "I thought you would never come. You will be late for the boat. And who do you have with you here?"

He quickly introduced us, and took off through the

main room to the rear, and returned almost immediately with his luggage.

"We will need a taxi for this lot, I will go down to the end of the lane and find a taxi," and he was gone.

Some minutes later we heard the taxi pull up, the door open and a man came inside and took one look at the luggage. "Mama Mia," he cried.

Alberto already had the larger case in his hands and was lifting it across the room. The driver took the smaller suitcase, and we helped with a backpack. By this time the aunt was in tears.

"Alberto, Alberto," she cried. Then hurrying over to him hugged him as if she would never let go.

He pulled apart, patted her cheek, and then swiftly turned to the door facing us, "Hurry along girls we are late."

We said our goodbyes, and as I hugged her said, "We will look after Alberto for you."

How three of us, the driver and the luggage all fitted into the old car I don't know, but we were soon winding down narrow streets, and lanes, avoiding the centre of town.

Once on the waterfront Alberto breathed a sigh of relief, especially when the ship came into sight. We were waved quickly through the gates and were soon beside the ship.

Alberto walked forward with his ticket and passport, and was directed back to a shed behind us. We had boarding passes so walked briskly straight up the gangplank. He didn't return for ages, and all we could see was his luggage at the bottom of the gangway.

Finally he appeared, and directed a steward waiting by the luggage to take it aboard. He was soon on deck and following the steward to his first class cabin, while we headed way down to the bottom deck to our humble cabin.

The bottom deck for passengers was under the water line and the cabins down there were very stuffy, but we had been lucky in having a porthole. Maybe because we arrived late, but our other friends were down here too.

We took off to our cabin to have a shower, and then down to our favourite bar 'The Pig and Whistle' for our usual Pimms before dinner.

We had the second sitting which meant we had plenty of time to admire the sunset each evening. The ship was full of immigrants going to Australia. I think they only paid ten pounds in those days, so it was quite an event for them to go to dinner. Well for so many years these migrants had suffered rationing, but while on board this ship food was plentiful and they never ran out.

We didn't see Alberto until later, and how he managed to sit at an officer's table I don't know. We didn't realize that back in those days, you just had to tip, and everything came to you so easily.

Catherine had decided not to sit at the same table as us so this gave us a great opportunity to meet more people. So she sat with an Officer, and I sat with the Doctor. Alberto was with one of the Engineers.

Our next stop would be Port Said in Egypt and this was I hoped going to be a highlight. There had been some trouble a couple of years ago in the Suez and with UN peace keepers still there separating the Egyptians and the Israelis, we were not sure if we would be able to go to Cairo, and of course see the pyramids. I was filled with great sadness that we were told at the last minute we could only go onto the wharf and the surroundings. The Captain did not want to be responsible for a shipload of passengers driving to Cairo in case there was an incident.

It would be some years before our wish to see Cairo would be granted. As neither of us at the time knew that I would marry and come here to live for three years.

We did have time to do some shopping, and came back with the large leather Pouf for which Port Said is so famous for, and I also managed to buy a small camel made out of leather.

The trip through the canal was amazing, so high and dry were the sides, and there seemed lots of 'Coolies' working carrying baskets of soil up and down the sides.

The canal had been damaged in the Suez Crisis and we had to be careful to avoid a few of the small submerged boats that were still there. It was sad to see how the men were working carrying everything on their shoulders, I don't think I had ever felt so sorry for anybody in my whole life.

It was better to go down to one of the lounges and not think about them, maybe write a letter home, to be posted in Bombay.

The night suddenly came upon us, and it was time to dress for dinner.

The same sad mood stayed with me until I reached the table, and then there was lots of upbeat conversation, about what people had bought while they were ashore.

We would soon call in at Aden but for a short while and just long enough to go to the shops, as no tours would be going further inland. We were warned not to buy cameras as on a previous trip somebody had bought a camera, but when they went to put a film in it found it was only a bare case, with nothing inside.

Aden was just a street full of shops and there seemed little to buy, so we thought it better to keep our money until we reached India. There were stories of lovely sandals, materials and best of all sapphires in Ceylon.

For years Catherine and I had wanted to buy a sapphire, as our mother had always worn one.

Unfortunately the voyage across from Aden was not pleasant it was very hot, and people started to fall ill on board. Several small children died and we dreaded the boat stopping at noon, as this was the time they would carry out the ritual of a burial at sea.

Suddenly the whole atmosphere on the ship turned from gaiety to wondering who would be taken out next.

Alberto seemed still to be in good spirits and when the Doctor suggested that Catherine and I should eat in his cabin instead of the dining room we gladly accepted. So each night we would go down to his cabin where his Indian steward would prefer to give us a light meal of mostly rice, and a sauce to make it more interesting.

By the time we reached Bombay we were all looking forward to eating on shore. We were taken on a short tour around the city, and here again I was witness to a strange sight, and not a pleasant one. Walking along to where the woman do their washing in long troughs, I commented on the birds hovering high in the trees.

"Why so many birds?" I asked.

"Better not to notice," we were told. "It is rather unpleasant and will only upset girls like you."

We dared not ask again, so kept looking at the ground until we were well past the trees.

It was not until years later that I learnt the practice of leaving the bodies of the dead outside. That fortunately no longer took place in Bombay, and I have never wanted to return there for that reason.

We were pleased to leave Bombay and hoped Ceylon would put some gaiety back on board, so when we finally came into the stream to wait for the tug boat to guide us in our mood changed.

Alberto had business ashore. During the time we had sailed from Aden, the Doctor and I had become quite friendly.

He had the day off and he invited me to go for a trip with him into the hills to see the tea plantations, and leave the others to go to the shops, and to meet them later at the Galle Face Hotel later in the day.

The Doctor was great fun to travel with as of course he had done this many times before, and probably with equally as many girls. He bargained with the driver like an old hand and we were soon out of the downtown area and exploring the countryside.

We drove high up in the hills and looked at the tea plantations, having a lovely lunch in the cool of the shady trees, such a refreshing change from the ship. It was all too soon before we had to return as arranged to meet Catherine at the Hotel.

The Hotel was an old fashioned building and had seen many expats over the years I am sure. The small expensive shops were a joy to look in, and the sapphires would have been difficult to choose from as there was so much choice.

We sat out around the pool and enjoyed a final drink before we were to return to the ship. Oh that ship had become like returning to boarding school. There had been so much sickness on board that it was not a happy thought for another ten days at sea before we reached Australia.

We were soon back on board and down to our cabin which seemed such a long way down the stairs from the deck.

Catherine wondered out loud for me to hear just how had Alberto become so rich in such a short time in Europe.

He showed us his cabin which had a large porthole always open, with a light breeze that would circulate its way through his cabin during the hot afternoons. He pointed out you should always know which side of the ship to book, most important when travelling out to India, or returning to India.

Well that did not trouble us as we were under the waterline but he was concerned when I felt faint, and offered his cabin any afternoon that I wished to lie down. For this I was grateful so he did have some feelings after all.

But I could not make out just what his feelings for me were, was I more like a frail sister that he did not want to see ill.

I became more and more unsure of myself when he was around, it was almost as if he had cast a spell over me.

Catherine did not like it, but maybe it was an over-reaction as there was a definite dislike between Alberto and her. But on the ship it was easier to be civil for all our sakes. He was most generous and always paid for our drinks in the 'Pig and Whistle' before dinner.

The days wore on and after a while it felt like being on the ship would go on forever. Some people enjoyed this comfort zone but not me. I tried to vary the day by sometimes sleeping on deck, but the temperature was constantly changing.

So after an early walk around the ship counting every

turn so once around the ship became at least twenty times around the deck.

Early in the morning you would meet some of the older people who found this the only time they wanted to move from their deck chairs. Some had travelled for years, and remarked how the passengers were changing on the return voyage.

There were so many immigrants on board and one felt sorry for them going to a new life. Why I don't know how our relations had spent six months at sea, boarding a small frail sailing ship called the "Charlotte" from Plymouth. In fact I had stood on the steps where there was a little plaque in the wall in Nelson to remind us that here they sailed to New Zealand in 1842.

Six months at sea, with small children and probably all their worldly goods that they were allowed to carry. To set out from Covent Garden by train to Plymouth and then to travel such a distance, only to have to live in a hastily erected sod hut in the back of Nelson.

The sod hut made of clay would have taken days to make, and then to move into one room with children and furniture.

The museum at Akaroa on the Banks Peninsula of New Zealand had given us an excellent picture of an early home. But this was much more glamorous than a farmers' cottage.

Our other relations had come out much earlier, the story of the old Sea Captain was that he had run away from home at the age of 13. But when we visited the village where he had come from on the English south coast, the Vicar could not find any mention of him in the Parish records that suggested that he may have had to run off to sea. How exciting having a Stowaway in the family. We had not thought of this, maybe he had stolen a hare or rabbit. Surely that was not a big enough crime, to be punished for by being banned from Mother England and sent to Australia or Norfolk Island. Far better to be free, even as a cabin boy.

My stowaway relation ended up becoming a whaler with Jimmy Jones of Kāpiti Island fame. Later he settled on a large track of land at the bottom of Lake Whakatipu and built a lovely farmhouse.

This house was a welcoming stopover for other travellers heading further south to Dunedin and Invercargill. But more for his own use as a stop off to his beloved Riverton, the Southern Riviera of New Zealand. It must have reminded him of his seaside home in England. Here he opened a whaling station, and later married another Whaler's daughter.

At long last we reached Fremantle, and took a bus into Perth to look at this growing city.

On returning to the ship to my amazement there was one of the girls I had flatted with in London on our arrival several years ago. She was so upset that she hadn't made the ship in time when it berthed. She had driven from a little country outpost of Tammin where she was now married to a run holder.

She begged me to return later in the year, as she was due to have another baby and was so lonely. She said there are no women around for miles and lots of unattached farmers, some quite wealthy perhaps you could be a neighbour.

I felt so sorry for her when the ship pulled out, and waved until I could see her no more. I was not tempted to spend the rest of my days living in the outback.

Our next port of call was Melbourne, and here an old school friend of mothers was there to greet us and take us home for the night. By chance she had a son home from the Islands where he worked for Burns Philip, the large trading company in the Pacific where my father had worked.

He was polite and kind to us both but being a whole five years older thought of us as two rather young girls, that he should show the town to. I think he was pleased when he returned us to the ship and waved goodbye. Little did he realize he would be seeing me again in six short months' time when I was to return to be a bridesmaid at a friend's wedding. The fare by ship was so reasonable and such a relatively short journey it would be a shame not to go to the wedding in Melbourne.

But on my return to the ship I saw two of Alberto's friends. Would I never be free of his men? I walked quickly down to our cabin and there the two men were waiting for me.

"You have a package for us I think," one grunted at me. So hurriedly I found one of the parcels in my suitcase and handed it over, and without so much of a thank you they were gone. I took myself back down to the bar with the little money I had and ordered a large brandy. Catherine had stopped to talk to the Doctor and hadn't noticed the men, thankfully.

Sydney was exciting to arrive at, as here again were old friends that I had made while skiing in Austria the previous year. Also there was a friend that I had travelled around Europe with for three months. He had kindly taken two days off to show Catherine and myself around.

We were both delighted when Alberto had told us he had a change of plans and had to do business in Melbourne.

I hoped that would be the last we would ever see of him.

But that was not to be so.

John was on the wharf in his navy blazer, and we were soon off in the back of his Austin soft top being given a first class tour of the city. He even took us home to meet his parents who were a little concerned that one of us may be their future daughter in law. We soon put his mother's mind to rest, and assured her we were on our way home to New Zealand, even though Catherine was staying on in Sydney.

Two days later we were back on board and who should greet us in the cabin but my two ski friends. They were so disappointed not being at the wharf on our arrival, but had been given the wrong arrival time.

We had lots of fun and chatter in the cabin, and they stayed on board and had dinner with us. I promised to return to Sydney sometime, better still why did they not visit me in Wellington.

Catherine and I had a tearful farewell, when our parents' friends collected her the next morning and waved us off as the ship left Sydney harbour for home.

The Wanganella was a great ship, with an air of old world charm. I had left the immigrants behind in Sydney and the ship had a festive air from our first night on, New Zealand bound. By this time my money was running very short, so I decided to stay away from the bars, and keep to myself.

By chance I had been standing with a group of Australian farmers as I left port. They were off to work in New Zealand and ready to enjoy their first taste of shipboard life. Lucky for me one had a plan, he wanted to know why I would not join him in the bar. I explained my financial situation and he laughed and offered to do a deal. "If I pay for your drinks, would you have pity on me when we reach Wellington and either have me to stay or for meals when I come to town?"

That was an easy answer, our mother was renowned for her wonderful roast dinners and good Kiwi hospitality. So he had an open invitation to visit us whenever he was in town.

He said he was to work in the Wairarapa and I explained it was just over the hill from Wellington, actually it was an awful drive and he would probably prefer to come by train. But I did not put him off.

So for the four nights on board I was his guest, but I am sure the others noticed that he always paid for my drinks.

It was not long before our days of leisure would be over as we only had one more night aboard before we reached Wellington Heads. The notorious Wellington Heads which had claimed so many ships in the early days when they were all under sail.

But we hoped we would have no problem, as the Wanganella had once made an unfortunate entry and ended up on Barrett's Reef for some weeks one summer back in 1947.

When we used to walk along the coastal path from the Bay to the Pencarrow Lighthouse we would look at her stranded high and dry on the reef.

But that morning we sailed in to Wellington, the sea was calm and we were soon steaming in past Seatoun, Eastbourne and the Bays. I could even see Lowry Bay where the family lived.

I could picture the parents driving into town around the harbour watching the ship as she steamed into Queens

Wharf.

The harbour of Wellington city looked beautiful as it can on a fine day and it reminded me a little of Monte Carlo. Well I was much travelled now, and could relate to other places I had seen in the eighteen months I had been away. Gosh it was only eighteen months so much had happened in that time. I would never be the same.

Oriental Bay looked as lovely as it always had, and the steep hills behind Thorndon Quay dark as usual with the pine trees that covered them.

Home at last and I wondered who would be on the wharf to greet me besides my parents. In no time we were coming in close to the wharf. Goodness everything looked so small, and such few people compared with other cities in the world, but it was home.

Chapter 14

Wellington

I looked up from the journal and wiped the tears from my eyes, my heart torn with mixed emotions as I read my sisters written revelations. Taking a deep drink of brandy, I steeled myself to read the next entry in the journal:

Wellington.

Arriving home was a bit of a disappointment, the wharf looked so small and everyone waiting below looked such a small group after the different ports we had arrived at overseas. There were the parents compliantly standing there in their best outfits behind a barrier of wooden stands that you could easily walk around.

After the usual farewells to our new and old friends, I walked down the gangplank to the wharf. This is where people in later years in different countries kissed the ground in a small thank you to say we are back home in the 'Promised Land.'

Mind you in the late fifties it was a 'Promised Land' for many immigrants escaping from the horrors of war in Europe waiting to be processed to see if they would become Kiwi citizens.

Australia was more open minded and a flood of Italians had arrived to work in Melbourne on the wharves, but most of the immigrants to New Zealand were from England and Holland.

They were nevertheless very lucky as they were also assisted financially and paid only ten pounds for a four week trip, whereas we paid at least hundred pounds to buy a return ticket.

I walked slowly over to the barrier, hugged my parents one by one and said quietly to my father on the spur of the moment, take my carry bag will you I have to go through Customs now.

All too easy really which Alberto had told me it would be, Alberto was always very confident and blasé when he was giving me instructions.

One helpful friend in Melbourne asked, "Please would you take my mother an electric fry pan. They are so much cheaper in Australia. In fact why don't you take one for your parents also?

Just remember to say to the Customs Officers when they come aboard you are Mrs. Doolittle's daughter."

Seemed a strange thing to say, and which Customs man did I say it too. The one on board or when I went into the queue onshore.

I entered the large wharf shed and here were a semi-circle of customs men waiting to look at our luggage. Our cabin luggage that is. My large green trunk was still in the hold. It was peculiar we were able to go into the hold once a week to take anything out or put something in we no longer needed. Mine had little of value in it just sheets, towels and winter clothes that had been worn in England.

"Next," cried out a voice and I walked forward and stood in front of the Customs Man. "Welcome home and how long have you been away?"

"Eighteen months," I said.

"Had a good time tripping around Europe I bet, you young things of today are so lucky. I saw enough of Italy to last me a lifetime during the war, this is the best place on earth," he stated convincingly.

"Are you sure you have nothing like liquor to declare?"

I replied, "If I had more than five pounds left in my purse I would be so lucky."

"Well off you go, your parents will be looking for you. Come back later today for your trunk it should be off the ship by then."

We walked out into the sunshine at 8.30 in the morning and across the wharf to the gate where my friends had arrived on their way to work.

"Some people have it lucky," they cried out to me. "We will come around tomorrow night to see you and hear all about your adventures. You had better look for work soon, so you are entitled to paid Christmas holidays. There are plenty of jobs in the paper at the moment. Bye for now."

My father came forward and proudly showed me my well-travelled car sitting on the wharf, "How did you manage to collect that without me being here to sign the papers?" I asked.

"Oh so easy, it is who you know in this world and not what you know, as you have probably found out during your travels."

So there was my car what a long way we had travelled together, what secrets and stories we both shared and now we were both back in little old Wellington.

A disturbing thought darted through my mind, I wonder if Alberto had managed to hide anything in it, as he had so many times previously when entering England.

Well I would soon find out if someone rang with that old signal. I hope my parents were not too alert to wonder why there would be overseas toll calls. Nobody ever rang from overseas, not even myself while I was away for so long. With anything urgent we always sent telegrams, at least until I found the night letter rate was better. Send it in the morning, and it would be delivered by hand in the mail the following morning.

I joined my parents but my mind was clearly somewhere else. "Still with us dear, or are you still away overseas?" asked father

"Sorry father, I was thinking of something else. You had better drive, my license is probably out of date."

So into the boot went my one rather battered and bruised suitcase, and into the rear seat went me.

The parents of course sat in the front and it all looked a little strange to see them in my car taking the lead driving.

We drove along the wharf where I had so many times taken my lunch and sat behind one of the sheds with a friend looking at the small boats.

From Queens wharf the Picton ferry boat left, and further north were the large ships from overseas, including the Port line boats, and the Blue Star line. The Rangitane which I had sailed on to London left monthly.

In no time we were driving out onto the Quay and soon we were heading along the waterfront past the Railway

Station and avoiding the railway tracks used for bringing produce to and from the wharf.

It was the days of high prices for wool and the farmers were the wealthiest people of the land. One such farming couple had been on board and it was a weekly party in the 'Pig and Whistle' for them and some of the luckier ones who were invited to their regular floating cocktail parties.

I think the only reason I received an invitation once was that I had been to school with their niece but they were a very gracious couple and I found that generally people who were much older were always interesting.

Over the ramp and now we were on the Hutt Road, a trip that had become a bore while at school and later. My lucky friends all lived in town, but being out at the Bay meant my life was previously ruled by the bus timetable.

It was alright after work, but later in the evening there was only one bus an hour, with the very last one leaving town at ll.30 pm. Giving one not much time to run and catch it if you had been to a school dance in the suburbs.

Well I won't have to worry about that again, now I had my own car.

On the short journey home along the coast, we had little to say as mother was deaf and to turn around to the back seat all the time was too difficult for her. So she suggested we would keep the conversation until we reached home.

Time flew and the harbour looked particularly lovely that morning, blue and calm which was not that often. Soon we were past the tanker wharf and into the quieter area looking due south. One more corner and we would be home.

We turned off the coastal road and there was home, I could see my bedroom window. The garden looked beautiful and everything was so inviting and just as I had remembered it.

It was lovely to be in my old room and look out over the tree tops toward the sea. I wondered if it would be too cold to swim well it was October and I always used to start swimming in October.

I thought it would be a good idea to have a walk after a cup of tea, just to make myself feel more at home. So I went downstairs and carried a tray outside onto the patio. The usual tray with Belle Fiore china cups and a plate of bran biscuits.

"I thought you would like those, one of your old favourites. Don't be surprised if the neighbours up the hill call in unannounced, they all want to see what you look like, and if you have changed. Well you know your voice sounded so different on that recording you sent us for Christmas. Everyone laughed and said it was like listening to the Queen's Christmas speech," mother proudly commented.

If I hurried with the tea maybe I could escape and take a walk along the hills and down to the beach until lunchtime. Everything seemed so small and quiet as if I had just dropped in from outer of space.

The silence was shattered by the telephone ringing, and father in his usual way stood up to answer it, probably someone on business anyway, he had taken the morning off to collect me and drive me home.

"One moment I heard him say, must be one of your shipboard friends didn't introduce himself, rather rude I thought," father growled.

"Hi," I said as I picked up the telephone, a long pause and then a rough voice on the other end. "You don't know me and you needn't know my name, a friend of Alberto's, he wants me to pick up something for him. You have it, name a time and a place and I will be there."

Quickly thinking of somewhere easy to find and not too obvious, I suggested the tanker wharf the largest place and it was usually busy with fishermen or cars just parked up looking at the view. "See you at 4 o'clock and if I'm late please realize it is not easy to just walk out having only been home for one hour."

"You better make it, I'm not coming all that way for nothing, you better think of a better place in future."

In future? There would be no reason for another meeting as there was nothing else to pick up and I certainly would not be leaving the country for a long time to come, or so I thought.

"Who was that? One of your friends to welcome you home dear?" my father asked.

"It is so important that you pick up the threads again, as we hope that you have come home to stay for a long time," mother begged.

"Yes, someone I met on the boat, he said he might have a good position for me in Featherston Street, in one of the offices there. I would like to work in that part of Wellington again as it is so close to all my friends and I could meet them for lunch."

"Speaking of lunch maybe I should help mother in the kitchen, I have learnt some recipes since I have been away you will be pleased to hear."

"I hope it not one of those dishes with lots of oil, like I used to eat in London in my day. Frankly I liked Italian food, but your mother will have to be led gently into Italian or Chinese," father mentioned.

"Yes, we ate a lot of Italian food, mainly because it was the cheapest food in London, but I will take it gently one step at a time." I went down to the kitchen and found mother making one of her famous bacon and egg pies. I couldn't think when I had eaten one of those last, probably not since I had left home.

"Need any help?" I asked, but I knew the answer would be no.

"Why don't you have a walk out into the garden dear, you will have to get used to no dog any more, sorry but after Dash died we decided that we would not have another dog."

"And you have missed the spring bulbs, but the rhododendrons are out especially that lovely pink pearl on the boundary," mother advised.

"Good idea, I will have a walk down to the waterfront and see if any of the new houses have started in the section next door."

It seemed strange to walk down the drive, the trees were just coming into leaf. I had never appreciated the beautiful old lime trees before, probably planted by one of the early settlers at the turn of the century. It was such a calm day and the tide was in, almost inviting for me to have a swim, but the breeze was a little cold, and as I looked across the Bay at Point Howard a cold shiver swept through me.

I had only been home a little over one hour, and already Alberto was aware that I was back at the Bay. I wonder who he is sending at 4 o'clock. It must be important for him to make a collection already.

It all must stop now, or it will go on for the rest of my life. How could I have been so stupid to be drawn into his web? If only he was coming to meet me, it would be easier to say no to his face.

I better walk back, I suppose it is going to be difficult to settle in, but they will have to realize that I left the Bay a very naïve 21 year old, and have returned only eighteen months later, worldly and wise.

Everything seemed just as I had left it, serene with a complete lack of traffic, so different from living in the heart of London. I suppose I had better see some of the neighbours, especially the family up the zig zag, they will want news of the last time I saw their daughter.

Entering the house the delicious smell of the pie made me quite hungry, and I hurriedly set the table. Should I put the welcome home gifts out now, or leave it until dinner? Better now it will cover up any pregnant pauses, as there are sure to be some.

Mother had put the first roses in her favourite vase in the usual place, how wonderful to be able to go out into the garden and pick flowers.

All those little things, I realized I had missed. Of course there were plenty of flowers to buy in London, but it was one of those unnecessary extra expenses that you never bought flowers, but saved every penny for exploring.

The old Windsor table looked exactly as it had before I departed overseas, polished so you could almost see your own reflection with the old mats with the hunting scene just the same. I must replace these with something new and bright, maybe for Christmas.

I wonder how they will like the silver candelabra I bought for their 25th wedding anniversary. Again thanks to Alberto I was able to buy them a beautiful one I had seen in a little shop just off the main gates to Windsor Palace. It was one of those weekends that I spent at a house party nearby. I must admit without Alberto's help that purchase would not have been possible on my salary of twenty pounds a week.

Now how was I going to mention my meeting for 4 o'clock? Better to leave it for a while and then suggest a long walk, neither of them would want to walk, so I would give them time for a long talk after lunch.

The candelabra was received with great appreciation and laughter, when I told them it had been taken to pieces, in case the customs wanted to look at it, and hidden in my ski boots. I needn't have worried, as there was no duty over anything one hundred years old or older, but I was to learn all about that later.

The afternoon flew by, and when I suggested that I would take a long walk before dinner, it was eagerly received. We had just about talked ourselves out, and I think they needed a rest from me for a while.

I set off with a shoulder bag with a sweater and my camera, and nobody took any notice of me carrying a rather large bag.

It took me about twenty minutes to walk around the bays, which I had done so often before over the years, especially on Sundays when I taught Sunday school in the little Church at Point Howard.

I arrived in plenty of time, walked around the disused road and looked for shells on the little beach, when I heard my name called. I turned and saw a man the same age as me standing on the road.

"Nice day," he said. "Had any luck looking for shells?"

"Afraid not, are you looking for me?"

"Yes, I believe you have something for me."

He walked down onto the beach and up to me. Looking

around to see if anyone was watching, he asked for the package. I took it out of my bag and handed it to him.

"Keep walking along the beach with me, I have a message from our friend," he said. "Is it too late for you to go up to the mountain skiing?"

"Well no, but I have no idea if there is any snow," I replied.

"Yes there is enough for you to make a trip, and as soon as possible," he demanded.

"But I have only arrived home today, and have no intention of going off so soon. Maybe in ten days when I have contacted my friends. Also I would like to speak to Alberto, as I am back home now, I have no wish to continue being at his beck and call."

"I don't think Alberto will be pleased to hear that, and you had better speak to him yourself. Maybe he will be on the mountain when you go. He is not in the country at the moment and he didn't mention being here for some time. But I will pass on your movements to him, he does not like having his arrangements changed."

With that he turned and walked back to his car parked on the road. Suddenly I felt that familiar cold shiver run down my spine, this was not going to be as easy as I had mistakenly thought. I looked out on the harbour to Wards and Somes Islands and the poles where we had often rowed our little boat to not so many years ago.

Ward Island looked so far away near to the entrance of Wellington Harbour. If only I could go back to those happy days we had all enjoyed in the Bay before my departure to England.

Slowly I retraced my steps along the beach and wondered if I would walk up the path to the church on the

Point. It would be closed and locked and I didn't feel like a steep climb up to the castle at the top of the Hill. Strange to build a castle here in New Zealand, it was unfinished of course and had become a site to look down the harbour from. The track lead on up to the top of the hill where it met the main road over to Wainuiomata and then down the valley to the coast.

The tide was in so it meant walking along the tiny path on the edge of the road. Everything seemed so small. Was the path always so narrow with cars passing us by all too close? Oh for the carefree days when I would walk, or ride along this road with not a care in the world. Now there was that shadow lurking over me and for the moment it looked as if Alberto had a hold over everything that I did.

Walking around the final corner past the black boatshed, the sun came out and shone on the nearby yellow boatshed. I had never really appreciated its architecture before, in fact we had never seen the doors of the shed open, let alone seen a boat inside.

Strange how you accept buildings that have always been there and never wondered what was inside.

The best thing for me to do would be to find a position in Wellington as quickly as possible. The Evening Post and Dominion were delivered every day, and tomorrow I would search for a position and then have an excuse to go into town for an interview.

I was fortunate I always found it so easy to find work, and my favourite area was Featherston Street. It was so central and I probably could get a lift into town with my father. If not, somebody usually picked me up as I walked along the road to the bus stop.

It seemed so lonely walking along the beach without

my dog.

He used to go everywhere with me. I met somebody in London who recognised me. "As the girl with the big black dog who was always walking along the road."

Strange how complete strangers talk to one another overseas, you feel as if you almost know them as friends. Instead somebody who commuted to work each day on a bus and on looking out the window saw me with my dog.

When I finally reached home, mother ran out with a big smile and informed me a dear old ski friend had rung to welcome me home, and she had invited him to dinner.

Good that would be a help through another meal, with an old friend that I had not seen since London days. In fact he was about to return to New Zealand shortly after we had arrived back from three months in Europe.

His parents were quite wealthy and he had gone out and bought all his family gifts in Bond Street. I had often walked down Bond Street looking at the private art galleries, and had never ventured into the jewellery shops let alone to actually purchase some gifts.

It would give me something to do in the kitchen and I offered to prepare a trifle which an old Italian neighbour had made whenever there was a gathering of people for birthdays or any other excuse. Dear old Mrs. Meo was long since dead, but I could still taste those trifles, she must have used a good glass of brandy on the sponge.

I looked in the bar for something to soak the sponge with and found only whiskey, oh well that would have to do.

There was the old turquoise Chinese cookie jar and I opened it on the off chance there would be some Brown Betty in it. But at the bottom were only crumbs. They had probably been there since the last batch was made, long before we had gone away.

Perhaps tonight being my first night at home, we would hear from Australia as to how my dearest sister Catherine was settling into her new Australian way of life.

Goodness the house seemed so large and empty, for the last two years there had hardly been one night that I would have had a bedroom to myself. It was strange to put my clothes back into the chest of drawers that definitely was a first in ages.

One just becomes so used to living out of a suitcase and really it was lucky that I had bought five new frocks in Oxford Street for wearing on the ship coming home. With summer coming up they would be useful for going to work.

In no time it was nearly six o'clock and Roger would arrive within the next half an hour. Goodness I wonder what we can offer him to drink. Wine was something we had never had in the house, and we had grown so used to drinking it in Europe.

My father must have read my thoughts, "I have put some beer in the fridge to cool down, I suppose Roger is used to drinking chilled beer overseas."

"Not at all, we used to go down to the pub at night, and being New Zealanders, the men used to drink it from the tap."

"I used to drink cider as it was cheaper, and you always had to think of whoever was paying for your drink," father recalled.

Mother had gone to a lot of trouble and I hoped it would be one of my favourites, and as we had had so little meat in London a crumbed cutlet would be marvellous.

The evening was a great success, the meal was perfect, and Roger kept the conversation flowing with tales of his time in London and Europe. Mother having not travelled was a little out of her depth with the conversation, but father enjoyed hearing all about his favourite city of London where he had lived for twelve years while he was studying at London University.

We were sorry to see Roger leave, as he had helped us all on my first night home. Tomorrow would be another day and hopefully it would not be too long before I was at work to save again and go to Australia next year to flat with my sister if she stayed on.

The next day I woke early with the sun flooding in through my bedroom window. It was so quiet, no noise of traffic, just the odd bus passing by at the bottom of the road. My bedroom looked out on some tall poplars and already they were in leaf. It is not until you have been away for some time, and then upon your return to the spot you have taken for granted for so long, that you really appreciate such a beautiful view.

I looked across at the spare bed and thought of the times that I had shared this room with my dear sister, and sometimes how we had talked long into the night of our hopes and dreams before we travelled to Europe. I was missing her already but realized that one day we would both marry, and maybe we would be living in different countries and not see one another for months, or even maybe years.

I was also missing Simon, especially after seeing Roger last night, they were so different and I wondered if I would ever see Simon again.

Perhaps I should surprise my parents with a cup of tea. Strange how we had taken turns in making the traditional cup of tea every morning. No time for that once we were away from home.

So I crept downstairs and put the hot water jug on, and looked for a tray and two cups and saucers. My favourite was blue and white china, a broken dinner set which had come from my grandmothers' home. There were more cups and saucers than dinner plates which must have been broken many years ago.

Strange how little things, like smells, china and taste brings back memories of happy times long ago.

I climbed the steep staircase, really it was so steep it was almost like a ladder and the tea cups were difficult to hold. Feeling stupid we had always used a tray before, why didn't I do that now? Too late, I was now at the top of the stairs and had to put them down on the floor to knock at the door.

A bright voice, "Oh good, I hope that is the maid with a cup of tea," father joked. "We did not like to wake you so have been sitting here reading on the terrace. What a lovely day, if you have no plans maybe we could drive around to the shops at Eastbourne and you may like to suggest something you have not eaten for a long time."

"How thoughtful you are, maybe we could visit your cousin while we are around there," mother suggested.

"I suppose my international driving license will be in order. Or maybe I should bring my New Zealand license up to date at the post office while we are there?"

It was a good feeling to drive again, and my little car seemed to know I was back at the wheel, it was almost like the car showing me the way. The car and I had had so many good times together and here it was now on the other side of the world.

We drove around each of the Bays, and I kept thinking, 'Oh this road is so small, it's not really wide enough for two cars, let alone a bus.' Those big red London buses that had ruled my life for fifteen years.

Eastbourne was a quaint little village, made up of a butcher, several general stores, two milk bars, a picture theatre and post office, a bank, bookshop, shoe shop and a drapery. Whilst at primary school all these shops were of great importance. Especially the fish and chip shop, and the pie shop where we were allowed to buy our lunch once a week from.

Our shoes were always bought at these shops, and our school books, and sometimes on a Saturday afternoon we would go to the picture theatre. A really safe quiet life in a small village, similar to being bought up in a small village in England.

Mother particularly liked the drapery shop where there was a small rack of clothes. Life was very simple and the only time one dressed up was to go into Wellington to one of the major stores.

After shopping we had an ice cream, I couldn't remember when I had last tasted an ice cream. We laughed while we ate it in the car and then drove along the waterfront to my cousin's house.

Lucky she was at home, and we were soon sitting out on her terrace having tea and cakes. She was a lovely cook and there was always something in her cake tin. It was a one way conversation as I touched lightly on the highlights of the voyage home, as other friends said nobody is really interested in your travels after the first sentence. You will find they want to tell you about the latest crop of tomatoes.

Suddenly I laughed as my cousin, commented, "It is

nearly time to plant our first tomatoes."

She looked at me and asked, "What is funny about that, may I ask?"

"Oh don't think too badly of me, but the thought of picking tomatoes is such a lovely thought, I haven't seen a vegetable garden in all the time I have been away."

We sat in the spring sun and laughed and it was good to be included in a family conversation as if I had not been away.

A cloud came over, blocking the sun and dampening my mood, sitting there quietly I wondered what they would say, if I told them the truth as to what I had really been up to the last year, driving around Europe smuggling drugs in my wee car. They would probably just look at me and say of course we do not believe you. How absurd, you must be joking.

***

With tears streaming down my face, I lowered the journal and reached for my brandy, I just couldn't read any more. It all was so sad, but at least I now understood my dear sister's actions and I could pass some more information onto David. Praying that justice would be done and Alberto, the cause of so much misery in the world, finally he would get his just desserts.

I wondered when or even if I would ever see David again.

Chapter 15

News Article

Crime Section

*Italian Drug Trafficker Found Guilty of Murder in the
South Pacific*

*British High Commissioner's Wife Found Dead in Palolo
Deep Lagoon*

UK Times, LA Times, Pacific News, August 1986

*Alberto Russo, New Zealand exporter, formerly of Italy
has been prosecuted today August 21st, 1986 in Los Angeles
for the death of the wife of the British High Commissioner
on a South Pacific Atoll.*

*Russo along with two accomplices was caught on
August 16th in Los Angeles after absconding from Apia.
New Zealand Police had managed to track him down
within days of Leticia Winchester's drowning in Palolo
Deep Lagoon, near Apia, Western Samoa.*

Russo has been found guilty of first degree murder and is now awaiting sentence in the Supreme Court of California, following which he will be transferred to San Quentin State Prison where he will carry out his sentence.

Russo is also wanted by Interpol on various drug charges and is suspected of being the infamous Mr Casino drug kingpin that has been operating worldwide.

Lead investigator, Detective David Harris was quoted saying, "the NZ Secret Intelligence Service have been watching Russo for some time and now have evidence on a number of rackets he has been involved in."

Leticia Ann Winchester was found dead in Apia, the capital of Western Samoa on August 7th, one day after she was murdered, at Palolo Deep lagoon, in Apia harbour.

Leticia and her husband Simon, the British High Commissioner in Western Samoa, had been living happily in the South Pacific for several years. Leticia nee Johnson, a New Zealander had met her British husband Simon while working abroad in London. They married on Mr Winchester's first posting to New Zealand and had enjoyed several postings with the British government, previously Bangkok, Stockholm, Cairo and Rome. Leticia is survived by her younger sister Catherine Seymour who resides in New Zealand.

UK Correspondent

***

Death Notice

Apia Times, 7 August, 1986

WINCHESTER, Leticia Ann (5 May 1934 – 6 August 1986).

It is with great sadness Leticia Ann Winchester passed away tragically at the age of 53 in her favourite place Apia, Western Samoa.

Leticia of New Zealand descent, is survived by her loving husband Simon (of Cornwall, England) and dearly beloved sister, Catherine Seymour (of Auckland, New Zealand).

The funeral service will be held on 9 August, 1986 at St Mary's Church at 9 am, followed by the wake at Vaisala, the residence of the British High Commissioner at 11 a.m.

By Leticia's request she will be left to rest in her favourite spot at Mt Vaea.

'Miss you forever, big sister, you will always be in my heart, and we will travel again together to that big happy place in the sky we always talked and laughed about, Love your Catherine'

All correspondence C/- Vaisala, British High Commission, Vaiala, PO Box 466, Apia, Western Samoa.

Chapter 16

Epilogue

While staying at Smeaton Catherine was surprised with David's arrival. He flew to the UK after the case was heard in LA finding Alberto guilty of the murder of Letitia. He suggested that they had a holiday together in Cornwall which he had never been to and one of Catherine's favourite places.

While they were there they walked the track behind Polperro along the cliffs to the next bay and here he proposed late one evening as the sun was going down. Catherine was delighted to say yes and he produced a ring he had bought in a small local shop. This ring he said would be replaced when Catherine choose an antique ring when they saw the right one. They walked back to the little house they had rented in the village near the local pub for a celebration dinner and to make plans to return home to New Zealand. This is what they did soon afterwards and returned to Waikanae to arrange for a wedding as soon as possible at St Luke's Anglican Church.

The End

Dramatis Personae:

David Harris	New Zealand Detective
Toni	Simon's chauffeur
Pae	Simon's housekeeper, Toni's wife
Mata	Simon's Cook
Alberto Russo	Leticia's New Zealand neighbour
Catherine Seymour	Leticia's only sister
Leticia Winchester	Catherine's only sister
Simon Winchester	Leticia's husband, UK High Commissioner
Stephen Seymour	Catherine's husband
Jack	Runs Palolo Deep, Apia
Sergeant Tui	Western Samoan Detective
Tim Sinclair	NZ Detective
Annette	Scottish cousin, owns Smeaton
Hamish	Annette's husband, Smeaton
Sally	Smeaton cook
Willie	Dutch expat in Samoa, plays bridge
Aunt Mary & Aggie	Own Aggie Greys Hotel, Apia
Nid	Bangkok Tour Guide
Orlando	Thailand bus trip tourist
Sophie	Orlando's daughter
Amanda	Catherine's Auckland friend
Lesi	Daughter of coffin maker
Mr White	Head of UN & best Village Judge
Ruth	Simon's secretary High Commission
Arthur	Australian on boat, shouts drinks

www.ingramcontent.com/pod-product-compliance
Lightning Source LLC
Chambersburg PA
CBHW021135110726
47900CB00002B/370